Welcome to ̶ home of bold men and daring women. A place where rich tales of passion and adventure are unfolding under the Big Sky. Seems that this charming little town has some mighty big secrets. And everybody's talking about...

Ethan Walker: The rugged rancher was known to have a temper, but was he a murderer? Everybody was confident he'd be convicted, but there was one person who wouldn't rest until Ethan was behind bars. It was Whitehorn's sweet little librarian...

Mary Jo Kincaid: She was sick of this trial. Why didn't they just lock Ethan up and throw away the key? It was enough to make a girl like her lose sleep. But hopefully it wasn't enough for people to figure out her connection to...

Lexine Baxter: Notoriously wild, the town bad girl had been missing for years—and yet the stories of her affairs kept multiplying. One thing was sure, her secret was safe with...

Nan Avery: Her murdered husband's infidelities were nobody's business but hers. Or so she thought. Sooner or later she'd learn that her secret was bigger than her pride. Because one man was determined to uncover the whole story...

Rafe "Wolf Boy" Rawlings: Legend had it that Rafe was as wild as the wolves that had raised him. If anyone would get to the truth, it would be him. Even if that meant going up against the woman he loved....

Montana ★ MAVERICKS

REBECCA DANIELS

Way of the Wolf

Published by Silhouette Books

America's Publisher of Contemporary Romance

Special thanks and acknowledgment to Rebecca Daniels
for her contribution to the Montana Mavericks series.

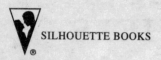 SILHOUETTE BOOKS

Recycling programs
for this product may
not exist in your area.

ISBN-13: 978-0-373-31093-7

WAY OF THE WOLF

Copyright © 1994 by Harlequin Books S.A.

Visit Silhouette Books at www.eHarlequin.com

Printed in U.S.A.

REBECCA DANIELS

will never forget the first time she read a Silhouette
novel. It was fifteen years ago, and she's been reading
and writing romance novels ever since. Born in
the Midwest but raised in Southern California,
Ms. Daniels now resides in Northern California's
San Joaquin Valley with her husband and two sons.
She is a lifelong poet and song lyricist who enjoys
early morning walks, an occasional round of golf
and scouring California's Mother Lode region for
antiques.

TYVMFE!—for Anne Canadeo, for having the tact of a diplomat, the mind of a scholar, the heart of a mystic and the soul of a dreamer. It makes for one hell of an editor. Many thanks.

One

"Looks like you got your man this time, huh, Wolf Boy?"

Detective Sergeant Rafe Rawlings stopped when he heard the familiar nickname and felt the strong tug on his jacket sleeve. He cringed, however, when he turned and found himself snared in Lily Mae Wheeler's iron grip. She smiled up at him, but Rafe remembered all too well the times he'd been victim of her vicious gossip.

"That's up to the jury to decide, Mrs. Wheeler. Will you excuse me, please?" he said politely, pulling the sleeve of his corduroy jacket free of her hold as tactfully as possible. "I've got to keep moving."

Rafe continued pushing his way through the crowd of spectators that lined the courthouse corridor. He didn't have time for idle chitchat—especially not with a meddlesome busybody like Lily Mae. He had more pressing things on his mind at the moment—like trying to stay as far from Raeanne Martin as he could. But he knew that wouldn't be easy. They would be sitting on opposite sides of the courtroom, but as far as he was concerned, that wasn't far enough.

Seven years ago, he had stood on the platform of the Whitehorn bus station and watched a shiny silver Greyhound carry her out of town and out of his life. She'd left for California, for law school and for a new life that didn't include him and he'd never expected to see her again. But three months ago, all that had changed. She was back now—looking stronger, more confident and more beautiful than ever. He'd had seven years to get her out of his system—to forget how smooth her skin felt, how soft her voice sounded. Seven long, torturous years to forget just how much he'd loved her.

"Hello, Detective Rawlings."

Rafe glanced down, surprised to find Whitehorn's demure and very proper, town librarian, Mary Jo Plumber Kincaid, standing in the crowd beside him.

"Hello, Mrs. Kincaid," he said, inwardly cursing his luck. He wasn't any more interested in small talk than he was in gossip, but the crowded corridor made it impossible to judiciously escape. Forcing himself to smile, he gave her a tiny, polite bow of the head. "I wouldn't have thought you'd be interested in all of this."

Mary Jo smiled, her cheeks blushing prettily. "Well, I might be relatively new to Whitehorn, but I'm interested in everything that happens in my community. And my husband, Dugin, has told me about Charlie Avery and all the stories about him. He worked by my husband's ranch when he died, you know."

Rafe smiled. "Yes, I'm aware of that."

The color in Mary Jo's cheeks deepened. "Of course, you

would be." As they moved with the crowd for a few steps, the smile on Mary Jo's face faded. "Uh, Detective Rawlings?"

"Yes?"

"I met him once—Ethan Walker, that is—in the library."

"I see."

"And I must say, he frightened me," she confessed, twisting the handle on her purse.

"Well, you don't need to be afraid any longer, Mrs. Kincaid," he said, noticing how the muscle near her jaw clenched tight. "Walker's not going to be able to hurt anyone else again."

"But he's…he's never confessed, has he?"

"No, that's true."

"But you think he'll be convicted anyway?"

"That's what the district attorney seems to think, Mrs. Kincaid."

"Oh, I hope so," she said with a shudder. "The thought of someone like him on the loose…" She thought for a moment, then looked up at him. "This Miss Martin, though—Raeanne Martin, his lawyer? I hear she's very good. You aren't concerned she might…well, you know, get him off?"

Rafe's dark eyes narrowed, marveling at the depth of still waters. In a million years, he wouldn't have suspected that this quiet, reserved librarian possessed such a peculiar interest, or such a morbid concern. "I think the prosecution has a strong case," he said diplomatically. "And the rest, I'm afraid, is up to the jury."

"Yes, well, of course you're right," she said, slipping the handle of her handbag over her arm.

Mary Jo stepped quietly aside and watched Rafe as newly hired *Journal* reporter Sandra Wilson rushed up to interview him. *Handsome,* she thought as she listened to Rafe deftly avoid the reporter's questions, *and smart, too.*

Her mind wandered back in time and a sly smile curved the corners of her pink lips upward. *Handsome and smart,* she mused, pleased. Certainly not traits he'd inherited from his father. But she didn't have to worry about him any more. Ethan Walker was the one that she had to be concerned about now. She thought of the man who stood accused of murder. Would he tell all he knew before the trial was over? She didn't think so. No man was ever anxious to admit he'd been made a fool of.

Ah, Mary Jo thought to herself with her smile widening, the male ego. What would she do without it? With flattery a man was putty in your hands. Add a little bit of blackmail and he would do anything you wanted.

"Okay," Sandra said with a frustrated sigh. "If you don't want to comment on the trial, what about Raeanne Martin's return to Whitehorn? How does it feel going up against an old friend? What kind of job do you think she might do?"

"Sorry, Sandy—" Rafe began.

"Don't tell me," she said, interrupting him with a shake of the head. Taking a deep breath, she joined him as he told her, "No comment!"

Rafe almost smiled, but then he spotted a sudden gap in the crowd. In one smooth motion, he made his move. "Ladies, I'm sorry," he said quickly as he stepped through the momentary break. "I really have to go. Excuse me."

Almost instantly, the crowd swallowed him up and he breathed a sigh of relief. He walked quickly, not anxious to be stopped again by any more reporters or curious spectators. The last thing he wanted was more idle chitchat—

or to be asked to comment to the press on his thoughts concerning Raeanne Martin's return. Besides, if he was to say what he really felt about Raeanne's moving back to Whitehorn, it would no doubt make headlines.

Damn—why did she have to come back? Why couldn't she just have stayed in L.A., stayed out of his life once and for all? After seven years, he'd managed to convince himself he was over her, but that hadn't made the past three months any easier.

He wasn't sure if it was some perverse act of providence, or just plain bad luck, that Raeanne Martin had been appointed defense counsel on this particular case. All he wanted was to stay out of her way, but as chief investigator for the prosecution, he would have to be in court throughout the entire trial and that would make avoiding her a little tough.

When she first moved back to town, he'd managed to keep their meetings to a minimum—short, casual encounters, impersonal and unimportant. He would have liked to avoid her completely, but that had been impossible. For all its big-city problems and urban sprawl, Whitehorn was still a small town and they were, after all, old friends. They had known each other since they were kids and to ignore her completely would have set too many tongues wagging. Everyone in town knew there was a history between them. They all knew Raeanne Martin had married his best friend.

Rafe stepped into the jammed courtroom. The spectators' section was nearly filled to capacity and the center aisle was packed. Of course, he wasn't surprised by the mob. The publicity about the trail had been building for weeks and it was only natural that all of Whitehorn wanted to be there to hear every grisly detail. Not that he blamed them, exactly. It wasn't every day that one of the town's most puzzling mysteries was solved.

Rafe had to admit that being called upon to investigate a homicide twenty-seven years after the fact wasn't exactly routine. He'd been found abandoned soon after Charlie Avery disappeared, over a quarter century ago, but he'd grown up hearing the rumors about it. Married, with two young children, Avery had hardly seemed the type to abandon his family and take off without a trace. But when week after week passed and no body turned up, no crime was uncovered, the rumors had begun to fly. There had been talk of drinking and bar brawls, of rowdy feuds and womanizing. For the next twenty-seven years, the folks around Whitehorn had speculated on what—or who—had caused Charlie Avery to desert his wife and children.

But nine months ago a horrifying discovery had been made and the community was still reeling from its effects. Human remains unearthed on the Laughing Horse Indian Reservation outside of town had later been determined to be Charlie's. Suddenly, a longtime missing persons case had become an unsolved homicide.

Assigned by Sheriff Hensley to the nearly impossible task of finding a killer almost thirty years after the crime, Rafe had discovered, to his surprise, that even though the trail to the murderer was an old one, it was far from cold. While it had been obvious that the killer had taken care to hide his tracks, there had been physical evidence found at the scene.

Near where a broken lipstick container and compact case had been discovered, a battered and badly tarnished Whitehorn High School class ring had been found. Of course, it had been impossible to trace the lipstick and compact, but the class ring had revealed a great deal. Engraved on the inside of the ring were the letters *E.W.*, and after meticulous probing through school archives and a careful process of elimination, that had led him directly to Ethan Walker.

But while the ring was damning, it hadn't been enough for an arrest. Still, it had placed Walker at the top of the list of suspects. A hotheaded teenager at the time of Avery's disappearance, Walker had been known for his explosive nature and the two men had a history. Avery had accused the Walkers more than once of rustling cattle from the Kincaid ranch and that had enraged Ethan. Rafe had interviewed a dozen or so witnesses who remembered seeing the two men arguing violently in the weeks before Avery's disappearance.

But it had only been after private investigator Nick Dean, whom Charlie's daughter Melissa had hired to investigate her father's death, helped trace the explosive used to bomb Dean's car to a lot purchased by Walker, that Rafe had the proof he'd needed. Ethan Walker was their killer.

And now, twenty-seven years after his death, Charlie Avery was about to exact his revenge. Ethan Walker was on trial for his life and the only thing that stood between him and the gallows was Raeanne Martin.

Rafe's thoughts turned again to Raeanne. She was a public defender now, but that hardly surprised him. She'd been defending the underdog since they were both in Mrs. Whitney's fourth-grade class. Only he'd been her underdog back then—the poor Wolf Boy all the kids feared and teased and ran away from. But Raeanne had never been afraid, had never feared Wolf Boy as the others did.

She had stuck up for him, had fiercely defended him against the others when they'd teased and taunted.

Now she would do the same for Walker. She would plead his case before the jury, make an ardent and impassioned argument before the court. Only this time Rafe was determined to see that argument fail. For as far as he was concerned, Ethan Walker was a murderer and he was going to hang.

Rafe made his way down the center aisle of the courtroom. He thought again of the quirky twist of fate that had brought him to this point. Solving the Avery case and delivering Ethan Walker to justice after nearly thirty years had been quite a coup for him. But victory never seemed to come without a price and his was going to be a big one. Seeing Raeanne in court every day wasn't going to be easy. It would mean being on a collision course with the past—a past he'd worked to forget.

"Well, here goes nothing."

Startled, Rafe looked up. Resting in a heavy wooden chair at one of the two counsel tables at the front of the courtroom sat Blue Lake County's district attorney, Harlan Collins.

"Nothing?" Rafe asked skeptically. He walked through the narrow gate in the railing that separated counsel from the spectators and took a chair beside the lawyer. "Don't you mean here goes something?"

"Actually, what I mean is here goes *everything*." Harlan took a deep breath and shook his head solemnly. "I tell you, I think my butterflies have butterflies."

Rafe smiled, the almost reluctant movement breaking the rigid line of his jaw. The two men had worked closely together in the past few months—Rafe as chief investigator and Harlan as chief prosecutor—and Rafe had come to have a grudging respect for the portly prosecutor. Rafe found his courtly, easygoing manner refreshing and had soon learned it masked a quick wit and a razor-sharp mind. But Harlan looked anything but easygoing this morning and that only made Rafe's smile widen.

"Now, don't tell me you're nervous," he said, nodding toward the stack of files piled on the table in front of them. "You look like you came armed for bear."

"Oh, I'm quite prepared," Harlan assured him, making a face. "But you never quite get over the jitters." Glancing back, he motioned toward the line of people filtering into the seats behind them. "And I could have done without the crowd. Nothing like having the entire community in attendance to watch you fall on your face."

"Well, you knew this would have them coming out of the woodwork," Rafe pointed out. "Let's face it, you can't solve a case that's kept tongues wagging around here for nearly thirty years without people being a little curious."

"I know, I know," Harlan conceded. "But did the whole damn town have to show up? The mayor's here, for God's sake and practically the entire city council. I saw you talking to Mary Jo Kincaid. She didn't even live in White-horn when Charlie Avery disappeared. What possible interest could she have in this case?"

Rafe looked back through the crowd to see Mary Jo, sitting in one of the middle rows, just behind the victim's family. He acknowledged her smile and wave with a slight nod of his head. Still waters, he thought, remembering her curiosity. "I don't know. Maybe she wants to write a book or something, or—" He stopped and turned back to Harlan, seeing the tension in his face and smiling again.

"Or maybe she's just got a thing for prosecutors…*old* prosecutors."

"I think the word you're looking for is *mature*." Harlan gave his bushy gray mustache an indignant twist. "And you're not helping."

"Sorry," Rafe said with a laugh, swinging around in his chair to face the front of the courtroom.

He checked his watch, feeling the muscles in his stomach tighten. He was dealing with his own butterflies, but they had nothing to do with the crowd. The mob in the courtroom didn't bother him. There was only one person whose presence was going to give him a problem. But that was something he'd have to deal with on his own. For when it came to his feelings for Raeanne, Rafe shared them with no one—not even her.

He glanced back through the crowd, toward the heavy wooden doors that hung open, allowing the throng of people and reporters to flow in and out of the courtroom. Like it or not, she would be walking through them any moment now and he would have to find a way to deal with it.

Taking a deep breath, he marshaled his emotions, concealing them well beneath the surface, in that secret spot where no one would ever think to look. He was good at hiding what he felt, at burying his feelings. God knew he'd had enough practice. He'd been doing it his whole life. Everyone in Whitehorn knew Wolf Boy was hard, Wolf Boy was tough and Wolf Boy didn't give a damn about anyone or anything. How he wished that was true.

The problem was, he did feel—more than he wanted, more than he should—but he never would allow it to show. If it bothered him now to see Raeanne, no one would ever know. He would tuck his feelings away, assemble them behind the rigid facade, confident that there they would never betray him. For in what seemed like a lifetime of loving her, he knew, she'd never suspected how he felt—and she never would.

Raeanne stared down at the swirling water in the bowl. She concentrated on moving air in and out of her lungs and forced herself not to think about the rolling and pitching in her stomach.

She let go of her death grip on the wall of the stall long enough to check the time on her wristwatch. Wonderful. She was off to a great start. Court was about to convene and if she didn't get in there soon, she was going to start the trial by being held in contempt.

Gingerly she stood up straight, rubbing her moist palms on the thin, smooth wool of her suit coat. She would be okay now, she told herself calmly. The rolling in her stomach had stopped and the queasiness had passed. She was ready to go in there, ready to get down to business, ready to—

Just then, another wave of nausea rocked her. With deep gasps, she began breathing in earnest, no longer concerned about being late. The way she felt at the moment, she would rather risk jail on contempt charges than walk into open court and lose what little was left of her breakfast.

In, out, in, out, she breathed. *In with the good air, out with the bad,* she chanted silently. In, out, in, out.

Gradually she began to feel better and she stepped out of the bathroom stall. Walking to the row of sinks that lined the opposite wall, she dampened a paper towel and cooled her forehead and cheeks. Glancing up, she stared at herself in the mirror.

The harsh fluorescent light showed every blemish,

every flaw and she wished now that she'd never looked. Her eyes looked sunken and hollow and her long, dark hair was disorderly. She should have worn it in a bun— anything to make her feel more professional and as though she might actually know what she was doing.

But of course Raeanne Martin did know what she was doing. If there was one thing she was sure of, it was her abilities in the courtroom. She would be fine once the proceedings had begun. Still, this was her first trial since she'd moved back to Whitehorn and it didn't help that the whole town had shown up to watch.

Picking up her heavy briefcase, she started for the door. In four years with the public defender's office in Los Angeles, she'd tried enough cases to have earned her spurs as a trial lawyer. She'd learned early in her career that nerves were healthy. They kept you on your toes, kept you sharp, alert. But the trial and the hometown crowd, were only part of the reasons for her nerves this morning.

Rafe Rawlings was going to be sitting in the courtroom today and the thought of his stern, dark eyes watching her every move made the blood run cold in her veins. She didn't particularly care what the town thought of her performance as a lawyer, but Rafe... What Rafe Rawlings thought of her mattered very much.

Raeanne would never forget the first time she'd seen Rafe Rawlings. He'd walked into Mrs. Whitney's fourth-grade classroom and every kid in the room had begun to whisper and titter. Well, every kid except one. She'd been unable to do anything but stare.

There wasn't anyone in Whitehorn who hadn't heard the tales of Emma Rawlings and her "wolf boy." Everyone knew the stories of how Rafe had been left in the woods as an infant, how he'd been raised by wolves, rescued from a wolf's den and adopted by the widow Rawlings.

Of course, the fact that those stories weren't true had done little to stop them from spreading. Rafe had indeed been found as an infant, abandoned in the woods beyond what used to be the old Baxter ranch, but there had been no wolves and no dramatic rescue from a wolf's den. He'd been affectionately nicknamed "Wolf Boy" by a rescue worker and because of that and his later fondness for the dogs he raised, the nickname had stuck, fueling rumors and spreading outlandish tales.

But Raeanne had never believed any of those stories. She'd hated it when the other kids teased and taunted him. It had broken her heart when they called him names and treated him like a freak with no feelings, no emotions. Raeanne had seen the look in his eyes and had felt his pain. She knew he had feelings and she knew he could be hurt. More than once she had seen the way he used that tough exterior to protect himself from being hurt and even as a child it had struck at something very deep in her. She'd wanted to shield and protect him, to take his pain away.

As the years passed and they moved from elementary to high school, the teasing of their classmates had turned into a begrudging respect for Rafe. Raeanne couldn't remember exactly when it had happened, but she'd found her own feelings for Rafe had changed, as well. The Wolf Boy legends might be untrue, but there was something feral and untamed about him. More than once, his dark, brooding image had filled her adolescent dreams. She'd imagined the most romantic of scenes with him—him holding her, touching her, kissing her.

But Rafe had never wanted her. Through the rest of

their school years together, he'd remained politely distant. And yet, try as she might, she'd never quite been able to get him out of her head. Even on the day she became Andy's wife, it had been Rafe who had filled her dreams.

Andy. Over seven years had passed since that awful night, since the night he'd been found floating facedown in that pool. Andy had died as he'd lived—rashly and carelessly. Drowned during one of his long nights of partying—dying as much from his unhappiness as from the water that filled his lungs.

Andy had lived the American dream—and the American tragedy. He'd been the high school football star, every girl's dream date, big man on campus. But the transition to real life had been difficult for him. After their wedding, he'd missed the limelight, the cheers from the crowd, the adoration of his peers. He'd begun drinking, hoping to find solace in the bottle and in the arms of other women. But it had done no good. Nothing he did could bring it back.

But that was ancient history now. Their brief, turbulent marriage was over and she wanted to put all those painful memories behind her.

She stood at the doors of the packed courtroom, catching sight of Rafe's dark, shaggy mane through the crowd. Why had she come back to Whitehorn? Why had she given up a job she loved, a life she'd created for herself, to take a giant step into the past? Had it been because she wanted a change, as she'd told all her friends? Or had it been her inability to forget about Rafe?

Taking a deep breath, she squared her shoulders and started down the center aisle toward the defense table. She had a job to do and dredging up old memories wasn't part of it. Ethan Walker was innocent of the charge of murder and it was about time she made the community of White-horn understand that.

"Any luck on finding…what's his name?" Harlan flipped through several pages in the open file in front of him. "Uh, where is it? Here. O'Brien?"

"Rusty O'Brien." Rafe shook his head. "We're working on it, but don't hold your breath. You know these cowboys—they drift from one place to the next. And it's been almost thirty years. Once he left the Kincaid ranch, there's no telling where he wandered."

"Are we even sure he's still alive?" Harlan asked.

"Fairly sure. At least he was up until a few years ago. He was arrested up in Wolf Point on a DUI. The sheriff there seems to think he might still be working some spreads up in that area—he was going to check it out for us. But like I said, don't hold your breath."

"Well, it's a long shot, but I still wouldn't mind talking to him." Harlan sighed, flipping the file closed. "He's the only one who worked with Avery that we haven't inter-viewed. You know how I hate loose ends." He tapped the table with the file. "Especially when the defense counsel is known for throwing curves from time to time."

Rafe sat up. "She is?"

Harlan smiled, tweaking the end of his mustache. "I called the D.A. in L.A.—you know, to see what he thought of her."

"And?"

Harlan chuckled. "He told me to watch my back. Told me she can melt you with those sexy legs of hers, but to watch her in the clinches." Harlan leaned back in his chair and his smile broadened. "Of course, a stab in the back just might be worth it. Hey." He sat up again. "You know her, don't you? I mean, didn't she marry a friend of yours or something?"

"Yeah." Rafe shifted his weight uncomfortably in the chair. "Andy Peyton."

"That's right." Harlan nodded, remembering. "Played football."

"Wide receiver."

"I remember now. Died a while back."

"About seven years ago," Rafe explained, remembering it as if it had happened yesterday. "Drowned in a swimming pool. I was still in a patrol car, was one of the first on the scene."

"Tough break," Harlan said, shaking his head. "So tell me, what's she like—Raeanne, I mean?"

"I don't know." Rafe shrugged, uncomfortable with the question. "You've talked to her. You know."

"Just a few times during jury selection and just about the case," Harlan pointed out. "What's she really like?"

Rafe ran a hand through his black hair, trying to think of something to say. How did he describe a woman who could get under your skin and stay there? Masking his discomfort as easily as he could mask his emotions, he turned to Harlan and shrugged nonchalantly. "Your usual women's-lib type—the young urban professional who's moved back to the country because it's now considered chic."

Harlan's eyebrows arched with surprise at his rather caustic description. "I thought I'd heard you two were friends, that you liked her?"

"I like her as well as I like any bleeding heart who takes home lost puppies, feeds stray cats and constantly roots for the underdog," he said simply, making the lie sound so believable.

"Well, she's got a real underdog this time," Harlan said, reaching for the file in front of him again. "But he's one lucky underdog."

Rafe looked at Harlan and made a face. "Lucky? I wouldn't exactly call the guy lucky."

"No? Then what would you call it?" Harlan asked. "The son of a bitch very nearly gets away with murder. Then, when he's finally caught, he claims he's innocent, that he's being framed and refuses to hire a lawyer. Says he can defend himself against 'trumped-up charges.' Puts *me* in the position of having to request the court appoint him a lawyer so the damn case doesn't get tossed back from the appellate court for retrial because he was denied adequate counsel." Harlan tossed the file back down and smiled, shaking his head. "Not only am I busting my hump to put the guy away, but as a taxpayer, I'm picking up the tab for the bastard's defense." He laughed loudly, giving Rafe a wink. "God, I love the American judicial system."

Rafe found nothing amusing about the situation and he glared at Harlan, disgusted. "Lawyers. You're all weird."

"Then what does that make cops?"

The sound of her voice behind him brought Rafe up short. Turning around, he came slowly to his feet. "Raeanne."

"Hi, Rafe," she said, smiling broadly and hoping like hell he didn't notice the quivering of her lip.

"Ah, my learned colleague," Harlan said, coming to his feet and graciously extending a hand.

"Mr. Collins," Raeanne said, slipping her slender hand into his soft, chubby one. "I don't suppose you've come to your senses and decided to forget all this nonsense?"

"What? And disappoint these good folks who've come here to see their local officials in action?" Harlan asked, gesturing grandly toward the spectators.

"Harlan, Harlan." Raeanne smiled. "I heard you were quite a showman."

"I was afraid you'd decided to throw in the towel," Harlan said, checking his watch. "Cutting it a little close to the wire, aren't we?"

"Not really," she said breezily, pushing aside thoughts of her queasy stomach. "I like making an entrance. Besides, I wouldn't miss an opportunity to see the legendary Harlan Collins in action."

"Legendary? My, my, I must say I like that. And flattery will, by the way, get you everywhere with me, my dear." Harlan beamed. "But from what I hear from my friends in Los Angeles, this old dog just might learn a few tricks from you."

"I'll see what I can do," Raeanne laughed. Turning back to Rafe, she said, "I ran into Emma the other day. She looks great, seemed as busy as ever."

Rafe smiled, thinking of the woman who had taken him in as an infant and raised him as her own. "Mom's too ornery to slow down. She must have been surprised to see you. I don't think she'd heard you moved back."

"No, she hadn't," Raeanne said, her smile faltering just a little. Apparently he'd found the news so unimportant he'd failed to mention it to his mother. Looking quickly away, she turned to Harlan again, reaching into her briefcase and extracting a sheet of paper. "I thought you might like a list of the witnesses I intend to call and their order— just so you can be ready."

"Well, yes, that would be nice," Harlan said, impressed

by the courtesy. He quickly scanned the names. "I see your client's name is missing."

Raeanne was aware of Rafe's dark gaze on her and she felt heat rise in her cheeks. "That's right."

"So I take it you don't intend to have him testify?" Harlan seemed to be deliberately keeping the tone of the conversation light, even though the business between them was anything but.

Being a good game player herself, Raeanne smiled with a confidence that was completely without foundation. "We haven't decided on that yet."

"I see," Harlan said, one gray, bushy brow arching with interest.

Just then a bailiff appeared, escorting Ethan Walker to the counsel table. The judge wouldn't be far behind.

"Ah…" Harlan smiled, rubbing his hands together. "We're about to begin. Good luck, my dear. You're going to need it."

"Oh, I never rely on luck, Harlan," Raeanne said with a sly smile. "Just reasonable doubt." She looked up at Rafe and winked. "Keep an eye on him. I don't think we can trust him."

"All rise," the court bailiff called. "Hear ye, hear ye. The county court of Blue Lake, in the state of Montana, is now is session. The Honorable Clarence P. Matthews presiding."

As the proceedings began and the formal charges were read, Rafe settled back into his chair. A mixture of emotions churned inside him, but it was anger that gained control. He was angry that she could still get to him, that she could still stir him up, unsettle him. He was used to being in control, but when it came to Raeanne Martin, he seemed to have none.

He watched her as she worked, as she addressed the jury, talked with her client, leafed through her notes. She was capable, confident and thoroughly at home in the courtroom, which only served to infuriate him even more. After Andy's death, she'd leaned on him, depended on him, *needed* him and for a while he'd thought he might have a chance. But he'd been a fool. She didn't need him, she didn't need anyone. To her, he would forever be one of her strays, one of her underdogs, one of her charity cases.

Rafe closed his eyes. Why couldn't she just have stayed away? Why had she returned and brought all the old memories to the surface again? She was part of his past, part of a fantasy he'd held on to for too long. He no longer had room in his life for dreams. He lived in the real world and in the real world the past was dead. Maybe he would always be curious about her because she was the one who'd gotten away, the one he'd never had. But the reality was, she would always be Andy's wife—Andy's widow.

He opened his eyes just then to find her looking at him from across the courtroom. A sudden surge of emotion swelled in his heart. Why was it so hard for him to let go?

Two

"Just promise me you'll think about it."

"There's nothing to think about," Ethan insisted. "I told you, you're barking up the wrong tree."

Raeanne dropped her head, feeling the dull throbbing at her temples spread to her nape. The first day of a trial was never easy, but this one had been exceptionally difficult. She just wanted to go home and crawl into bed, pull the covers over her head and never get up.

The judge hadn't done her any favors today. His rulings had been swift, harsh and usually in favor of the prosecution. And despite Harlan Collins's impeccable charm and easygoing style, he was as tough as they came. She'd had to be on guard constantly. Add to that the fact that there hadn't been a moment today when she wasn't aware of Rafe watching her with that cold, dark gaze of his and it was a miracle she'd been able to concentrate at all.

She closed her eyes, willing the pounding in her head

to go away. At least she could be grateful that he'd left immediately after court was adjourned for the day. She just wasn't up to another awkward meeting with him.

The courtroom was nearly empty now, except for the clerk, the bailiff and a few lagging spectators. The deputies from the jail would be in any moment now to put the shackles on Ethan again and escort him from the courtroom to his cell for the night and that wasn't nearly enough time for her to get through to him.

Turning her head, she stretched the tight muscles of her neck and shoulders. Between Rafe Rawlings's watchful stare and Ethan's stubbornness, this was turning out to be one hell of a day.

"Okay, look," she said finally, with a long, tired sigh. "I'll come by the jail later. Get some rest and have something to eat. We can talk about this then."

Ethan Walker's strong, etched features cracked a half smile and his dark eyes narrowed. "First they frame me with these phony charges, then they send me a lawyer who's still wet behind the ears and thinks she can tell me what to do. You know, little girl, I was making my own decisions while you were still messing in your drawers." Seeing two marshals step into the courtroom from a side door, he rose slowly to his feet. "And I've decided we're not going to talk about this again. The subject is closed."

Raeanne said nothing, waiting instead while the officers slipped the shackles on his wrists and ankles. But once that was done, she rose to her feet. Stepping close, she looked up into Ethan's rugged face. She understood why people called him stubborn—stubborn, tough and unreasonable. He could be all those things. But there was a decency behind those lean, hard features and a kindness he couldn't quite keep from showing through. She'd let him push her, but only so far. She wasn't about to let herself be backed into a corner. He wasn't the first difficult client she'd had and no doubt he wouldn't be the last. She'd tolerated his obstinate pigheadedness during the pretrial stage, but they were in trial now and all bets were off. This was serious business and it was time he understood that.

"I'm going to say this only once," she said in a low voice, "so I want you to listen. This is a courtroom, not a cattle ranch. You're in *my* territory now and until this trial is over, *I'm* the one calling the shots. We talk about what I say we talk about. Is that clear?" Ethan's eyes widened in surprise, but she didn't give him time to respond. "You're a smart man, Ethan. Be smart enough to let me do my job. It's going to take more than you saying you're innocent to convince those twelve people on the jury—a lot more. And like it or not—" she reached down and began stacking her files together "—I'm the best chance you've got to do it."

Ethan stared down at her for a moment, his blue eyes narrowing. "Sunflower seeds."

Raeanne blinked, staring up at him in surprise. "I beg your pardon?"

"I want sunflower seeds. Roasted, with lots of salt. Bring some with you tonight."

Raeanne smiled. It wasn't exactly a promise to fully cooperate, but from Ethan Walker, it was as close as she was going to come. "See you later."

She watched as the deputies led him out, the shackles restricting his movements and causing him to shuffle rather than walk. He was full of anger and she had the uneasy feeling he was hiding something from her. And she was sure a jury would see it as well. Like it or not, angry people with secrets looked guilty. Of course, she understood that as an innocent man Ethan had every right to be upset and angry at having been accused of a crime he hadn't committed. But anger could be a powerful motivator in people, oftentimes making perfectly sensible people do pretty despicable things. Killing someone in a fit of anger wasn't exactly a rare occurrence in homicide cases and the prosecution would have plenty of witnesses to testify to Ethan's short temper and angry outbursts.

She tried her best to stuff the last of her files into one of the two already crammed accordion satchels she'd brought with her. She wished she could pack away her thoughts about the trial as easily. They were troubled and they weighed heavily on her mind. Ethan's short temper was one reason she hadn't been able to decide whether she wanted him to testify or not.

She thought of seeing him at the jail this evening, imagined their conversation and began plotting her strategy. Ethan had already made up his mind about testifying—he simply wasn't going to do it! As far as he was concerned, it was up to the prosecution to prove his *guilt*, not up to him to prove his *innocence*. And Raeanne had to admit that, given his pigheaded way of thinking, that made sense. But too many times she had seen juries interpret a defendant's decision not to testify as a silent admission of guilt.

So what did she do—put Ethan on the stand and run the risk of an angry outburst during cross-examination, or let him have his way and not testify and let the jury think what they would?

The throbbing in her head increased a degree and the

empty feeling in her stomach reminded her just how long it had been since she'd eaten—and managed to keep anything down. Wondering what the Tuesday-night special at the Hip Hop Café was, she began gathering up her things—coat, briefcase, purse, satchels, notes, pens, et cetera, et cetera, et cetera. Good Lord, she thought as she juggled the armload of supplies, how was she ever going to get all this stuff back to her office?

Rafe watched as long as he could. When he first stepped from the clerk's office and saw Raeanne walking toward the elevators just ahead of him, his impulse had been to duck inside the office and wait until she was gone. After the long day in court, the last thing he'd wanted was time alone with her. But watching her struggle with the huge armload of files seemed so callous.

Without his consciously being aware of it, his pace quickened and he began to catch up with her. They lived in a small town, he reminded himself again as he saw one of the stuffed satchels she balanced start to slip. They were bound to run into each other from time to time. Sooner or later he would have to deal with it.

"Oh, no," Raeanne groaned, feeling the load in her arms begin to list dangerously. Completely helpless, she felt a satchel start to fall.

"Got it."

Raeanne turned just as Rafe reached around from behind to catch the heavy packet before it hit the floor.

"Oh, thank you…" She let the words out in one long breath, pushing an errant strand of hair out of her face.

"Let me help you with those," he said, tucking the satchel under his arm and reaching for the other.

She watched in a sort of trance as he relieved her of her burden, too tired to even try to stop him. She marveled at her luck—or rather her lack of it. This really wasn't her day. She was exhausted and she had about a million things to do before she could go home and get some rest. The very last thing she needed right now was to be alone with Rafe Rawlings.

"I don't even want to think how long it would have taken me to sort all this out if it had fallen," she said, struggling to keep her tone light. "I guess I should have made two trips, but I was just so tired."

"It's been a long day," he commented quietly, trying to pretend he didn't see the exhausted look in her eyes. She seemed so small standing there, so vulnerable, as if she might need someone to lean on, someone to help. Bending down, he pressed the call button for the elevator. "Headed for the parking lot?"

"The office," she told him with a small shake of the head. "I've got some things I want to go over before I see Ethan at the jail tonight."

Rafe nodded, reminding himself to stay away from the jail tonight. He purposefully directed his attention away from her, concentrating on keeping his eyes glued to the closed elevator doors. But he didn't need to see her to react to her presence. He could feel her standing beside him.

Only a few hours ago she'd had him on the witness stand, grilling him on the evidence he'd found at the scene, on the details of his investigation and the methods they'd followed to trace the explosive used to blow up Nick Dean's car to Ethan Walker. It hadn't been easy to sit there and answer her questions, to have her meticulously pick apart everything he said. She'd watched him with such cool skepticism, such controlled reserve, he'd felt like a bug under a microscope.

The corridor grew quiet as they waited, the silence stretching out around them like a thick, ominous fog. Rafe could hear her soft breathing beside him and he swore violently under his breath. Was that damn elevator ever coming? All he wanted was to get downstairs and away from her as fast as he could.

"Sounds like you've got a long night ahead of you," he said suddenly, no longer able to stand the quiet.

Raeanne nearly jumped at the sound of his voice. "It seems like they've all been long lately."

"Yeah," he said, giving her a brief glance before quickly shifting his gaze back to the doors again. "I know the feeling."

For one horrifying moment, he thought they would lapse into silence again. However, as his mind scrambled for something else to say, the elevator finally arrived. With a quiet sigh of relief, he stepped to one side to allow her to pass, then followed her inside.

Raeanne stepped reluctantly into the elevator. She wasn't entirely sure how much more of this strain she could take. It had been awkward and difficult to cross-examine him earlier, but as bad as that had been, it had been better than this. What was the matter with her? Where was her self-confidence, where was her self-assurance? She felt so awkward, so stupid and her mind had suddenly become completely devoid of anything to say. If nothing else, Rafe had always been her friend and they'd always been able to talk—at least about superficial things. Had they changed so much that a simple conversation was now impossible, or had fatigue dulled all her senses?

Like the corridor, the elevator was deserted and Rafe

silently pushed the button on the control panel for the lobby. He couldn't help noticing how even under the harsh overhead lighting her skin looked flawless and perfect and that only served to make him more uncomfortable. Clearing his throat loudly, he turned to her, about to speak, only to realize she was about to say something herself.

Raeanne laughed nervously when they both started to speak at the same time. "Oh, I'm sorry."

"That's all right," Rafe assured her, surprised to realize he was actually smiling. "Go ahead."

"No, that's okay. It wasn't important," she insisted, thinking anything was more important than the inane question she'd been about to ask concerning the weather. "What were you going to say?"

He shrugged. "Nothing really. I just wondered if you didn't find Whitehorn a little dull after the big city."

Raeanne laughed, motioning with her chin toward the files he held for her. "I haven't had a lot of time to get bored." She paused for a moment and when she spoke again her voice was reflective. "The cold was a little hard to get used to again, but it's funny, you know? Now that I'm back, it's as though nothing's changed. I almost feel like I'd never left."

Except now she didn't have a husband, he thought darkly. Now she was strong and independent, with a promising career and life of her own. Her future was bright and needed nothing from a Wolf Boy with no past. "So you plan to stay for a while?"

The elevator stopped at a lower floor to allow several more people to board, but Raeanne hardly even noticed them. She was looking up into his dark eyes, thinking of all the times she'd seen them in her dreams. "It's home. My friends are here, my family."

"And Andy's family," he said.

Raeanne smiled sadly, thinking of the modest, unassuming couple, who had quietly gone to pieces at the loss of their only son and of the guilt she felt whenever she visited them. "Yes, and Andy's family." She shook her head, dispelling the unpleasant memories. "Emma tells me she's hired a ranch hand?"

"Yeah." Rafe smiled, shaking his head. "And it was like pulling teeth. But the place was getting too much for her to handle alone and I don't really have the time to help out like I used to." He rolled his eyes. "But you know her, always wants to handle everything herself. She wasn't easy to convince."

Raeanne laughed. "I can imagine. How about Call?" she asked, remembering the giant shepherd-mix hound that had been the latest in his long succession of dogs. "Do you still have him?"

Rafe shook his head. "No, Call died about a year ago."

"Oh, no," she said, looking up at him. For a moment she'd thought she saw something in his cold, black eyes—a flicker of emotion, a flash of regret—but it had been so quick, so brief she could have been mistaken. "I'm sorry."

Rafe shrugged. "He was old. He'd led a good life. I have his daughter, though. Crier. She's expecting her first litter."

"Oh, that's exciting," Raeanne said, nodding. Call, now Crier. She thought of the names of his dogs over the years—Whisper, No Place, Lone Boy, Bad Girl. Had she ever noticed what sad names those were before? Or what questionable mongrels all his dogs had been?

"I see your dad down at the drugstore from time to time," Rafe continued, scattering her thoughts. "I suppose your folks were glad to have you back. Especially with the holidays coming and everything."

Raeanne drew in a deep breath. She'd put her parents through a lot. It had been difficult for them to stand on the sidelines and watch her marriage crumble. They'd worried about Andy's drinking and about his abusive behavior, but they'd never interfered, never pressured or pushed her. They'd just been there for her when she needed them. She let out the breath in one long, slow sigh. "Yeah, it's been nice. I've missed Montana Christmases, too. Oh, say! Do you know who I ran into the other day?"

The elevator stopped again to allow several passengers off and a number of others to enter, but Rafe and Raeanne barely took notice. They automatically stepped closer as the elevator became crowded, deep in conversation about old friends and the latest gossip. When the doors quietly opened at the lobby, they followed the crowd out, crossing over the gleaming golden Blue Lake County seal embedded in the courthouse's shiny marble floor. At the doors, Raeanne peered outside and slipped into her coat.

"Brrr...look at it out there." She shivered, pointing to the tan corduroy sport coat Rafe wore over his blue chambray shirt and striped tie. "Don't you have a coat? You're going to freeze out there." She reached for the files he held. "Let me take those now."

"I'm okay," he insisted, shrugging off her concern and pushing open the door. "I'll walk them over for you."

He didn't realize until he'd stepped to one side to allow her to pass him that he'd let a perfectly good opportunity to get away slip through his fingers. Five minutes ago, all he could think about had been getting as far away from her as he could, but now…well, now he didn't want to think about what had him changing his mind.

"Oh, I forgot," she was saying, pulling her coat around her tight. "You big, tough Montana cowboys are immune to the cold, right?"

"You call this cold?" His breath created a long white plume as he spoke. "Hell, lady, this is practically spring." He paused, then made a face. "But do you think we could walk just a little faster?"

"Cowboys," she said with a smile, hurrying down the steps after him.

They dashed along the street, rushing over the wet pavement and carefully stepping through the dirty mounds of snow left behind by the snowplows. The public defender's office was housed in a crowded corner of the second floor of Blue Lake County's administration building. Depositing Raeanne's files on her desk, Rafe gazed around her tiny cubicle.

"I don't think I've ever been in the public defender's office before," he said, noting that the photos on her desk were of her nieces and nephews and not her dead husband.

"No? Well, by all means, let me give you the grand tour," she said, gesturing toward her crowded bookcase, tiny window and cluttered desk. "Does the county know how to lavish comforts on its hardworking public defenders, or what? I hope you're impressed."

His dark eyes shifted, gazing at her from across the small office. "I am."

The look in his eyes had heat rising in her cheeks. "Oh, right." She quickly looked away. "I know what cops think of lawyers."

"What?" Rafe smiled, feigning innocence. "I don't know what you mean."

"Oh, I think you do," she said, her dark brown eyes narrowing.

His smile broadened. He'd forgotten how much he'd enjoyed her wit and her sense of humor. It had been so awkward and difficult between them at first, standing in the corridor waiting for the elevator. He'd thought that maybe there had been too many changes in the past seven years for them to ever be able to talk again. But it seemed that once they broke the ice, once they got over those first few clumsy moments, all the old feelings had come back— maybe too many of them.

He picked up a heavy law book from her shelf and began flipping through the pages. "You know, he'd be proud of you—Andy, I mean. All that you've accomplished."

The smile faded slowly from Raeanne's face. Andy hadn't exactly encouraged her interest in the law. She remembered too many times, when he'd been drinking, that he'd mocked and ridiculed her career goals. She closed her eyes against a familiar surge of guilt. "Do you think so?"

"Of course." He sensed her discomfort immediately. Was talking about Andy still too painful for her? He returned the book to the shelf and sat down in one of the chairs facing the desk. "You doubt it?"

She shrugged, slipping into her chair. "I don't know. Andy never thought much of women having careers," she said, remembering all too well his drunken cracks about women and keeping them in their "place"—a view she'd come to believe came from his insecurities about a woman being strong and successful. "I think he would rather have had me just stay home and raise kids."

Rafe showed no sign of the rush of emotion that swelled in his chest. He picked up a paperweight and began casually tossing it back and forth between his hands. "Maybe that's because it's what he thought he could give you."

Raeanne met his cool gaze from across the desk. "But what about what I could have given him?"

The sudden warble of the telephone cut the silence, sounding unusually loud and harsh in the small office. With a brief, confused shake of the head, Raeanne picked up the receiver. She listened intently, picking up a pencil and jotting down a few notes.

"Well, thanks for trying, Wes," she said, a frown causing the lines between her brows to deepen.

"Trouble?" Rafe asked after a moment.

Raeanne leaned back in her chair and tossed her pencil on the desk. "When is it ever anything else?"

"Wes Simon?" he asked, recognizing the name of the public defender's chief investigator.

"Yeah," she sighed, sitting back up. "I'd hoped he could get Nan Avery to agree to an interview with me, but she's not being very cooperative."

"What? Charlie's wife?" he said with a surprised laugh, abruptly catching the paperweight and putting it back on the desk.

"Yeah. What's wrong with that?" she asked, a little too defensively.

"Nothing, I suppose." He shrugged, picking up on the tension in her voice. "A little insensitive, maybe."

"Insensitive?" she repeated, offended now. "How do you figure?"

He looked at her and shook his head. "You're Ethan Walker's lawyer. Can you blame her for not wanting to talk to you?"

"No, of course not." She found his cynical, combative tone thoroughly annoying. "But I think she could at least understand why I'd be interested in talking to her."

"Frankly, if I was Nan Avery, I'd tell you to take a flying leap."

She gave him a cool look. "Well, I don't doubt that you would," she said, irritated by his flippancy. "But I'm hoping Nan Avery is more interested in getting to the truth than you apparently seem to be." She paused for a moment, challenging him with a look. "If she's got nothing to hide, she's got nothing to be afraid of."

"That's stupid," he said, hating that cool courtroom manner of hers. "Your client murdered her husband. You honestly expect her to help you?"

Raeanne bristled, coming slowly to her feet. Stupid? No one called her, or the job she did for her clients, stupid. For a moment there, she'd almost thought she had reached him, that he might actually have been impressed by her and by her accomplishments, but now he just sounded like…like a pigheaded cop.

"Would you rather I subpoena her?"

"Lawyers," he snorted, glaring at her from across the desk. "Is going after the victim's family something they teach you in law school, or do you just get some kind of thrill messing with innocent people's lives?"

"Oh, and you're not messing with Ethan Walker's life?"

"Ethan Walker isn't innocent."

"That's bull," she said in a firm, unflagging voice. "There's more to this so-called *feud* between Ethan and

Avery than a class ring and a few sticks of dynamite. And I've got a feeling Nan Avery knows what it is."

"If you're talking about all those old rumors—"

"What I'm talking about, Detective Rawlings—" she picked up the pencil and jabbed it in his direction to emphasize her point "—is that it's been *alleged* that my client killed Charlie Avery and despite what you and the rest of the Whitehorn Police Department seem to think, a person is still innocent until proven guilty—*even* in Blue Lake County."

The emotion in her voice sent an icy finger traveling down Rafe's spine. Raeanne was never better, never more passionate, never more articulate, than when she was defending one of her strays. The same passion she'd once used to defend Rafe from the kids at school, she now used to defend creeps like Walker.

But it had been so different with Andy. She'd never pitied him, never gone running to protect him. She hadn't needed to. She'd looked up to Andy, admired him.

Rafe recognized the familiar gnawing in the pit of his stomach. How many times had he wanted Raeanne to look up to him, to think of him as her hero?

He thought of her skill in the courtroom, how strong and competent she'd appeared and the anger swelled in his chest. For some thoroughly irrational and totally absurd reason, her strength and competence made him furious, made him want to strike out and to hurt. He didn't want to be lumped together with all the rest of her losers and charity cases. He wanted to be someone special in her life and it made him angry and frustrated to know that would never happen.

He came slowly to his feet, bringing his palms down flat

on her desk and leaning across it. "Ethan Walker murdered Charlie Avery," he said in a cold, unemotional voice. "And now he's going to pay for it. And there isn't anything your bleeding heart can to do stop it."

"Oh, no?" she asked through gritted teeth.

"No," he said coolly. "The prosecution's case is airtight, the police investigation is flawless and there are no loopholes, no technicalities, no rabbits you can pull from your hat to change that. So go ahead, give the jury the best argument you can—plead and implore them, paint the prettiest picture you can, it's not going to do any good. Slime is still slime and like it or not, lady, Walker is guilty on this one."

Raeanne leaned forward until they were practically nose to nose. She knew all too well the reputation Rafe had for being intimidating, but she wasn't about to be pushed around. "Stick around, Detective Rawlings. We'll just see about that."

Three

It had been there. Damn it, it had been there. She'd seen it and she'd felt it—at first, anyway. It had been in his eyes, in the tone of his voice and in the way he looked at her. It had been there, she was sure.

Raeanne sat at the small Formica table in the crowded Hip Hop Café sharing a much needed drink and a deliciously greasy meal with four of her female co-workers. Out of the twenty attorneys in Blue Lake County's public defender's office, the five of them represented the entire female population of the office, which made them a close-knit group.

But Raeanne had trouble concentrating on the lively conversation of her friends. It wasn't the raucous atmosphere or the melancholy country tune wailing from the jukebox that had her mind drifting. Actually, the noise and clutter of the Hip Hop were what she'd been in the mood for after the long, tense day she'd had. What had her

troubled and unable to concentrate was Rafe and the
argument they'd had in her office.

After he stormed out, she'd stood at her tiny window
and watched him in the street below. Bracing himself
against the frigid wind, he'd walked down the street, past
the courthouse, toward police headquarters. A hard knot
of emotion had twisted in her stomach as she watched his
tall frame disappear around the corner. It had all happened
so fast. One moment they'd been talking—carefree and
easy, like two old friends—and the next…well, the next it
had been as if they were the bitterest of enemies.

Raeanne closed her eyes, blocking out the ambient
noise and hearing his harsh words in her mind. They had
been cruel, unfeeling words, letting her know in every way
possible how little he thought of her and the work she did.
She knew everyone thought of Rafe as tough and unyield-
ing and that no one else would have been surprised by his
harsh appraisal. But it had always been different between
them—or at least she had thought it was. She'd seen the
compassion beneath that macho exterior of his, seen the
feelings, even though he tried to mask them.

Only there had been no compassion in his cold, dark
eyes today. He'd leaned across her desk and glared at her
as though she were the lowest form of life, as though he
despised her and all that she stood for.

Did he hate her? Did he see her only as the widow of
his best friend?

Raeanne opened her eyes and took another bite of her
hamburger. No, she thought, oblivious of the taste of the
food in her mouth. He didn't hate her. He'd been angry
when he left, they'd been arguing. But before that, it had
been different. Before that, she'd seen *it*.

It. That was how she'd come to think of it—that strange awareness, that mysterious intuition, that puzzling feeling she got whenever they were together. It was something she'd felt as far back as she could remember, something she'd never actually been able to see or explain, but something she was convinced was there. It was just…

If it hadn't been for…*it*…she might have gotten over him long ago, she might have been able to forget and move on. She was too much of a realist to allow schoolgirl dreams to cloud her judgment. Rafe had never shown her any encouragement, never given her any reason to think he had feelings for her. But something had started the wheels in motion, something had encouraged her and spurred her on, something had kept her coming back when there were no visible signs of hope.

She'd felt it—felt something between them from the first, something strong, something special. It was what had kept her coming back, what had made her refuse to give up and it was what she had felt again in her office today.

How many times had she called herself crazy? How many times had she tried to convince herself it was all in her head, a figment of her imagination, something she wanted rather than what was really there? But then she would see him, talk to him and it would start all over again.

She knew Rafe had trouble expressing his feelings. He'd spent a lifetime hiding behind Wolf Boy—a ridiculous front that made him think he was different from others, impervious to human emotions. But she'd never believed that image of him, any more than she did the outlandish stories about him being reared by a pack of wolves. As far as she was concerned, Rafe Rawlings was a man, with all the desires and all the needs of one. He might not be able to express his feeling, but she'd sensed they were there.

And that was why she'd never been able to forget, why his image still haunted her and why she couldn't get him out of her head. It wasn't what Rafe Rawlings said to her, it was what he didn't say. It was the way he looked at her, the tone of his voice, the look in his eyes.

It had been there when they were students at Whitehorn Elementary School, it had been there the night she became Andy Peyton's wife and for a while today in her office it had been there.

Was she just a fool? Were her instincts about him real, or was she just seeing things that weren't really there?

"Are you going to finish those fries?" Karen McGuire asked, giving Raeanne's sleeve a little tug. "I'm still hungry."

"Hmm…what? Fries?" Raeanne stammered, her troubled thoughts scattering. Glancing at her plate, she made a face. She'd been ravenous when the meal came, but now the giant hamburger and country fries looked anything but appetizing. Shaking her head, she shoved the plate toward Karen. "No, help yourself."

"You hardly touched your food," Cinda Cox said accusingly, reaching for her glass of wine. Cinda was the mother hen of the group and worried about each of them. "I thought you said you were hungry."

"I ate enough," Raeanne mumbled, rubbing at her temples. Her headache was back.

"You've been working too hard," Helen Stein said as she reached across the table for a french fry.

"She's right," Cinda agreed. "You get finished with this Walker thing, you should think about taking some time off."

"Oh, right," Raeanne said drolly. "I'm sure that would go over real big with administration. I've been on the job exactly three months and already I want a vacation."

"It's been my experience that nothing goes over very big with administration," Cinda said dryly, draining her glass of wine in one gulp. "But seriously, you should really try and relax a little."

"Relax," Raeanne murmured with a tired smile. "I'm not sure I remember how to do that anymore."

"We all need to do something different. When was the last time we all went anywhere just to have some fun?" Debbie Browning asked, picking a sprig of parsley off her plate and tossing it across the table toward Cinda. "I mean, look at us, will you? It's nearly eight o'clock, none of us has a home life and all we do when we get together is talk shop." She shook her head, disgusted. "It's pathetic."

"What's pathetic is that if we didn't talk shop, we wouldn't have anything to talk about at all," Karen complained. "I mean, when was the last time any of us spent some time with a man?"

There was a collective groan from all of them.

"Well, now, wait a minute," Debbie pointed out thoughtfully. "When you say spend time with a man, exactly what are you referring to?"

"I'm not talking about paying the paperboy," Karen said darkly.

"Or having lunch with your dad," Helen added.

"So we're talking about a *man,* actually over the age of sixteen, who isn't married, or gay and who isn't a client? Is that right?" Debbie asked.

"You mean there are still some of those around?" Helen asked cynically.

"See what I mean?" Karen laughed, leaning back in her chair and crossing her arms over her chest. "We're all pathetic."

"Well, maybe not all of us," Cinda said cryptically, turning a knowing eye on Raeanne. "If I'm not mistaken, one of us had quite a recent exposure."

"What's this?" Karen demanded, perking up.

"Oh, no," Raeanne groaned, narrowing her eyes and glaring at Cinda. She knew what was coming. "I'll get you for this."

"Oh," Cinda went on breezily, unaffected by Raeanne's threat, "just that one of us actually had a man in her office today. You know, for a little private confab?"

"You mean a full-grown heterosexual single male?" Karen gasped.

"In the flesh," Cinda announced proudly. "One of Whitehorn's finest, I might add."

"You don't mean Detective Sergeant Rafe Rawlings, do you?" Karen asked.

"What?" Debbie gasped, turning to Raeanne in surprise. "The infamous Wolf Boy?"

"Don't call him that," Raeanne moaned, realizing she still felt the need to stick up for him. "And he just helped me carry some files over from the courthouse."

"Who cares what the excuse was?" Karen said, pouring them all some more wine. "It worked, didn't it? You were actually alone with Rafe Rawlings. Are you aware that the majority of women in this town would be willing to commit a major felony just to be hauled into jail by that man? So come on, give us all the gory details."

"All the what?" Raeanne said, feeling herself go warm all over. "There are no details. Nothing happened. He's an old friend, that's all. We went to school together. He's Harlan Collins's chief investigator on the Walker case. That's it."

"That's it?" Karen said dubiously. "You sure you two don't have a little *investigating* of your own going on the side?"

"You guys stop this," Raeanne insisted. But, to make matters worse, she felt the color in her cheeks begin to deepen, which only added fuel to their fire.

"Look at her, she's blushing!" Cinda howled, pointing. "There *is* something going on with you two, isn't there?"

"There's nothing going on," Raeanne said.

"Oh, no, nothing…" All four women chimed in together, raising their glasses and clinking them together.

"We're just friends," she insisted.

"Just friends!" her friends hooted, falling back in their chairs.

"That's it," she stated flatly. There was more hooting and laughing and in frustration, Raeanne raised her voice. "That's all there is!"

But by this time, all control had been lost and there was no talking sense. Giving in to fatigue, high spirits and wine, she picked up her glass, toasted her friends and joined in their laughter.

"See, I told you. We're pathetic," Karen cried, wiping the tears from her eyes. "We're hopeless. We can't get a man and Raeanne has one and doesn't even know it."

Just then Debbie spotted Winona Cobbs weaving through the tables toward them. "Oh, look, there's Winona. She'll help us. Let's ask her what she sees for us."

Short, stocky, eccentric Winona, with her Stop 'n' Shop, was something of a fixture around Whitehorn. For the majority of her seventy-odd years, she had lived in her trailer just outside town, collecting and selling her "treasures," which most people just called junk. But Winona's greatest treasure was her gift for palm reading and just about everyone in town had at one time or another had their fortunes told by her. Her predictions were sometimes kooky and most of the time they were offbeat, but there were times when she was eerily correct.

"Hey Winona!" Debbie called, waving her hand. "Over here!"

Winona deftly maneuvered her considerable girth between the crowded tables. Smiling broadly, she pointed to the nearly empty bottle of wine. "My, my, my… Doesn't it look as though the spirits are lively tonight?"

"But, Winona, we need help," Debbie moaned. "Look into your crystal ball and tell us what you see in our futures. We need some men in our lives."

"Lord help them, they want men," Winona lamented, turning her eyes heavenward. "Although God knows what for. They're not good for much. I've never known a man yet that didn't just complicate a woman's life." She shook her head. "No, no, trust me, you're better off without them."

"But, Winona, what about love?" Debbie asked. "What about romance?"

"Romance? You mean five young, modern professionals still want that? I'd hoped all that had gone out of style when we burned our bras," she said teasingly, joining in their high spirits.

"Well, it's making a comeback," Cinda explained. "After all, winter nights in Montana are so cold. Tell me there's someone tall, dark and handsome out there who will help to warm me up."

"Well, okay, but I can't make any promises," she warned. Playing along, Winona squeezed her eyes tight and hummed for a couple of seconds. "Nope," she said, stopping abruptly, a smile tugging at her thin, crinkled lips. "There's nothing. Blank. You're all hopeless."

The women wailed before breaking into laughter.

"Join us for a glass," Cinda said, grabbing the bottle of wine and holding it up to Winona.

"Oh, no, thank you, ladies," she said, raising a hand. "Never touch the stuff." She touched a knowing finger to the side of her nose, winking. "Dulls the senses, if you know what I mean." She glanced down at Raeanne, slipping a familiar arm around her shoulder. "Glad to see you back around these parts again. It's been a long time."

Raeanne's smile faltered a little. She was surprised by Winona's recognition. Driving out to the Stop 'N Swap and having Winona tell your fortune was almost a rite of passage for kids who grew up in Whitehorn and like everyone else, Raeanne had participated in the ritual back in high school. But that had been years ago and she would have hardly expected Winona to remember.

"Well, it's good to be home again," Raeanne mumbled, feeling just a little uneasy.

"Ah, yes, home," Winona said, nodding and bending close. "A happy home. You know, we all look for happiness," she said in a low voice. "But first we need a clear path. Oftentimes we let old conflicts clutter the way and emotional scars sometimes can make us stumble and fall short." Winona straightened up, stretching her creaking joints and sighing heavily. "Yes, we're all looking for happiness. It's really what we want—deep down, I mean. But you have to clear the path first. Resolve the conflicts and clear the path."

She patted Raeanne maternally on the shoulder and waved to the others. "Well, good night, my lovelies."

Raeanne thought about Winona's words long after the diviner had left and the conversation at their table had turned to other things. She knew a lot of people thought Winona Cobbs was little more than a kook, an odd duck who had lived alone for far too long. They saw her "visions" as delusions and her fortune-telling as little more than wishful thinking. But Raeanne had read the reports of the criminal cases Winona had assisted on and the help she'd given the police on those cases couldn't be denied.

But just what vibes had Winona been picking up on tonight? She had talked about old conflicts and emotional scars.

Raeanne thought about Rafe, about the years she'd spent in love with a man who didn't want her and about the way she'd felt the day she realized her marriage to Andy was a mistake. God knew she had her share of past conflicts and emotional scars, but were they blocking her way to happiness?

Raeanne finished the rest of the wine in her glass. Winona had said the path to happiness had to be cleared, but with so many painful memories and so many past mistakes, would her way ever be clear?

Raeanne pulled into the narrow drive and coasted to a stop. It was late and she wasn't sure she had the energy needed to take her out of the car and up the steps into the house.

After the Hip Hop, she'd visited Ethan at the jail and while she felt they'd made some progress, there was still a long way to go. Again and again she had pressed him to explain the hostility between him and Avery, why the two of them had hated each other so much and what it was they had been seen arguing about so many times before Avery disappeared.

Ethan insisted their arguments had been about the cattle-rustling charges Avery had made, but Raeanne was convinced there had to be something more, something Ethan wasn't ready to talk about, something he was hiding. But what it was and why Ethan refused to tell her, she couldn't guess—especially tonight.

With a tired sigh, Raeanne grabbed for her purse and her briefcase and stepped out of the car. She crossed the drive and had just started up the narrow walk toward the porch when she came to an abrupt halt. Standing before her on the sidewalk was a huge black dog, its dark eyes glowering at her and a low growl rumbling from its throat.

"Lobo, don't be a bully."

Raeanne jumped at the sound of Rafe's voice. She looked up, to find him perched on the top step of her porch. "Didn't feel you got in enough licks in my office this afternoon, so you brought your dog by to finish me off?"

"If I'd wanted to do that," he said dryly, coming slowly to his feet, "I'd have brought one of the mean ones. Lobo here is a pussycat."

Pussycat? Raeanne glanced down at the giant dog in front of her, with its strong jaw and powerful build. Somehow she doubted that. Still, with his tail wagging back and forth now, he did look much friendlier and she relaxed a little.

"I take it you're here to see me about something?" she said, slipping her purse over her shoulder. With her hand free, she reached out hesitantly and patted the dog's large, flat head.

"Yeah, but I was just about ready to give up," Rafe said, checking his watch. "Late night tonight."

Lobo nuzzled Raeanne's hand and she scratched behind one thick, pointed ear. "Afraid I'm not giving the taxpayers of Blue Lake County their money's worth?"

Rafe hadn't missed the sarcasm in her voice and he knew he'd had it coming. "I never doubted it for a minute."

Raeanne stepped around Lobo and started up the porch steps. At the top, she stopped and looked up at Rafe. "Then what are you here for?"

"I forgot to tell you something earlier," he said, motioning to Lobo, who had followed Raeanne to the porch. "Something I wanted to say."

Raeanne's shoulders slumped. "Look, Rafe, if you're interested in going another couple of rounds, I'm not in the mood." She walked to her front door and slipped the key into the lock. "If you've got something else to say to me, catch me before court in the morning."

"This won't wait."

She turned back to him slowly and took a deep breath. "I'm really not up for another argument."

"Good," he said, glancing down at the dog. "That'll make this a lot easier."

"Make what a lot easier?"

He lifted his gaze and looked at her. "Apologizing."

Raeanne felt a little tremor rumble through her. An apology? She wasn't sure what she'd expected from him—another argument maybe, more harsh words or accusations, but certainly not an attempt to make amends. "You came here to apologize?"

"I felt lousy about the way we left things earlier."

She looked up at him. Even in the glow of the porch light, his eyes looked dark and searching. "I didn't feel too good about it, either."

"I'm…I'm sorry," he said, stumbling over the words. He took a few steps forward. "Look, I said a lot of stupid things before." Lobo nudged his leg and he reached down and stroked the dog's neck. "Things I guess I didn't really mean."

"Are you saying you've changed your mind about Ethan?"

He laughed. "I said I was sorry, not delusional." The smile faded slowly from his lips. "I guess what I'm trying to say is that I realize we're on separate sides of the fence on this thing. You've got your job to do and I've got mine. It's silly for us to try to argue it out. How about we just leave that for the jury to do." He offered her his hand. "Deal?"

Raeanne could appreciate the point. It was, after all, the right and practical thing to do. They were both adults, both professionals who just happened to be on opposite sides of an issue. It was something that happened all the time in her line of work. To take it personally was not only foolish, it was unreasonable.

Only try as she might to pretend otherwise, this time it was more than just business for her. While she appreciated his showing up on her doorstep, appreciated the apology and his efforts to put things in perspective, she couldn't help feeling a little let down. He wasn't just another business associate to her, he was Rafe Rawlings and anything concerning him she took personally—very personally.

"Yeah, okay," she said in a tight voice, slipping her hand in his. "Deal." She felt uncomfortable holding his hand and withdrew hers awkwardly. "Uh…would you like to come in for a while? Have some coffee?"

What he wanted was to forget about that stupid argument, to forget about Ethan Walker and Charlie Avery, about Andy and the past and sweep her up into his arms. He wanted to mean something to her, something more than just a loner with no past. But that was impossible. What he had to do was learn to see her, be around her and try not to think about those things.

"No thanks," he said, shaking his head. He turned and started down the steps, signaling for Lobo to follow. "Get some rest, Counselor. You've got your work cut out for you."

Raeanne watched as he crossed the snowy lawn to his pickup parked at the curb. He unlocked the door, holding it open for Lobo, who bounded into the cab in one powerful leap. Within moments, they were gone, the taillights of the truck disappearing into the maze of lights and traffic.

She knew she should be pleased that he'd apologized, pleased that he had cared enough to set things straight between them. And yet all she felt was a cold, empty feeling in the pit of her stomach. He'd said some terrible things to her this afternoon—harsh, angry words. And yet, in an odd, crazy sort of way, the apology had been even worse.

At least his anger had been some indication that what she thought mattered to him, that at least he cared enough about her to get angry. But tonight…tonight there had been no emotion in the cool, clipped professional tone he'd used to explain away their conflict, no sign of any caring or concern.

She turned and slowly walked into the house, feeling more defeated than she could ever remember. She hadn't been happy about the argument, but the apology just might make her cry.

Raeanne turned the idea over in her mind as she watched Melissa North help her mother out of the row of seats and into the courtroom's center aisle. She'd been trying for weeks to get Nan Avery to agree to an interview, but Charlie's widow had ignored each inquiry her investigator had made, each politely written request she had mailed. But Raeanne suspected that if she was to walk over to the woman now and personally request an interview, Nan Avery would have a difficult time ignoring that.

An extremely proud woman, Nan Avery had escaped to California years before, leaving behind the humiliation of being a deserted wife. But with Ethan Walker's arrest, she had returned to Whitehorn to watch the trial of the man accused of his murder. Staying at the sprawling ranch of her daughter and son-in-law, Melissa and Wyatt North, she attended the proceedings each day, stoic, proud and faintly bitter.

Raeanne remembered how Rafe had ridiculed her frustration with Nan's refusal to be interviewed by the defense. It had been two weeks since he walked her to her office, since they argued and he'd offered her his apology. She'd seen him almost every day in the courtroom since then and he'd meticulously kept his word. Each day he'd been polite and professional—treating her to the same cool courteousness he did all the other court personnel. She'd told herself dozens of times in the past fourteen days that this was best and yet she couldn't help feeling hurt. They had a history, a past and to be relegated to the same treatment as other acquaintances was not an easy thing for her to accept.

Raeanne watched as Mrs. Avery started down the aisle toward the corridor. Dealing with a victim's family was never something Raeanne looked forward to. Understandably, the families of crime victims always harbored a degree of contempt for the defense team and no matter how polite or how tactful you were, the episodes were often emotional and difficult. Raeanne had come to accept that it was part of her job. Still, she had to admit it wasn't a part she'd come to relish.

It had been a long day in court and a difficult one. Forensic anthropologist Tracy Hensley's testimony had been long and complicated, as she'd explained how the bones were examined, how they were identified as the remains of Charlie Avery and exactly how the cause of death was determined.

The blow to the back of the head that had killed Charlie Avery was a key point in Raeanne's defense plan. She wanted to make it very clear to the jury, through Tracy's testimony, that the trajectory of the fatal blow had been at an angle that would have made it very difficult for someone of Ethan's height to accomplish. With careful skill and despite the prosecution's attempts to stop it, Raeanne was able to inform the jury that it was Tracy's opinion, based on the evidence she'd examined and the angle of the injury, that it would have been difficult for someone of Ethan Walker's height and stature to administer the fatal blow.

Just as she'd expected, Tracy's testimony had a considerable impact in the courtroom and that didn't make the prospect of approaching Nan and the Norths any easier for her. But time was running out. The gloves were off now. She had to find a way to poke as many holes in the prosecution's case as she could, or Ethan wouldn't stand a chance with the jury.

"Excuse me, Mrs. Avery?" Raeanne said politely, catching up with them at the door of the courtroom. "If you have just a moment, I'd appreciate—"

"No, I'm sorry, Miss Martin, I don't have a moment,"

Nan Avery said coolly, cutting her off. "And I would appreciate it if you and the representative from your office would stop harassing me."

Raeanne's gaze darted across to Melissa North and then to her husband, Wyatt. She saw none of the contempt in their faces that was so obvious in Nan's.

"I'm sorry if you think I'm harassing you," she said, careful to keep her tone respectful and considerate. "I don't mean to. It's just that this is so important. A man's life is at stake. I would simply like the opportunity to talk with you for a little while."

"As I've told your people before, I have no interest in talking to you," Nan reiterated, slipping her arms free of her daughter's hold. Turning, she confronted Raeanne, face-to-face. "And, frankly, I'm surprised at you, Miss Martin, taking a case like this. How do you do it? How can you sleep at night? Helping someone like…like *him,* who could kill another human being, then just walk away."

"Mrs. Avery," Raeanne said quietly, "I'm just trying to get at the truth."

"The *truth?*" Nan snorted. "You mean just twist the truth." She shook her head, her eyes narrowing. "No, I won't let you do it. I won't let you take my family's name and drag it through the mud, I won't let you embarrass me and my children any more than we have been already. We've provided the town of Whitehorn with enough gossip over the years. I refuse to give you any more." She turned and walked proudly from the courtroom. "Please don't bother me again."

Even though the courtroom was nearly empty, Nan's cool dressing-down had attracted the attention of the few spectators who remained. Raeanne drew in a deep breath and turned to Melissa.

Even though Melissa Avery North had been several grades ahead of Raeanne in school, they'd known each other and they'd been friends. Knowing Melissa and liking her, just made Raeanne's job all the more difficult.

"Look, Melissa, I'm sorry. I really don't want to upset her," Raeanne said apologetically.

"I know." Melissa nodded, smiling. "And I know you're just trying to do your job. It's just…" She paused, shrugging a little. "This whole thing…it's brought back a lot of memories—bad ones. It's been pretty hard on her."

"I understand and truly, I don't want to make it any worse," Raeanne said, reaching into her briefcase and pulling out a business card. She handed it to Melissa. "If she changes her mind, give me call. I'd hate to have to subpoena her."

Raeanne watched as Wyatt and Melissa caught up with Nan and escorted her the rest of the way to the elevator. Raeanne sighed, feeling tired and defeated. Tomorrow was Friday and she looked forward to the weekend break. She hated feeling like a bully, feeling like the bad guy just because she had a job to do. The last thing she wanted was to cause Nan Avery and her family any further pain. They were good people and they'd been through enough already. But she wasn't about to give up. Nan Avery was a fiercely proud woman and Raeanne was convinced she was hiding something behind all that pride. And the fact remained that Ethan's life depended on her and at the moment it was more important for her to do a good job than to worry about what the Avery's thought of her.

She gave a tired sigh, starting back to gather her things. But as she turned, she caught sight of Rafe. He was standing near the judge's bench, talking with a court bailiff and it was obvious they both had witnessed the entire episode with Nan Avery.

The two weeks since they'd talked in her office had been difficult ones for her. To see nothing in his eyes, to have him watch her with no more interest than he did anyone else...

The way he was staring now. Raeanne quickly looked away, making her way back to the defense table. She began to gather up her things, telling herself it was better this way. His indifference was preferable to other emotions he seemed able to stir in her.

"Miss Martin?"

Looking up, she was surprised to see one of the deputies who had earlier escorted Ethan from the courtroom. He was a young man—clean-cut and good-looking, with dark hair and dark eyes and a serious, somber expression.

"Yes?" she said guardedly.

"Your client..." he started hesitantly.

"What is it?" she demanded, growing uneasy.

"Uh, he, uh..."

"Is everything all right?" she asked quickly, rising to her feet.

"Oh, yeah. He just asked if I could remind you to bring him more sunflower seeds."

Raeanne breathed a sigh of relief, remembering the huge bag of salted seeds she had brought several weeks ago. For one horrifying moment, she'd thought...

She shook her head. She was ashamed to admit it, but for a moment she thought Ethan might have done something really dumb—like try to escape. He was normally so stubborn, so hotheaded—arguing with her on each and every point. But the past several days, he'd been so compliant, so agreeable and his sudden change in attitude had bothered her. Past experience told her that could be a sign of trouble. When a client lost interest in his own trial, it could mean he wasn't planning on being around for the rest of it.

But she shook off the troubling notion, looking up at the young officer and smiling. "Sunflower seeds. Yes. Yes I will. Thank you."

The young officer smiled back at her, showing her a perfect row of gleaming white teeth. "Did you want me to give him a message—your client, I mean?"

Raeanne thought a moment. "Not really, thanks. Just tell him I'll be by the jail tonight."

The young man nodded, but made no attempt to leave. "I sat in for a while today," he said finally, shifting his weight from one foot to the other. "On the trial."

"Oh, you did?" Raeanne asked, aware of Rafe's dark gaze watching from across the room. "What did you think?"

"I thought you were great," he blurted out, his cheeks flooding with color. "Ethan seems like a decent guy. He's lucky to have you in his corner."

"Well, thank you. I appreciate that," Raeanne said, knowing the young officer had no idea just how much she did. The encounter with Nan Avery had left her pretty low and more than a little discouraged. The young man's smile had been so genuine and the compliment so sincere and unsolicited, it was all she could do to stop herself from gushing with gratitude.

"I...I'm starting law school myself—next fall, over in Billings."

"Really?" Raeanne smiled. She could see Rafe's tall frame at the edges of her peripheral vision and it made her feel awkward. "That's great. What kind of law are you interested in?"

"Criminal." He shrugged. "Defense, maybe, like you. I'm not sure."

"Well, good," she said absently, trying not to think about the dark eyes watching her. "I hope everything works out for you."

"Thanks," the young man said, a broad smile breaking across his face. "Who knows, maybe we'll be working together someday."

"Maybe," she answered with a laugh. "Good luck."

The officer nodded, turning to leave. "Same to you. And don't forget the seeds."

"I won't."

She watched as the young man disappeared through a side door to the holding cells. When she turned back, she was a little disappointed to find that Rafe had disappeared, as well. Slowly she gathered up her things and walked down the corridor to the elevators.

She felt depressed and alone. For years she'd told herself she wanted to know where she stood with Rafe and now it looked as though she did. She thought of him standing in the courtroom, watching her with his cold eyes and unemotional expression. At least, before, she'd been left with some hope. Now, all hope was lost.

Four

He watched her from a distance. Standing in the lobby of the Blue Lake County jail, Rafe peered through the glass partition beyond the main reception desk, through the wired window of a worn wooden door and into the prisoner interview room. He could see her inside, sitting at a table across from her client—back straight, head bent, hand clutching a short yellow pencil. Even in the bare, dingy setting of the interview room, she looked perfectly at ease and in command.

She was listening intently to Ethan, her head bending close to catch every word, as though she were contemplating and analyzing everything he said. From time to time, she would stop, just long enough to make an occasional note on the legal pad in front of her and then she would resume her position again.

Nothing had changed, he thought darkly, drawing in a deep breath. His whole life he had watched her and here he was watching her again—always from a distance, always on the outside. For as far back as he could remember, there had been something that stopped him from getting close, stopped him from making a move. When he was a kid it had been the teasing and the Wolf Boy tales and later it had been Andy and the marriage that followed. But even though the stories and the teasing had stopped long ago and Andy and the marriage were gone, little had changed. Now, a courtroom, a client and professional differences had replaced the old obstacles and put him on the outside again.

Raeanne Martin seemed to possess a strange power over him. She could stir emotions in him, fill him with a desire he wanted to forget, a longing he wanted no part of. He'd wanted to curse at her, wanted her to stop being the person she was, stop being the woman he found himself wanting day after day, year after year.

Rafe released his breath in a long, slow sigh. It was late and he'd been up since dawn. He should leave, should turn around and get the hell out of there while he still could. Maybe he'd drive out to his mother's ranch—check on Crier and the litter of pups she'd just had. Or maybe he should just return to the small, cramped apartment above a dry cleaner's that he kept. But neither option held much interest. Besides, he didn't want to be alone, didn't want to go to bed. He'd only lie there and think back on the day, only remember things he'd rather forget.

Rafe thought of the courtroom and of the exchange he'd witnessed between Raeanne and Nan Avery at the close of the day. He'd heard Mrs. Avery's cool, abrupt words. He understood the woman's bitterness, sympathized with her pain and her pride, but that hadn't made it any easier to watch her strike out at Raeanne. He'd seen the expression on Raeanne's face—the empathy and the distress. It had been all he could do to stop himself from barreling across the courtroom to come to her defense.

He almost smiled—almost—and ran a weary hand through his long hair. Nothing had changed. Maybe nothing ever would. He was still standing on the sidelines of her life, watching, waiting for a sign, or for a signal that she needed him, waiting for the moment when he could ride up on his white horse and rescue her.

Only Raeanne wasn't a woman who needed rescuing—not by anyone and certainly not by him. She was perfectly capable of taking care of herself and she'd proven it to him over and over again. If he could only make himself remember that.

He glanced back through the glass barriers. Raeanne was standing now, looking down at Ethan and talking. How many nights had he lain awake in his bed, trying to forget, trying to convince himself he didn't care? He felt a familiar rush of anger—anger at a woman who needed nothing from him and anger at a stranger who had abandoned him and left him only a legacy of questions and doubts.

"Something I can do for you, Rafe?"

Rafe jumped, glancing down at Sergeant Ollie Benson with an uneasy scowl. "I...uh...I'm just waiting."

Ollie turned his head, following Rafe's gaze through the yellowed venetian blinds to the occupants of the small interview room beyond. With a crook of his head, he looked back at Rafe. "She's a looker, ain't she?"

"Yeah," Rafe mumbled, unreasonably annoyed by the innocent comment. He thought of the young deputy who had stood and talked with her in the courtroom earlier, re-

membered the unpleasant and unwelcome burst of jealousy
it had caused. "She's okay."

"Okay?" Ollie snorted, giving Rafe a suspicious look.
"Boy, your eyes need fixin'? I'd say she's a mite better than
okay." Ollie reached down and picked up a glittery piece
of tinsel that had fallen from the tiny Christmas tree
perched at the end of the counter. Examining it carefully,
he tossed it over one of the small branches, which were
already sagging under their load of decorative ornaments.
"Nosiree, when they look like that, I don't mind it one little
bit when they come to visit their clients."

"She down here very often?"

"To see Walker?" Ollie shrugged, gathering up a pile of
papers lying on the counter and tapping them into a neat
pile. "Three, maybe four times a week." He stopped and
looked up at Rafe, two gray, bushy eyebrows arching with
curiosity. "Think maybe she's got a thing for him?"

Rafe glowered down at the short, round sergeant. "No,"
he said crossly. "What the hell are you talking about?"

Ollie shrugged, feigning wide-eyed innocence. "Well,
you never know. Some women really like a man in the joint."

Rafe shook his head. "You've been down here too long,
Benson. You've lost it."

"You might be right, Rafe," Ollie snorted, obviously
pleased with the fact that he could tweak the cool, collected
Wolf Boy every now and then. Still chuckling, he picked
up the stack of papers and headed for an ugly brown file
cabinet. "You just might be right."

Rafe ignored Ollie's clowning, instead glancing back at
Raeanne. Ollie was right, she was a looker and there wasn't
a doubt in his mind that every man who laid eyes on her
would agree.

He thought again of the young officer in the courtroom. Rafe had thought he'd gotten beyond his discomfort at seeing her with someone else. After all, he'd spent years watching her with Andy. And while it hadn't been easy to stand back and see them together, Andy had been his best friend—one of the few true friends he'd ever had in his life—and for the sake of that friendship, Rafe had learned to endure the pain of seeing him with Raeanne.

Of course, on their wedding night it had been a different story. It taken a considerable amount of whiskey before he managed to successfully block out the images of the two of them together in his head.

But that had been Andy and that had been different. Seeing this…this *kid* with her had been something else entirely. Rafe remembered the fierce wave of possessiveness that had engulfed him. It had surprised and disturbed him. He had no reason to feel protective of her. There was nothing between them. She could talk to whomever she wanted, it was no business of his. And yet the incident bothered him, just as the one with Nan Avery had.

What a fool he was, he thought darkly, watching as a uniformed officer appeared at the door of the interview room to escort Ethan back to his cell. Once again he'd found himself wanting to be her white knight, wanting to rush in and save her when she was more than capable of saving herself.

He watched as she slipped into her long wool coat. It was well after nine o'clock and a cold snow was swirling outside, but she still wore the same pale gray suit she'd worn in the courtroom. As she started down the corridor, past Ollie and the main reception desk, she looked up and spotted him.

Raeanne glanced across the reception area and felt all the air slip from her lungs. Another tense encounter with Rafe Rawlings was not what she needed right now. She didn't have the energy and after the day she'd had, she didn't have the fight. She glanced around. Was there any possible way she could avoid him?

She took a step forward, then hesitated. Her large brown eyes stared up at him and Rafe felt a pressure building in his chest. It was obvious she wasn't pleased to see him and he took it like a bullet to the chest. The trial of Ethan Walker had put a strain between them, had put them on opposite sides of the judicial fence. But it had been just the latest in a long string of people and events that had served to put time and distance between them. Their past was like a lost and forgotten highway, littered with memories and blocked by uncertainty. But standing beneath the bleak, dreary lighting of the jail's reception area, Rafe couldn't seem to make himself remember all of that. He slowly walked toward her. She looked weary and alone, helpless and utterly vulnerable. She looked nothing like his enemy and everything like his friend.

"You look tired," he murmured.

"Is that your subtle way of telling me you think I'm wasting my time down here?" she asked, her chin rising defensively. She heard the sarcasm in her voice, but didn't care. He looked strong and solid standing there, rugged and handsome in his flannel shirt and warm down vest and that made her mad. She didn't want him strong, she wanted him miserable, as she was.

"No," he said carefully, noticing her dark lids and drawn expression. Raeanne was tall and slender, but tonight she looked so small, so...defenseless. He could see faint circles of fatigue below her eyes and felt the muscles in his stomach tighten. "Apparently it's my not-so-subtle way of saying that it looks like you've had a long day."

Feeling like a battle-weary warrior whose foe has just held up a white flag, she exhaled slowly. "I'm sorry," she mumbled, giving her head a shake. "You're right, it has been a long one."

"Heading home, or back to the office?"

"I just have to pick up a few things from the office, then I'm heading home—finally." She sighed, glancing down at her wristwatch and groaned loudly. She thought of the pages of trial transcripts that still needed reviewing before morning and the two large bags of Christmas presents she'd intended to get wrapped. "I didn't realize how late it was. You know, it's a good thing I don't have a cat. The poor thing would starve waiting for me to get home."

As if responding to a silent, mutually agreed-upon command, they both turned and slowly started for the door.

"Ollie says you're down here a lot," he said in his normally guarded tone.

"You checking up on me?"

"No." Rafe smiled, just a little, his mouth feeling strange and out of practice with the movement. He pulled his leather gloves from the pocket of his jeans and looked down at her. "Would you mind if I was?"

The quiet tone of his voice had the steady rhythm of her heart stumbling just a little. "I guess that would depend."

"On what?"

"On what you suspect me of."

He shook his head. "Lawyers," he said with a small laugh. "So suspicious."

"Only because cops are always looking for trouble," she retorted.

"Well, I'm not—not tonight, anyway," he added, holding up one gloved hand in a gesture of innocence. "Ollie just mentioned that he sees you visiting Walker a lot."

"We don't get much of a chance to talk in court," Raeanne said, rubbing at her tired, scratchy eyes. Cops rarely understood the unique relationship between attorney and client and Rafe Rawlings had been sounding an awful lot like a cop lately. "I like to come down and go over the day with him, make sure he understands everything, answer any questions he might have."

Rafe regarded her carefully, thinking about Ollie's tasteless crack. "Do you give all your clients such consideration, or is this just something special with Walker?"

"Oh, it's pretty much the standard service," she said dryly, thinking it was a strange question for a cop to ask. "But I understand being locked up and on trial for your life is a scary thing. It helps to have someone to talk to."

"Ethan Walker doesn't exactly look scared to me," he said sarcastically.

"Oh, he's scared all right," she said simply, ignoring his cynicism. "He's not nearly as tough as he makes out."

"Bull. Walker's as tough as nails."

She looked up at him, shaking her head. She was too exhausted to argue. "So typical."

Rafe looked down into her eyes. They had the same lost, forlorn look Lobo's had had when he found him starving by the roadside. "Oh, what's this? What's so typical?"

"You," she said. "So typical of a cop to see only what's on the surface."

"Oh? And your lawyer's sensitivity is going to tell me Ethan's really just a big, cuddly teddy bear under that tough hide?"

"No," she said, having to smile just a little at the analogy. "But he is a human being, with feelings and emotions and beneath that thick hide and those rough edges is one scared man."

"Well, if he is, he's got good reason to be," Rafe told her.

"Which is exactly why I like to come down and just sit with him sometimes," she said, making her point. She looked back to the empty interview room, then glanced at Rafe. "We talk, but mostly I'm here because I know how he feels, even though he can't seem to tell me."

Rafe quickly looked away. How many times had he wanted to tell her what was in his heart? How many times had the words stalled in his throat?

They walked a few steps in silence, past Ollie's tired-looking Christmas tree and Rafe wondered if she'd ever suspected, if she'd ever guessed how he felt. He felt a mixture of emotions forming in his throat—a tight knot of anger mingled with frustration and a desire held too long at bay. He swallowed hard, pushing the emotions back. "So I guess all that insight into your client makes for the late nights, then?"

"It's just trial mode." She shrugged, suppressing a yawn. "You'd think I'd be used to it by now. There always seems to be something that needs doing."

"Are you anxious for it to be over?"

She looked up at him. "That all depends, I guess."

"On?"

"On what kind of verdict the jury brings back."

Rafe gazed down at her, remembering their fierce difference of opinion on what that verdict should be. He remembered how angry he had been in her office, angry at her strength, at her convictions.

But now she looked anything but strong. She looked soft and extremely susceptible—nothing like the cool, competent lawyer she was in the courtroom. It made him want to reach out, to touch, to comfort, to offer her some of his strength.

But the knot in his throat tightened and had him turning away. "Looks like it's finally stopped snowing," he said, pushing the thick glass door open. "But I'll bet the roads are still icy."

Raeanne pulled her coat more tightly around her and shivered at the blast of frosty air that met them at the door. "Damn, it's cold," she muttered, teeth chattering. "It almost makes me miss California."

"Looks like you brought a few bad habits home with you," he said, pointing to her soft leather pumps. "Your feet are going to freeze in those—that is, if you don't fall down first."

Raeanne looked down at her shoes, remembering the pair of insulated boots she'd forgotten by the front door when she rushed from the house this morning. "You're right. I guess I forgot."

"Come on," he said, offering her his hand. "I'll help you."

Raeanne stared down at his proffered hand, uneasy about taking it. He'd said nothing about the argument they'd had in her office, nothing about the strain that had existed between them since the start of the trial. She felt uncertain and awkward, unsure of what to do. Was she just suppose to forget about it? Pretend it had never happened?

Reluctantly she took his hand, allowing him to maneuver her cautiously down the concrete steps and through the snow-and-ice-slick parking lot to her car. Waiting while she unlocked the door, he pulled it open for her.

"Thanks," she said, slipping in behind the wheel. The

snow had stopped and the black sky was alive with stars. She looked up at him, saw his tall frame silhouetted against the night. Like Ethan Walker, Rafe was a tough, hard man. But she'd managed to crack Ethan's tough outer shell. She'd tapped into his core of emotions. But Rafe's hold on his feelings was stronger and much better guarded. In all the years, she'd never broken through, never penetrated his cache of emotion.

She looked up into his eyes. He might be able to bury his feelings deep, but she knew they were there. She felt them, just as she felt the cold December wind that raged about them.

But she couldn't live on hunches or sensations, couldn't survive on hopes and ideas. She needed something real, something solid, something she could touch and hold on to. And that was something he would never give to her.

She reached for her seat belt, quickly looking away to escape his dark gaze.

"Well, good night," he said, taking a step back.

"Good night." She reached for the door, starting to pull it shut.

"Uh…Raeanne?"

His hand on the door made it impossible to close it. "Yes?"

He stared down at her. He wanted to tell her how much he hated the strain between them. He wanted to tell her that he thought about her all the time, that he wanted her to think about him. But her eyes were so big, so brown and they searched his face so earnestly.

"What is it, Rafe?" she asked. The look on his face had her heart pounding in her chest.

"I'm…I…" In frustration, he pushed himself away from the car, releasing his hold on the door. "Drive carefully."

"I will."

She stared up at him. Whatever she thought she'd seen in his face was gone now. Whatever it was he'd been about to say, he'd changed his mind. His expression was stone-cold, closed tight against any emotion, any sign of feeling.

She'd allowed herself to be taken in again, let her hopes begin to rise, only to be let down again. She'd been a fool. To hell with Rafe Rawlings, to hell with Wolf Boy, to hell with intuition and instinct, to hell with—*it*.

She slammed the door shut, twisting the key in the ignition and tossing the car into gear. She pulled away a little too fast and the rear tires skidded causing the back of the car to fishtail. In the rearview mirror, she saw him, standing alone in the darkness.

Rafe swerved to avoid the cat, which stood in the middle of the road with eyes ablaze, hypnotized by the headlights of his sturdy four-wheel-drive truck. As he turned the wheel back to correct his course, one of the truck's oversize tires hit a pothole filled with dirty, slushy water, sending him jerking violently against the door.

"Damn!" he swore, cursing the cat, the pothole and the wet, muddy road.

But his mind wasn't on his driving or the condition of the road. He was thinking about Raeanne.

He'd almost done it again, almost been taken in, almost made the same old mistake. He thought about how she had looked, how soft and vulnerable.

But it had all been an illusion. He'd been seeing what he wanted to see, what he needed to see. He couldn't seem to make himself understand that Raeanne Martin didn't need him, that he had nothing to offer her, nothing she wanted.

Just then, his police radio crackled loudly, but he barely took notice. It was his custom to monitor the radio—on duty or off—and its sudden outbursts were something he'd gotten used to a long time ago. But when it crackled again, there was something that had him sitting up, something that had him taking notice.

The address broadcast over the frequency had caught his attention—311 Coyote Path. He recognized the numbers immediately.

It was Raeanne's address.

Rafe braked hard, the huge tires of his truck skidding noisily on the wet, cracked pavement. He turned the wheel sharply, spinning all four wheels around and headed back for town. He grabbed for the handset, radioing the dispatcher for details, but his mind was already moving too fast to listen. He wasn't interested in details or response times, he wasn't concerned about procedures or protocol. All he knew was that Raeanne was in trouble, she needed help and wild horses weren't going to keep him away.

Five

Raeanne trembled, the shaking having nothing to do with the wet sleet soaking through the soft leather soles of her shoes and causing her toes to go numb with cold. The two squad cars parked nose to nose in front of her house had their lights flashing, turning the snow that blanketed her neighborhood a brilliant shade of red.

She looked down at the scattering of pine needles and ribbon strewn across the porch steps and the lawn, the meager remnants of the beautiful Christmas wreath that had once adorned her front door and felt her stomach roll uneasily. Ugly streaks of black and red paint formed unintelligible letters and words, marring the beveled glass and varnished wood where the wreath had once hung and a lone string of Christmas lights now dangled forlornly from around the frame of the door.

Bending down, she picked up a small shred of ribbon, rubbing its satiny smoothness between her fingertips. Who would do such a thing? she thought, repulsed by the sense-lessness of the act. What kind of sick mind got a thrill out of destroying something just for the sake of destruction?

"There's a can of spray paint and some Magic Markers over there underneath the bushes," Terry Gaines said, his breath blowing out in a long pink plume as he spoke. He'd been driving a squad car for the Whitehorn Police Department for only six months and he took his job very seriously. "Tracks in the snow lead off down the street. You don't remember seeing anyone around when you drove up?"

Raeanne shook her head, shivering. "No, not really. I don't remember. But, to be honest, I really didn't pay that much attention." She squeezed her eyes tight in an effort to block everything out. "I—I didn't even notice anything was wrong until I was halfway up the steps."

He nodded, making a notation in the small tablet he held in his gloved hand. He pulled a long black flash-light from his belt and clicked on the beam. "I'm going to give the back—"

But the screeching of tires from the street behind them drowned out his words and had them both turning around. Raeanne recognized Rafe's truck immediately and her heart lurched violently in her chest.

"I heard the call on the radio," he said, ignoring Gaines and walking directly to Raeanne. "You all right?"

"I'm fine," Raeanne said, feeling ridiculously better now that his comforting arms held her lightly, his strong hands on her upper arms. "A lot better than my house."

Rafe turned around, taking in the torn and broken Christmas decorations and the defaced door and walls. Feeling her tremble beneath his touch, he turned back to her. "You're freezing. Why don't you wait inside?"

Raeanne shook her head. "It hasn't been checked out. I called from a neighbor's. They told me on the phone to wait until the officers had a chance to check inside."

Rafe's dark eyes shifted to the officer. "You haven't done that yet?"

"We were just about to," Officer Gaines explained defensively.

"Forget the inside," Rafe told him curtly. "I'll take care of it. Look around back, let me know if you see any sign of a break-in." The officer nodded, taking off around the side of the house with the beam of his flashlight zigzagging in the darkness. "Come on," Rafe said after a moment, giving Raeanne's arms a slight squeeze.

Raeanne let him guide her up the steps, carefully avoiding as much of the debris and wet paint as they could. She tried not to think about the painstaking care and the time she'd spent stringing lights and putting up holiday decorations only days before.

Her weekend had started out so miserably. The stress of the trial had been getting to her and she knew she'd been letting the strain with Rafe bother her more than she should. Desperate for a diversion, she'd forced herself into the holiday spirit and gone Christmas shopping. She'd bought ridiculously extravagant gifts for family and friends and enough Christmas ornaments and lights to decorate several households.

The shopping had proven a satisfactory distraction and, still caught up in the holiday spirit, she'd stopped on her way home and picked out a huge Christmas tree. She'd spent the rest of the weekend trimming her tree, hanging her wreath and garlands and stringing lights outside the house.

But now the lights that had framed the porch and her

living room window crunched beneath her feet, lying broken amid shredded pine boughs. But it wasn't until she reached her front door that the despair hit.

"Are you all right?" Rafe asked, hearing her strangled gasp.

"My door," she moaned, pointing to the wet, dripping streaks of paint trickling down the glass and defacing the rich wood grain. She looked up at him, shaking her head. "Why would someone do that?"

"Why do sickos do anything?" Rafe asked, reaching for her house key. Releasing his hold, he set her away from him. "Stay here for a minute. Let me check things out inside."

He stepped in the door, his eyes carefully scanning for signs of broken glass or forced entry. He made a swift but thorough check of the small wood-frame house, doing his best to ignore the warm furnishings and appealing decor. He returned to the porch just as Terry Gaines was climbing the front steps.

"What have you got?" he asked, stepping from the small foyer onto the porch.

"No sign of anything—no paint, no break-in." The officer shrugged. "Not even any footprints."

Rafe turned to Raeanne, holding open the door. "Why don't you go inside and get warm? I'll stop in after I finish up out here."

Exhausted, Raeanne nodded, walking past him and into the warmth of the small foyer. As the door closed behind her, she slipped out of her wet shoes, kicking them into a corner beside the insulated boots she'd forgotten that morning. Hugging her coat around her, she tiptoed down the short hallway toward her bedroom, stopping just long enough to reset the temperature on the heater's thermostat. The natural-gas-burning monster leapt to life, shooting air through the vents and causing them to creak and moan ominously.

In the bedroom, she searched through the drawers of her chest until she found a pair of warm, woolly socks. Slipping them on over her numb toes, she then stepped into a pair of well-worn slippers.

The combination of the socks and slippers looked crazy and out of place with her long wool coat and sedate business suit, but she was beyond being concerned about appearances. By the time she headed back down the hallway toward the living room, warm air was streaming from the heater vents and she slipped out of her coat. She had just hung it on a large brass hook on the hall stand when she heard a tap on the door.

Seeing Rafe's familiar silhouette through the paint-spattered window, Raeanne opened the door and motioned him inside.

"You all right?" Rafe asked, leaning just inside the threshold.

"Well, I'm warmer, anyway," she said, pointing at the bulky socks and old slippers. "Come in and warm up. I've turned up the furnace."

"Thanks," he said, rubbing his gloved hands together as he stepped through the small entry and into the living room. "That heat feels good."

"Find anything out there?"

"Nothing, really," he said, slipping off the gloves and stuffing them into the pocket of his vest. "It doesn't look like they intended to break in. Just mess the place up."

"Well, they managed to do that pretty good," Raeanne said dryly.

"Could have been worse," he said, stepping across the

soft carpet to the huge Christmas tree in front of the picture window. "But it looks like you might have scared them off when you drove up." He poked at one of the small crystal ornaments, causing the cut-glass edges to catch the light and sparkle. "Gaines said you didn't see anything?"

"No, I didn't," she mumbled, noticing that despite the tree's size, he looked big and imposing standing beside it.

"Probably kids," he said with a heavy sigh, turning back to her. "Taggers, people who vandalize buildings and such, usually with paint, though the main object is destruction. We've been seeing some of that lately. We're going to increase patrols in this area, though, just to be on the safe side." He looked back at the tree. "This is nice."

She smiled. "Thanks."

"You do it all by yourself?"

"You sound surprised."

"I guess I am," he confessed.

She laughed. "It's been seven years since I had good old-fashioned traditional Christmas. I guess maybe I went a little overboard."

He nodded. "Not much on tradition in L.A.?"

"Not much on snow, anyway." She shook her head, shrugging just a little. "It's hard to believe Christmas is just a few days away. This trial has really screwed me up."

"Planning on spending it with your folks?"

She smiled. "Well, I'd hoped to have them and all the relatives here for Christmas dinner. You know, show off my culinary skills a little, give Mom a break." She paused, thinking. "But with the trial and everything and now this…" She pointed outside, at the mess on her porch. "I don't know. But how about you? I'll bet Emma's been baking up a storm. She still make her almond cookies and fruitcakes?"

"I guess." He shrugged, shaking his head. "I just try to stay out of her way this time of year."

"Well, it wouldn't be Christmas without them," Raeanne said, remembering the years Rafe had delivered the holiday goodies to her family's door for his mother. Every year she had hoped he would accept her invitation to come inside, but he never had.

The play of emotions across her face had his stomach tightening again and he cleared his throat, uneasy. "I'm afraid those lights outside are goners," he said, pointing to the strands of broken and drooping lights they could see through the glass that once framed the window. "Should be replaced."

Raeanne peered through the glass, taking in a deep breath. "Such a mess," she murmured.

"Well, at least it will clean up," he told her optimistically, but he clenched his jaw tight. At the jail, she'd looked so lost and vulnerable, but now, standing in the warmth of the comfortable little house and staring at the results of such a senseless act of destruction, she just looked frightened.

For all her modern ideas, for all her sophistication and professionalism, she was really such an innocent. As far back as he could remember, she'd seen good in everyone. Maybe that was why he'd always wanted to protect her. He knew about cruelty, he knew that sometimes there wasn't anything good to find. He'd experienced fear and pain firsthand and he'd wanted nothing more than to protect her from all that.

The need to reach out swelled like a tidal wave inside his chest. He wanted to grab her, to shield her with his strength, protect her with his power. He wanted her to lean on him, depend on him, wanted to make the fear and hope-lessness disappear from her eyes once and for all.

"Raeanne," he said quietly.

Raeanne turned away from the window and looked up at him. "Yes?"

"There's something I…something I think we should talk about."

"Wha—" Her voice broke and she swallowed hard. Could miracles happen? Could he finally be opening up to her, sharing his feelings? "What is it?"

"I want…" He cleared his throat. "I think maybe it would be a good idea if…well, if I hung around outside tonight."

She blinked, confused. "What do you mean?"

"You know, stake the place out," he said, reaching for his gloves and slipping them back on again. "Just to be on the safe side, in case our friends decide to come back."

Raeanne came crashing back to reality with a hard thud. She'd thought…she'd hoped… But it no longer mattered what she'd thought, it didn't matter what she'd hoped—it was obvious she'd been wrong. She gave her head a small shake in an attempt to cushion the blow. "You said it was a bunch of kids," she pointed out, making a conscious effort to keep any trace of emotion from her voice. "Why would they come back?"

"I said it was *probably* kids," he said, hating that unemo-tional courtroom voice of hers. "How do we know for sure? It could be…something else."

"Something else?" she repeated. Suddenly the room felt uncomfortably warm, even though gooseflesh rose on her arms. "What are you talking about?"

He looked down at her, his dark eyes narrowing. Why was she making this so difficult? Didn't she know that all he wanted was to keep her safe? Why couldn't she just accept the fact that he wanted to help? Why couldn't she trust him to know what was best for her?

"There are a lot of people in this town who don't like it that you've been poking your nose around, asking a lot of questions, stirring up a lot of trouble."

"Is that right?" she said, folding her arms across her chest. "So you're going to stake out my house because some redneck got his feathers ruffled?"

"You're representing a killer. A lot of people think Walker's gotten away with murder for too long as it is. They want to see him pay for what he did."

"Then there are a lot of people in this town who are going to be disappointed," she pointed out deliberately.

He glared down at her, his breath coming in deep gasps. "Did you forget everything about *real life* living in L.A.? This isn't California. People here don't like it when criminals go free. They don't like it when a bleeding-heart lawyer defends one loser after another—even if she is a hometown girl. It makes people mad."

Loser. The word had her seeing red. She was stupid to think he might understand, stupid to think he had any compassion—or any feelings at all.

"What are you saying? You're afraid they're going to run me out of town on a rail?" she asked, her voice heavy with sarcasm. "Come on, Rafe. This is Whitehorn, Montana, not Dodge City."

"Fine, go ahead and make fun of the dumb country cop," he told her, his hands curling to fists at his side. "But see how much you laugh when one of these rednecks decides to take the law into his own hands."

"My clients are entitled to the best defense I can give

them," she told him coolly. "That happens to be the law. And *nobody* is going to scare me away from doing my job."

"Well, somebody left you a little message tonight," he said, jerking a thumb toward the vandalized window. He took a step closer, glaring down at her. "And maybe next time they won't be satisfied to scrawl a few messages across your door."

"If you're trying to scare me, it's not working."

"I'm not trying to scare you. I'm just trying to do my job," he said, carefully controlling his voice. He drew in a deep breath. Anger mixed with frustration and he swore violently under his breath. "You could be in danger, whether you want to admit it or not. And it's my job to protect you."

"I can protect myself," she said, walking to the small desk in the corner. Retrieving a key from the ornamental ceramic jar sitting on top, she unlocked a side drawer and pulled out a black .32-calibre Beretta 90.

"A gun," he said, his bland tone masking his surprise.

"Don't worry," she said caustically. "It's licensed."

"You'd use a gun?"

"If I had to," she said, cocking the pistol. "Just because I don't strap it to my side, or shoot the place up from time to time, like the rest of you crazy cowboys, doesn't mean I'm afraid to use one."

Crazy cowboys. The words hit him like a physical blow.

She was right, he was a crazy cowboy. That was how she thought of him and that was what he was—crazy to think she'd needed him, crazy to think she ever would. In a weak moment, he'd been taken in again. He'd heard the report over the radio and came barreling over to her house like the cavalry riding to save the wagon train. He'd had one thought in mind—protecting her. Only…she didn't need his protection, she didn't want his help, she simply didn't need him.

"I give up," he said, stalking back across the living room. "I'll be outside, whether you need anything or not."

Raeanne stared after him as he stormed through the foyer and out the door. "I won't!" she called out, but he had already disappeared down the steps. "I won't," she said again, in quiet voice.

She wouldn't need him for anything, because what she wanted from him, he would never give.

Damn him, she cursed silently, turning the lock on the door and walking slowly down the hallway, toward her bedroom. Tears burned in her eyes and a heavy knot of emotion swelled in her throat. Damn him and damn her, too, for being such a fool. When was she finally going to get it through her head, when was it finally going to sink in? There was no special feeling, no special link between them.

Realizing she still held the gun in her hand, she held it up, finding its brutal black lines and cold feel oddly beautiful, in a perverse sort of way. Cold, hard steel—that was her protection, she thought, slipping the gun into the drawer of her nightstand. As cold and as hard as Wolf Boy's heart.

She slipped out of her suit coat, tossing it carelessly on the bed and ambled toward the bathroom. The evidence on Rafe was in and she didn't need to be a legal expert to realize her case didn't look good. She was ready to admit defeat, ready to stop relying on dreams and face the fact that if Rafe Rawlings had wanted her, he'd had more than enough time to do something about it. How much more proof did she need? Once she'd thought she could let her feelings for Rafe go unresolved, let them just linger out there in a permanent state of limbo. But she'd been wrong. She'd tried that once and it had been Andy who paid the price for her mistake.

Winona had said there were old issues she needed to resolve. Maybe this was what she'd meant. But how did she do that? How did she just forget the feelings of a lifetime and how was she supposed to live with the resolution?

Mary Jo slipped into the courtroom, which was nearly empty at this early hour. She found a seat toward the back and settled in. A smile broke wide across her face. She couldn't be more pleased. The trial was going just as she'd hoped. The prosecutor was throwing his stones and Ethan was doing very little to dodge them.

Raeanne Martin, however—she was another story. The woman was quick and smart—maybe too smart for her own good. Still, Ethan was stubborn and as long as he kept his mouth shut and didn't spill the beans, there was little his lady lawyer could do to pull the truth out of him.

The truth. Mary Jo's smile widened. Just what would the fine folks of Whitehorn do with the truth? It would almost be worth sticking around to find out—almost.

Mary Jo looked up as Rafe walked in and the smile faded from her lips. Wasn't it ironic that, of all people, she had Rafe to thank for the way the trial was turning out? But she also knew that the handsome young lawman could turn out to be her worst enemy. As he walked by her though, she couldn't resist speaking to him. And she had other plans—plans that didn't include getting mixed up in a murder investigation.

* * *

"You were right." She reached out and touched his sleeve.

Rafe stopped to find Mary Jo Kincaid beaming up at him. It was early and much of the courtroom was still empty. "I beg your pardon?"

"About the prosecution's case," she explained. "On the first day of the trial, you said the prosecution had a strong case. You were right."

Rafe remembered how she'd commandeered him that first day in the corridor and her curious array of questions and concerns. "Well, let's hope you feel the same way once the defense gets through with their case."

"Oh, I'm sure I will," Mary Jo said breezily. "After all those witnesses who saw Ethan arguing with Mr. Avery and the testimony about the cattle rustling and all. I mean, how could the jury not convict him?"

Rafe's eyes narrowed. "Well I don't see how they could, either, if they've followed this case as closely as you have, Mrs. Kincaid."

Mary Jo's eyes widened and color rose to her cheeks. "Well, I find all this all so fascinating. Real human drama, you know?"

Rafe stood and watched as she gave him a cute little wave, slid down one of the rows of spectators' seats and sat down. She interested him, mostly because he couldn't quite figure her out. As a cop, he was used to categorizing people, stereotyping them—creeps, criminals, pimps, perps, liberals, losers, et cetera. But he couldn't seem to get Mary Jo Kincaid to fit in anywhere. While Ethan Walker's case had caught the interest of a lot of people in Whitehorn, the curiosity of this quiet, demure librarian seemed oddly different. After all, it wasn't as though she were like Lily Mae Wheeler, who made gossiping about others a way of life. And yet, each day for over two weeks, Mary Jo had conscientiously attended the proceedings. What was it about a twenty-seven-year-old murder that had her so interested? Why was she so curious about the fate of a man she'd never met?

He was still thinking about Mary Jo when he started back down the aisle. But after one step, he was brought up short when he felt his boot come down on an unsuspecting foot.

"Excuse—" But whatever else he'd planned to say just drifted from his mind as he turned and looked down into Raeanne's face. It took him a moment to recover from the shock. "I'm sorry," he then said, automatically reaching out a steady hand. "Are you all right?"

Raeanne clutched at his arm, steadying herself and taking a few painful steps. "Is the prosecution so uncertain about its case you feel you have to cripple me now?"

He gave her a deliberate look. "Actually, I'm operating at a bit of a disadvantage this morning. I didn't get much sleep last night."

Raeanne remembered the dozen or so times during the night she'd peeked out her window to see Rafe's truck parked at the curb in front of her house. "Too bad. I'll bet there are some kids out there with paint on their hands who got a full eight hours."

Rafe glared down at her. He wouldn't have minded debating the pros and cons of playing it safe, but he was interrupted by a tug on his arm.

"Was that my son I saw who nearly steam-rollered over you?" Emma Rawlings's round, weathered face beamed, full of life and energy. Turning to Rafe, she gave him a playful swat. "I thought I'd raised you better than that."

"Ma," Rafe said, flinching as she swatted. "What are you doing here?"

"This trial is open to the public, isn't it?" Emma snapped, her rough tone edged by true affection. "Well, I'm the public. Besides, I've been hearing how this young wisp of a girl is giving you big strong men a run for your money. I thought that was worth a trip into town to see for myself." She turned to Raeanne and gave her a hug. "How's it going, darlin'?"

"Well, when I'm not being accosted by the prosecutor's chief investigator, it's going pretty good," Raeanne lied, slipping her arms around Emma's sturdy frame.

"I told your father I would stop by the pharmacy on the way home and tell him everything." She gave Raeanne a stern look. "I've heard you've banned your poor parents from coming to watch."

Raeanne grimaced guiltily. "It's true. It makes me too nervous."

Rafe's eyes widened with surprise. He wouldn't have thought anything could rattle her in a courtroom. "Careful, Counselor, it sounds like you're not very proud of what you do."

"Oh, I'm proud, Rafe," Raeanne said, trying very hard not to let the tasteless remark upset her. "I'm just not perfect. Believe it or not, I sometimes get a little jittery when I know someone I care about is watching."

He glared down at her. Could she have made her point any clearer? He'd been watching her for weeks in court and she'd looked anything but jittery.

"Well," Emma said quickly, with a wave of her hand, "I know they're awfully proud of you."

"I know they are, too," Raeanne said.

"And if this one keeps giving you a hard time, just let me know," Emma advised her, motioning to her son with a nod of her gray head. "He gets a little too full of himself from time to time, but I can still put him in his place. They're never too old to get a scolding from their mothers."

"I'll keep that in mind," Raeanne said, watching the look mother exchanged with son. Only last night Raeanne had decided Rafe Rawlings was incapable of feelings, that the emotional, vulnerable side she'd once believed he hid behind the Wolf Boy facade didn't exist at all. But there was love for his mother in his eyes, despite his impatience, despite his irritation and despite how he tried to hide it.

"Oh, you don't have to worry about the lady lawyer, Ma," Rafe said, as he began to back away. "She can take care of herself. Ask her about the friend she keeps with her for protection."

"What's this?" Emma asked, but he was already down the aisle and through the gate to the counsel table at the front of the courtroom. Emma turned back to Raeanne. "You have a friend living with you?"

"No," Raeanne said, thinking of the Beretta she'd returned to the desk drawer this morning. "It's nothing, Emma. Just Rafe's idea of a joke."

"Not a very funny one, I take it."

Raeanne looked down at the woman who had taken in an abandoned baby and raised him as her own. Emma had raised her son to be strong and tough in order to face the hard realities of his birth. But she had also raised him with a mother's love and tenderness. It was easy to see the strength his mother had given him—but what had happened to all the love?

"You're right," Raeanne said, smiling down at Emma. "Not a very funny one, I'm afraid."

Emma reached into her old canvas handbag, pulling out a foil-wrapped package. "Christmas is in a few days. This is for you and your folks."

Raeanne gazed down at the shiny package, with its bright Christmas bow. "Almond cookies?"

"And a fruitcake," Emma added. "What else?"

Raeanne hugged her again, feeling the sting of tears in her eyes. "Thank you, Emma."

Emma sighed, glancing at her son, who sat with his back to them at the counsel table, with Harlan. "You know, I think Rafe half believes those foolish old stories about himself—so tough, so cold, different from everyone else. A wolf boy." She snorted, glancing back up at Raeanne. "Such nonsense. Men—how they complicate our lives." She gave Raeanne a small squeeze. "I'm glad you decided to come home again. This is where you belong." She turned and started down a row of seats. "Now go and teach those men a thing or two."

Raeanne smiled and turned to the counsel table. But when she caught Rafe's dark gaze from across the courtroom, the smile faded slowly from her face. Maybe it had been a mistake to move home again, to try to make a life for herself among all the memories and mementos of the past. Things had been so strained between them, so difficult and not just because of the trial. Did he blame her for Andy's death? Was that where all the hostility came from? Had they grown to be such different people that they could no longer be friends? They said you could never go home and she was beginning to think that it was true.

She pulled her gaze away, feeling a dull, empty ache

inside. She set her briefcase down on the table, lifting her heavy files out and slipping the package of Emma's Christmas goodies in their place. The courtroom was nearly filled with spectators now and the noise level had risen considerably.

She scanned the list of witnesses scheduled to testify, knowing Harlan was getting very close to resting his case. That only depressed her more. She was still trying to put her case together and she hadn't decided whether to put Ethan on the stand.

"Excuse me, Raeanne?"

Raeanne jumped at the faint tap on her shoulder "Melissa! H-hello," she stammered in a raspy voice, surprised to find Melissa North standing behind her. She came quickly to her feet.

"I talked to her," Melissa said quietly. "My mother, I mean."

Raeanne's heart lurched violently in her chest. "Yes?"

"She's agreed to meet with you. Could you be out at our place tomorrow, around noon?"

"Saturday at noon. Absolutely," Raeanne assured her, thinking maybe miracles could happen after all. "And, Melissa?"

Melissa stopped as she turned to leave. "Yes?"

"Thank you."

Six

Raeanne bit into the crescent cookie, its powdered-sugar coating fluttering down her chest and dusting her dark teal parka with a sprinkling of white. She released the steering wheel just long enough to brush it away, thinking of Emma and her yearly Christmas baking. She'd missed the holiday tradition of exchanging home-baked gifts during the years she lived in L.A., missed the closeness of family and friends.

She swallowed, popping the rest of the cookie into her mouth and savoring the rich, delicate flavor of almonds and butter. Tradition was important to her, even though she knew that would probably come as a surprise to some people in Whitehorn.

Some people? Or just Rafe?

Despite the fact that they'd known each other for years, she was beginning to feel they didn't really know one another at all. She knew he saw her as a cold, hard-nosed professional—a career woman who needed no one and nothing else.

She almost had to laugh—but not because there was anything funny about that, but because it was so sad. If only he knew how needy she could be, if only he knew how frightened and alone she felt. Yet maybe it was her fault, too. It had been important to her that he know she was capable of taking care of herself. He was so strong and so forceful, she'd couldn't imagine him wanting anyone who wasn't the same way.

She thought of the things he had said about her clients and the job that she did, how arrogant and unfeeling he had been. Was that how he really felt? Did he really have so little respect for the job she did, or was it just that he had no respect for her?

She took a deep breath, clearing her lungs and giving her head a little shake. She wasn't going to think about all that now. Whether Rafe Rawlings thought much of it or not, she had a job to do and it deserved her full attention.

Raeanne eased her foot onto the brake, slowing the car to a crawl and maneuvering around a large depression in the road. She almost wished now that she'd listened to her dad. He'd offered her his truck when he came by earlier to help her clean up her front porch. He'd pointed out that it was better equipped to handle the wintry country roads than her sedate Volvo sedan. But Raeanne had refused. When she was fifteen, she'd learned to drive in her dad's creaking, cumbersome old truck—which had been no small feat. With no power steering, no shocks, a sticky clutch and an engine that sounded like a beast from hell, it wasn't exactly a joy to drive.

Just then she was bounced abruptly against the door and she heard the sound of scraping as her bumper caught the edge of a muddy pothole. Making a face, she braked again and slowly continued on. Montana ranchers drove trucks. The country roads could be treacherous, especially in the winter.

She carefully steered around a puddle that took up most of the rutted drive that led through the North property to their luxurious ranch house. At least it wasn't snowing, she thought as she squinted up at the sky. As much as she'd missed the beauty of a winter landscape while she lived in L.A., she hadn't missed driving in snow and sleet.

As she inched along, she kept a running check of the time on the clock in the dash. Impatience had her wanting to hurry, had her wanting to gun the engine, to race over the rough road and get to the North ranch any way she could, but the fact was, even at the snail's pace she was going, she'd be there in plenty of time.

Patience, she cautioned herself. Just be patient. But it wasn't easy. Ever since Melissa North told her yesterday in court that Nan had agreed to an interview, Raeanne's mind had been racing. She'd been up most of the night, going over questions, developing a strategy, outlining a game plan. The woman would be hostile, but that was to be expected. She'd dealt with her share of hostile witnesses before. But this wasn't a courtroom and a certain amount of tact and finesse would be necessary. She didn't want to appear too pushy, or too anxious. And she certainly didn't want to give Nan Avery any idea that the entire case for the defense might very well hinge on what she had to say.

Raeanne thought about Ethan, about his dark moods and surly temper. The Walkers had lived in Whitehorn for years—scraping out a living on their small ranch out on Mountain Pass. They had always been a wild lot and there were others in Whitehorn who'd had run-ins with them from time to time. But those had been minor fracases, nothing serious, nothing like Ethan's run-ins with Charlie Avery.

Raeanne shook her head. She still had trouble putting it all together. Ethan had been just a kid when Avery was killed. What would make someone like Charlie Avery go after a teenager? It just didn't make sense. And while the Walkers might be eccentrics, they were far from being killers. Cattle rustling was a serious charge in these parts, but would it have been enough to get a young Ethan angry enough to kill?

No, Raeanne decided. Something was missing. There had to be something more and someone had to know. Was it Nan Avery? And would she be willing to tell?

Raeanne glanced down at the clock again, then a distance up the road. It wasn't much farther. She would be early, but that was all right, too. She'd hoped to have time after the interview to drive to the site on the Indian reservation where Charlie's remains had been discovered. After FBI forensic anthropologist Tracy Hensley's testimony earlier in the week, there were some questions in her mind as to exactly how the body had been disposed of and she wanted to recheck the location herself.

Her mind turned again to Ethan, sitting in his cell at the county jail. She'd hoped to have time later to visit him, too. She'd decided not to tell him about the interview—not right away, anyway. Besides, she wanted to see what she learned from Nan first.

They'd come a long way in the weeks since the start of the trial, she and Ethan and even though he said little and he could be gruff and obstinate, Raeanne was convinced he'd finally come to trust her—as much as he could trust anyone.

Still, he could be difficult and despite her careful probing, he'd opened up very little on the subject of Charlie Avery.

Her tire sank into a mud-filled pothole, jostling her roughly against the seat belt and sending her thoughts fleeing. The ranch house was just ahead and a knot of apprehension began to form in the pit of her stomach. The almond cookies she'd been munching on suddenly came back to haunt her, their richness making her feel queasy and uncomfortable.

She pulled into the large circular drive, bringing her car to a stop near the large stone steps that led to the wide covered porch that stretched the length of the house. There were several trucks parked along the drive, but she paid little attention to them. She was too busy thinking about how she would handle the situation, what she would say.

She stepped out of the car and straightened her long parka, making sure all trace of the powdered sugar was gone. It had taken her a long time this morning to decide what to wear. She wanted to keep things casual and relaxed, but it was still business—serious business—and she felt a certain degree of decorum was in order. Thinking jeans or slacks would be too casual, despite the wintry conditions, she'd finally decided on a long denim skirt and a pale blue chambray blouse, worn with a pair of rugged leather knee boots.

Retrieving her briefcase from the back seat of the car, she took a deep breath and climbed the steps up the porch. Pushing the small button beside the door, she heard the faint sound of a bell from somewhere inside the house. She told herself to relax, to breathe evenly, but she still felt jumpy.

She stared at the beautiful Christmas wreath hanging on

the Norths' door, remembering the torn remains of her own holiday wreath, which she and her father had cleaned up from her steps and porch. She thought of the vandalism of her home, of Rafe arriving and of the harsh words they'd exchanged. He'd told her someone in Whitehorn might want to hurt her. Had he honestly believed that, or had he just been trying to frighten her? But just then the door opened and her thoughts scattered like the torn remains of her wreath.

"Hi, Raeanne," Melissa said, pulling the door open wide and motioning her to come in. "Thanks for coming."

Raeanne walked inside, the warmth from the house surrounding her immediately. A huge Christmas tree stood silent and beautiful in the living room and the smell of cinnamon and bayberry filled the air. "I should be the one thanking you."

"I didn't do anything," Melissa insisted, helping Raeanne out of her parka and hanging it on a hanger. "Not really. My mother doesn't mean to be difficult or anything. It's just that this whole thing has been so hard on all of us."

"I understand that," Raeanne said, meaning it. "And I promise, I'll try and make this as painless as I can."

"I know you will," Melissa said, smiling. "I believe you when you say you're interested in getting at the truth. I'm interested in the same thing. That's why I hired Nick Dean in the first place. I have to tell you, I don't know whether Ethan Walker murdered my father or not. I know the police think he did, I know my mother does, too. And if he did, no one wants to see him punished more than me. But if he didn't…" She stopped, letting her words drift for a moment. "If he didn't, I want to find the person who did."

Raeanne regarded Melissa Avery North carefully,

feeling tremendous admiration for the woman. In a gesture that belied the professionalism she was determined to maintain, she reached out and touched Melissa's arm, giving it a reassuring squeeze. "I want that, too."

"So," Melissa said, taking a deep breath and patting Raeanne's hand, which rested on her arm. "They're waiting for us in the den. Shall we go in?"

They? Raeanne picked that up as soon as Melissa said it, but she just assumed she was referring to her mother and her husband. It wasn't until she walked down the short hallway and stepped into Wyatt North's masculine-looking den that she realized that wasn't what Melissa had meant at all. Nan Avery sat straight in a wing-backed chair before a roaring fire and behind her chair stood Rafe.

"Raeanne," Melissa was saying from behind her, "you know Rafe, of course."

"Of course, but I don't understand," Raeanne said, confused. She stopped, looking first to Rafe, then Nan Avery. "What is he doing here?"

"Mrs. Avery asked me to sit in on the interview," Rafe said, stepping slowly from around the chair. "Do you have a problem with that?"

Actually, Raeanne had a lot of problems with that, but she merely turned and looked at Melissa, who shrugged apologetically. "It was the only way she'd agree."

"I see," Raeanne said, turning back and glancing down at Nan, whose stern expression had stiffened. "I have no problem with Rafe being here. But you really have nothing to fear from me, Mrs. Avery," she said, struggling to keep the anger out of her voice. "It wasn't necessary to involve the police."

"Rafe is here as a friend," Nan said in a tight voice,

twisting the small hankie she held in her hands. "I asked him to come because I trust his judgment."

"I see," Raeanne said. She didn't like being pushed into a corner, but her options at the moment appeared limited. She could create a scene, start making demands, but what good would it do? She'd only end up blowing any hope she had of getting information out of Nan. And while there was a likelihood that Rafe's presence would inhibit Nan's comments, the alternative was to leave with nothing. In the courtroom, she'd always prided herself on knowing when to press a point and when not to. This was a time not to. "Okay, then, shall we get started?"

Rafe had seen the look on her face when she walked in and saw him and it had felt a little like a hot branding iron on his flesh. After seven years he knew he couldn't love her any longer and after weeks of trial he wasn't even convinced they were still friends. But he hadn't thought she hated him.

He'd known when Nan Avery asked him to come that Raeanne wouldn't be happy about it. He had expected her to be angry, had prepared himself for it, had even begun to look forward to taking on her fiery wrath. What he hadn't expected was that cold look of contempt in her eyes. He could take her anger, but he wasn't sure he could take her disdain. He'd always said he wanted her out of his life. Now, maybe, he'd finally done it. Maybe he'd finally pushed hard enough, finally gone far enough to push her away for good.

He watched her as she talked with Mrs. Avery and felt a heavy weight on his chest. She sat on a straight-backed chair, listening intently to what the woman had to say. He remembered watching her at the jail and how she'd listened to Walker with the same intense concentration. Only this time the soft light of the fire shone on her hair, making the long brown strands look warm and golden. She sat with her hands in her lap, resting atop a blank legal pad. She held a long black pen and as she listened, she absently wove it in and out between her slender fingers.

There was nothing confrontational or insolent in her manner, nothing inappropriate or impolite. She displayed none of the stereotypical behavior he'd come to expect from cutthroat defense attorneys on the attack. He was completely impressed and he felt it was probably lucky she wasn't questioning him. Feeling as he did, he would no doubt have told her anything she wanted to know.

He remembered again the look she'd given him when she first walked in the room and felt himself go cold all over. Even standing before a roaring fire, he'd felt the chill of her scorn. Not that he blamed her. He'd said some pretty awful things to her lately—stupid things, things he hadn't really meant. It had just been so much easier to be angry, to be cruel, than to tell her how he really felt.

"You were there last week, when Pete Riddick testified?" Raeanne asked, leaning forward just a fraction as Nan nodded. "Mr. Riddick had said it wasn't unusual for your husband to stop in at the Sundowner Saloon a couple of times a week, is that right?"

"Yes," Nan said, nodding again.

Raeanne's sharp ear heard the slight edge in Mrs. Avery's voice. She'd kept the questions fairly general up to this point, in an effort to get Nan to relax and open up a little. But that was all about to change. The questions she now needed to ask were sensitive and very personal. It would be important to tread carefully.

"This was something that didn't bother you?" she asked, purposely keeping her voice at a monotone. "Having your husband frequenting a bar?"

"Why should it?" Nan snapped defensively. "I mean, the man had a right to relax after a hard day, didn't he?"

"Oh, absolutely," Raeanne assured her quickly. "I just imagine there are a lot of wives who wouldn't be so understanding. After being home all day long with two small children, they'd want their husbands home.

"But were you aware of the fight your husband had with Ethan Walker at the Sundowner? I mean, before Pete Riddick testified about it?"

Nan turned back to her, her face stiffening. "Well, I'd seen bruises, if that's what you mean."

That wasn't what Raeanne meant and Mrs. Avery knew it. But if she wanted to play games, Raeanne was more than willing to go along with her. "So you're saying you knew they came from a fight with Ethan Walker, is that right?"

"I guess," she mumbled. She shook her head, twisting the hankie. "It was so long ago, how can I be expected to remember?"

But she did remember, Raeanne thought. She remembered exactly where Charlie's bruises had come from and why. Raeanne would have bet her life on it—or rather she was betting Ethan's. Still, she understood the woman's reticence and she smiled pleasantly.

"You're right, it was a long time ago," Raeanne agreed. "But do you happen to remember if you knew what the fight was about?"

Nan took a deep breath, rolling her eyes. "He might have said something—about the cattle rustling, I think. Something like that. I don't remember."

"I see," Raeanne said, taking her pen and making a short notation on the tablet. "So you knew there were hard feelings then between your husband and Ethan because of the…rustling."

"Of course I knew," Nan snapped. "We were married. We shared everything."

"Calm down, Mama," Melissa said, reaching out a comforting hand. "It's okay."

"I'm sorry, I'm sorry," Nan said, closing her eyes and sighing heavily. Taking another deep breath, she looked back to Raeanne and made a sweeping gesture with her hand. "Go on."

Raeanne glanced up at Rafe, who stood leaning against the hearth. She'd half expected him to spring into action at any moment, to go on the attack and jump down her throat for bullying Mrs. Avery and yet for the past thirty minutes he'd stood quietly watching her every move with his cold, dark eyes.

She glanced back to Nan, giving her another pleasant smile. "I guess what I want to know is if you ever got the impression that there was something more to the fight between your husband and Ethan—more than the cattle rustling, I mean."

"Of course not. What more could there be? Ethan Walker was just a boy," Nan pointed out, leaning forward to make her point. "My husband wasn't in the habit of getting into fights with teenage boys."

"Oh, I understand that," Raeanne said, nodding. "But it does seem strange, though, doesn't it? I mean, he argued only with Ethan, not any of the other Walkers. Could it have had anything to do with Ethan's sister, Marilee?"

"Just what are you trying to imply?" Nan demanded.

"Nothing," Raeanne said quickly. "I was just speculating."

"Well, there's nothing to speculate about. None of this was Charlie's fault," Nan maintained. "Ethan Walker was a hothead, even as a boy."

"That's what I understand," Raeanne said, feeling a little as if she were walking a tightrope. "Did your husband ever say anything to you about Ethan?" She laughed a little, hoping it sounded natural and not nervous. "About what a pain in the neck the kid was, or anything like that?"

Nan thought for a moment. "He might have said something once. I don't remember what, exactly." She looked at her daughter, then turned and looked up at Rafe. "He'd been drinking. I'm—I'm not sure he even knew what he was saying."

"Did your husband drink very often?" Raeanne asked casually, but her hold on the pen tightened.

"Once in a while," Nan said, defensive again. "A lot of people do, you know."

"So it was never a problem for him—alcohol, I mean?"

"Of course not," Nan snapped. "It wasn't a problem. Charlie drank sometimes, but he just did that to unwind, that's all. He used to work hard, put in long hours. He needed a little help relaxing."

"Mama, please. You're getting upset again," Melissa said, moving to the arm of her mother's chair and slipping a supporting arm around Nan.

"Maybe we could take a break," Raeanne suggested. She desperately wanted the interview not to stop, but she sensed that Nan was closing up.

"Maybe that would be a good idea," Rafe said, stepping away from the hearth and glancing down at Mrs. Avery. "There's no hurry with this, you know."

"No," Nan insisted. "I want it over with."

Rafe turned to Raeanne. He lifted an arm up and rested it on the mantel, his dark eyes alert and attentive. "I guess the ball's still in your court, Counselor."

"Okay, then," Raeanne said, taking a deep breath. "I've just got a few more things here. You said you thought Mr. Avery had said something about Ethan. You can't remember what that might have been?"

"It was nothing, really," she insisted again. "I just remember him saying something about putting him in his place."

"Putting Ethan Walker in his place?" Raeanne repeated.

"Yes, Ethan Walker," Nan snapped back. "That is who we're talking about, aren't we?"

Raeanne thought for a moment. She had reached the point of no return—or maybe she'd already gone a little beyond it. It was apparent that Nan Avery was becoming more agitated and more defensive with each question and while Charlie Avery's widow had opened up a little, the lid could snap closed at any moment. There was no sense in holding back. She might as well bring out the big guns.

"Mrs. Avery," she said in a matter-of-fact voice, "what was your relationship like with your husband?" From the corner of her eye, she saw Rafe step away from the hearth, but she consciously kept her eyes glued to the woman in front of her.

"I beg your pardon!" Nan Avery gasped.

"Would you say you had a good marriage?" she asked. "Did your husband ever give you any reason not to…trust him?"

"What are you implying?" Nan demanded, leaping to her feet. The delicate lace hankie she'd been clutching in her tightly clenched fists drifted to the floor. "Just what is it that you're trying to say?" She turned to her daughter, who was trying to comfort her. "I don't know what she's talking about."

"I know you don't, Mama," Melissa said in a soothing voice. "Don't get upset."

"I'm already upset. It's those awful rumors again. Those awful, hateful lies about Charlie and—" Nan pushed Melissa away, turning to Rafe. "I don't want to answer any more questions. I don't have to, do I? She can't make me, can she?"

"Of course not," Rafe said. He looked at Raeanne, who was already gathering up her things. "I'm sure Miss Martin won't mind."

"Not at all," Raeanne said quickly, zipping her briefcase closed. "Thank you, Mrs. Avery, for agreeing to see me. I appreciate your taking the time." She looked at Melissa, who was helping her mother back into the chair. "Thank you. I'll see myself out."

Raeanne slipped out the door and down the hall, stopping just long enough to retrieve her parka. She was out the door and down the porch before she realized Rafe was behind her.

"Raeanne, wait!" he called, catching up to her as she reached the door of her car. He reached for her arm, stopping her. "Can't you wait a minute?"

"Look," she said, spinning around and knocking his hand away, "I'm not in the mood for another sparring match with you. I've got too much to do."

"Sparring match?" he asked, noticing how the cold winter temperatures had brought up the color in her cheeks. He thought about how soft it would feel beneath his touch, how silky and smooth. Awareness of her assailed his senses and he felt his body react. "Is that what we do? Spar with each other?"

"Well," she asked, pulling her car keys from her purse, "what would you call it? We don't exactly have conversations anymore."

He smiled a little, hoping to lighten her angry mood. "Couldn't we just think of it as lively debate?"

She gave him a killing look and started to pull the car door open. "I've got to go."

"Wait," he said, the smile fading from his lips. He reached out and pushed her car door closed again. "Couldn't we just try—to talk, I mean?"

"What have we got to talk about?" she snapped impatiently. "Do you want to tell me again how slimy my clients are, or give me another lecture about the moral corruption of lawyers?"

He recoiled, remembering the stupid things he'd said to her out of anger. "Stop it."

"What's the matter, Rafe? I thought you said you wanted to talk." She glanced down at her watch. "I've got to go."

"What's the big hurry?" he asked, her caustic tone leaving him stinging. "A date? I wouldn't think you'd have much time for socializing with the way Walker's trial is going."

She gave him a scathing look. "Go to hell."

She yanked open the door again, but before she could toss her briefcase inside, he slammed it again.

"Look," he said, drawing in a deep breath. Jealousy was something new to him and it had him lashing out, talking stupid. "That was..." He shook his head. "I'm...I'm sorry."

Raeanne knew it had been a difficult admission for him. "So much for conversation," she said wryly.

"Debate."

She smiled, in spite of herself. "Whatever," she said, reaching for the door handle again. "I really have to get going."

"Where you headed?" he asked, purposely keeping his tone casual and conversational. He'd gone overboard with that comment about Walker and he didn't want to make that mistake again.

"I thought as long as I was out in this direction, I'd drive to the reservation. There are some things I want to check out at the place where Avery's remains were found."

"I'll take you," he offered, pointing back to his four-wheel truck. "You'll never make it in that...that *yuppie-mobile* you drive."

"I'll be okay," she said, pulling the door open.

"You'll get stuck," he declared, thinking of the rough terrain and the rugged logging road.

"No, I won't," she said adamantly, not liking his tone.

"Yes, you will," he insisted. "And then you'll freeze your briefs off out there."

"I'll be fine," she told him in a tight voice, telling herself she wasn't going to let herself get angry.

"Stop being so stubborn," he said, raising his voice.

"Then stop bullying me," she said, raising hers.

"I'm not bullying you."

"Yes, you are."

"No, I'm not," he insisted, but he stopped and took a deep breath. "I'm...I'm just..."

"Sparring?" she inserted smugly.

He looked down at her, his lips parting in a small smile. "Yeah, well, maybe this time."

"See you later, Detective," she said, tossing her briefcase across the seat.

"Raeanne," he said, stopping her as she started to get in the car.

"Yes?"

He stared down at her, seeing the face of the woman he knew he'd never stop wanting. He wanted to tell her how impressed he'd been with the way she handled the interview, how taken he was with her sensitivity and her professionalism. He wanted to tell her she had sympathy and understanding, style and finesse. He wanted to tell her how much he liked seeing her, how much he enjoyed sparring with her and teasing her and just standing there staring at her.

But, as always, the words wouldn't come. He felt them become tangled and confused and his nerve start to cower and collapse. And so, like a hundred times before when he'd been afraid of revealing too much, he opted for silence and revealed nothing at all.

Raeanne watched the play of emotions across his face. It was happening again. There was something there—in his eyes, in his face, in the very way he looked at her. Once again she felt that old feeling, sensed he wanted to tell her something. "Rafe, what is it?"

"Nothing," he said quietly after a long moment. He shook his head, letting out a slow breath. He knew that for all his bravado, he had his own brand of cowardice. He could face bullets and brawn, outlaw and outcast, but the eyes of Raeanne Martin, the feelings she stirred in his heart, had him heading for cover every time. He released his hold on her arm and turned away. "Forget it. Never mind."

Raeanne watched as he started for his car. Anger coursed through her veins. She didn't want to forget it, she wasn't about to "never mind." They'd been going through this little routine for too long and he'd walked away from her too many times. But not now, not this time.

She stalked after him, grabbing his arm and spinning him around to face her. She glared up at him, her breath coming in huge, heavy gasps. "No, you don't. You were going to tell me something. What was it? What were you going to say?"

Rafe felt emotion thick in his throat. He wanted to say everything, he just didn't know where to start. Words were like emotions for him—deep and hard to find. They represented too much and he'd lived with silence for so long. Vanquished and defeated, he merely shook his head.

Raeanne felt the sting of tears burn her eyes. She raced back to her car, slamming the door. She'd been a fool for the last time, she decided. The very last time.

Rafe stood and watched the small sedan bounce and rebound down the drive until it disappeared in the distance. This wasn't the first time he'd been unable to tell her how he felt. He knew his silence would never win her love, but he hadn't realized until today that it just might make her hate him.

Seven

The road narrowed to little more than two muddy ruts in the frozen ground. She was lucky that it hadn't snowed in several days, otherwise the trail would have been impassable. The car rocked wildly, throwing Raeanne hard against the side of the door. The small logging road that cut through the rugged Laughing Horse Indian Reservation to the spot where Charlie Avery's skeletal remains had been found was narrow and rough and Raeanne hoped like hell she wouldn't get stuck.

She'd been to the site before—but that had been several months ago, soon after she'd been assigned Ethan's case and before a foot of snow had blanketed the entire area. Everything looked different to her now.

She glanced down at her copy of the map she'd taken from her file, drawn by a sheriff's deputy during an initial stage of the investigation. Glancing quickly back up, she scanned the landscape again. If she wasn't mistaken, she was where she was supposed to be—or at least close.

The road grew worse, causing both her and her car to bounce wildly. When she heard the loud grinding noise that sounded when a large rock made contact with something on the bottom of her car, she decided enough was enough. She'd gone as far as she could with the car and would have to make it the rest of the way on foot.

Bringing the car to a stop, she sat for a moment, getting her land legs again after the rough ride. She shifted the car into Park and turned off the ignition, letting the silence of the area surround her.

It was a desolate place, wooded and lonely, miles from anywhere or anything—a spot perfect for keeping the secrets of a killer for years on end. She opened the door, stepping out onto the cold, hard ground. Despite the clear sky and the sunny afternoon, a chill ran up her spine. Somewhere in the distance there was the lonely cry of a bird—a forlorn creature lost from its flock, diverted from its journey south and now destined to weather a frigid winter in this harsh, icy environment.

Carefully she made her way up what remained of the road, which ended somewhat abruptly near a bluff. Below, she could hear the quiet trickle of Beartooth Creek as its icy waters cut a narrow swath through the snow. It was mostly frozen now, as was Lovers Lake, nearby, where Andy had taken her ice-skating once with a group of friends.

She thought back to that day. She and Andy had only just started dating and she'd gone thinking Rafe would be there, too. But of course he hadn't. She'd been terribly disappointed and Andy had spent the whole afternoon drinking beer and showing off.

Raeanne stopped, bracing herself against a strong and decidedly unpleasant pang of guilt. Andy. Her life would have been so simple if she just could have loved him. Maybe she could have helped Andy keep his drinking in check and maybe he wouldn't have become so abusive.

"No, no, no, no," she said aloud, shaking her head. Her voice sounded small and lonely, reverberating through the trees. "I will not think about that now. I will *not*."

She did her best to push the troubling memories aside. After her encounter with Rafe, she was having a hard enough time concentrating on business. The last thing she needed was to start rehashing her entire life with Andy.

She thought about the episode at the Norths' ranch, thought about how Rafe had looked at her and the things he had said. He'd done it to her again—started to tell her something, only to change his mind at the last minute. It was driving her crazy. Maybe that was why she'd confronted him, why she'd tried to push him, to force him to talk. But she should have known that wouldn't work. No one could push Wolf Boy Rawlings and it was time she just accepted it.

She took a deep breath, feeling lonelier at this moment than she had in her whole life. At the bluff, she turned and made her way toward a clearing off the road, as her small map indicated. Her eyes scanned the area, looking for something familiar—but nothing seemed to be. Frustrated, she turned the map one way, then the other, but nothing seemed to help. With the snow, everything looked different.

The place had a quiet, eerie feel and it sent a shiver up her spine. She suddenly got the uncomfortable feeling that she was being watched, that she wasn't alone.

She turned her head slowly, a cold, dead feeling spreading through her veins. Standing just up the ridge to her left were two timber wolves—their icy black eyes watching her every move.

Raeanne didn't dare move, didn't even breathe. A wave of panic rendered her mind momentarily useless and her ears rang with the sound of her own strangled breath. Should she try to run, should she try to make a break for the car? What was she supposed to do?

She slowly let out her breath, the air leaving her lungs sounding like the roar of the wind in the quiet forest. She moved one foot, intending to make a slow turn, but the ears of both wolves perked up. The closest one took several steps down the ridge toward her and Raeanne froze again.

Involuntarily a quiet sob escaped her paralyzed lungs, the sound causing the ears of her curious companions to perk up again. She watched in horror as they carefully wandered down the ridge toward her.

"They won't hurt you."

Raeanne spun around at the sound of a voice behind her, nearly stumbling. When she saw Rafe's tall, muscular frame walking up from the road, her entire body sagged with relief.

"Rafe," she said in a breathless gasp, her hand covering her pumping heart. "Wh-what do I do?"

"Just stay calm," he told her, stepping with a sure foot over the rough terrain. "They're just curious."

He stepped in front of her, staring across the snowy expanse at the pair of inquisitive animals. Raeanne peeked around from behind him, her legs trembling so badly they threatened to collapse beneath her.

She didn't know exactly what it was he did—a look, a gesture, a nod of the head—but something passed between. Some kind of sign or communication traveled between man and animal, causing the two wolves to turn and disappear beyond the ridge.

"You frightened them," he said, turning around to face her, taking her by the arm.

"*I* frightened *them?*" She choked the words out, her eyes widening. "They scared me to death. That one was so big and looked so mean."

"He was just protecting his mate," Rafe explained, watching the color returning to her cheeks. "He didn't want to see her hurt."

"Oh, and you were able to tell all that from just looking, I take it."

"I was raised by wolves—or don't you remember?"

"Yeah, right," she said, rolling her eyes. She felt better now and the sarcasm felt good. "I forgot about the Wolf Boy mysticism—communing with nature and all that."

Rafe ignored her sarcasm. "What are you doing over here, anyway?"

Raeanne took a deep breath, feeling her heart slowly begin to quiet in her chest and gave him a deliberate look. "I told you. I wanted to see where Charlie Avery's bones were discovered."

"That's what I thought," he said, watching as annoyance replaced the fear in her eyes. "So what are you doing wandering around up here?"

Raeanne shook her head, the hand on her hip betraying her impatience. "Aren't you listening? I already told you."

"You told me you were looking for the place where Charlie Avery's bones were found."

"That's right."

"Charlie Avery's bones were found over there." He pointed to a grade twenty feet behind her, in the opposite direction.

Raeanne followed the line of his gaze, spotting a small piece of yellow police tape hanging from a tree limb that had once cordoned off the area. She stared at the dangling tape for a long moment, not realizing until she turned back to Rafe that her jaw had actually dropped open. But when she saw the amusement in his eyes, it snapped shut again. She felt a little like Alice after she drank the magic potion, shriveling and shrinking to just inches in height.

"Oh," she said meekly, feeling more than a little foolish.

He regarded her for a minute, watching the wheels turn and her expression go from angry to abashed. "You okay?"

"What do you mean, am I okay? Of course I'm okay," she snapped, yanking her arm away. But she wasn't okay, she was embarrassed and it had her testy and defensive. "I'm fine." She turned and started for the spot he'd indicated, stumbling as she went. "Just fine."

Rafe let her pass, watching as she stalked off. He wasn't sure exactly why he'd followed her out here from the Norths'. He'd gotten into his truck with every intention of returning to town, but for some reason he just hadn't been able to.

He'd told himself he was merely concerned for her safety, that he was concerned that something might happen to the car, or to her and that she'd be stuck out here alone. But those weren't the real reasons. There was unfinished business between them and it bothered him.

"You're not going to see much," he said, turning and following her. "The snow has pretty much obliterated everything."

"I'm not really looking for anything in particular," she mumbled, scanning the small clearing. "I didn't remember much of what it was like around here. I guess I just wanted to get the feeling of the place."

"So what kind of feeling do you get?"

She stopped and gave a careless shrug. "I'm not sure."

Rafe kicked at a snow-covered branch that had fallen to the ground. "It's a lonely place."

"Yeah," Raeanne agreed, thinking it didn't seem nearly as lonely as it had before Rafe arrived. "And apparently the perfect place to hide a body." She watched him as he bent down and picked up a small rock and threw it over the bluff. "Why did you follow me?"

"You mean besides to rescue you from a pack of wolves?" he said lightly. "Or point you in the right direction?"

Embarrassed, she had to smile at his reply. "Thanks, by the way," she said with a deep sigh. Breaking off a small twig from a low-hanging limb, she began breaking it into tiny pieces.

"Anytime," he said.

She looked up at him, tossing the small bits of twig to the ground. His dark eyes showed nothing.

Why had he come? He wished he could answer that himself. He turned and walked to the edge of the bluff, looking out across the landscape to the densely wooded horizon. "That's where they found me," he said, ignoring her question and pointing out across the plateau. "In the woods over there."

Raeanne walked over to where he stood, gazing over the countryside. "Isn't that part of the Kincaid ranch?"

"Yeah, near where the old Baxter place used to be."

"Baxter," Raeanne repeated slowly. "I remember my mom and her friends talking about the Baxters. Wasn't it a Baxter that was rumored to be Charlie's..."

"Yeah," Rafe said when her words drifted off. "The daughter—Lexine."

"Lexine Baxter," Raeanne murmured. "What was it about her that got people talking so?"

"From what I remember hearing, plenty," Rafe said, glancing back out across the panorama. "When I was little, Tracy Hensley's dad used to come out and talk to my mom a lot—you know, about people around these parts, stuff like that. I think he was doing a book or some kind of research, I don't remember exactly. But I remember hearing them talk about Lexine. She was pretty wild."

"Really wild? Or wild for Whitehorn?"

Rafe smiled. "From what I remember, I think old Lexine could have held her own even in L.A."

"That wild, huh?" She laughed, not taking offense at the jab. "But you know how people around here love to talk."

He looked back at her, his eyes narrowing. "Better than most."

The bitterness in his voice surprised her. "But those stories about you were so ridiculous. I mean, look back at it. A baby raised by wolves? That's nonsense. No one really believed any of that."

"A lot of people did at the time. You forget, people used to be afraid of me."

"Kids," she said dismissively, with a shake of the head.

"Not just kids."

"There are people who think Elvis runs a karaoke bar in Missoula, too," she drawled. "So what does that tell you?"

He turned and stared down at her. "There are some who are still afraid."

She looked up at him, seeing something flicker in his eyes. Uneasy, she glanced away, making her way down, away from the bluff. "I would bet that has more to do with the fact that you're a cop than you being some kind of wild wolf boy."

"You were never afraid."

She turned and looked back at him. He hadn't moved, just stood staring at her from a distance. She didn't want to talk to him—not about the past. "No, I wasn't."

He turned and started down the bluff toward her. "Why?"

"Why what?" she asked uncomfortably. "Why wasn't I afraid?"

"Everyone else was," he said, coming close.

"Rafe," she said with a small, nervous laugh, "why are we talking about this? It's silly."

"Is it?" he asked simply. "I still want to know. You were always different. You never teased or heckled me, you never made fun. Why not? Why weren't you afraid of me?"

"This is ridiculous," she insisted, but the quiver in her voice threatened to betray her true feelings. "Why would I have wanted to tease you?"

"Because I was different. Because everyone else did."

"This isn't even worth discussing." She stumbled back a step, feeling uneasy and uncomfortable. She didn't want to talk about this and didn't like that he was pushing it on her. They could barely speak about the present without arguing—what good would it do to dredge up the past?

"Even Andy," he went on. "He even admitted he used to be afraid of me, used to tease and run away—before we became friends."

"I'm going," she said, gesturing with a sweep of her hands to indicate that the subject was closed.

"Why? Because I mentioned Andy? Does it bother you to talk about your husband with me? We were friends, or have you forgotten?"

She glared up at him. Andy... He was a large fragment

in their littered past and even seven years after his death, he still stood between them. "You used to be my friend, Rafe—before Andy, before everything else."

"Was I?" he asked, reaching out and grabbing her by the elbow. "Was I really?" He glared down at her, his dark eyes wild. "Why did you want to be friends with Wolf Boy, when everyone else ran away? How come I frightened everyone else away and not you?"

Raeanne glared up at him, angry that she was the one being confronted now. What was she supposed to tell him, what did she say? How could she explain the special place he'd always had in her heart? What could she reveal without revealing too much?

"I thought it was mean," she said finally, after a long silence. "I thought it was cruel what they said to you, the names they used to use. It made me feel sad. I knew it hurt you and it hurt me, too."

Her words were eloquent and thoughtful, but Rafe took no solace in them. Instead, they felt like a piercing sword in the chest. The pain was crippling and he felt he would bleed for the rest of his life.

He saw the emotion in her face, saw the sympathy and the compassion in her eyes, but it made him feel cold and defeated inside. It was as he'd guessed, as he'd always suspected. She'd felt sorry for him. She'd championed his cause out of sympathy—sympathy for the poor boy without a past, for the child whose mother had thrown him away, the baby who'd been suckled by wolves and weaned on the wild.

"I never wanted your pity," he told her in a bitter voice, tightening the hold on her arm.

Something in Rafe's black eyes flared—a spark, an

ember—and Raeanne felt a shiver travel down her spine. It had been something harsh, something angry, but also something hot and alive.

"Pity," she repeated, struggling against his hold. "I never pitied you."

"Didn't you? A stray, with no background? The mistake someone had just tossed away?"

"It wasn't like that," she insisted, trying to wrestle her arm free.

"A wolf boy to be pitied and apologized to," he continued, his voice growing harsher.

"Stop it," she demanded.

"A misfit," he continued, sneering. "A loser you could defend and make excuses for."

"Stop it!" she screamed, finally pulling herself free. She looked up at him, her chest heaving with emotion. "Stop it right now!"

"Maybe you should stop," he said, anger and pain making him go a little crazy. "Maybe you should stop feeling so sorry for me." He reached out suddenly, grabbing her again. He used both hands this time and the force of his strength brought her crashing against him with a violent jolt. "Think about it," he said in a low voice. "You're alone out here with me. There are those in town who would fear being alone with a man who'd been raised by wolves." He wrapped his arms around her, bringing her close and holding her tight. "Maybe you would do good to fear me just a little."

Rafe brought his mouth down hard on her soft lips. He was angry and hurt, the thought of her pity making him furious. He wanted to make her feel his pain and to understand his anger. He wanted to be rough to show his contempt, wanted to be crude to pay her back for her charity.

But when he felt the velvety softness of her mouth against his, something changed. Raeanne was in his arms—the woman he'd wanted for longer than he could remember—and the realization had his anger melting away. What he'd only imagined, he now could touch. What he'd only dreamed about, he now could feel and taste. He forgot about pity and charity, forgot about sympathy and sorrow and picking up strays. The bitterness scattered from his brain, like dry, forgotten seeds scattering in the winter wind. Without the anger, he was left with only needs and an ache inside that he'd carried with him for far too long.

Raeanne wasn't afraid, she was terrified. His mouth had captured hers with a force that took her breath, that mastered her will and sent her thoughts fleeing. He'd never kissed her before—not once, not even on her wedding day. But his lips settled over hers now as though they'd been made for that purpose. For years she had waited, for a lifetime she'd anticipated and now she knew the dizzying reality of his kiss.

She stopped struggling against him and turned the battle inward instead. She'd held her feelings in for so long, sharing them with no one else. But as if a floodgate had been opened after a long winter's rain, needs flowed from her in a torrent, carrying her so far, so fast, she feared she'd never find her way back.

Rafe forced her lips apart, tasting her magic and feeling himself grow dizzy and weak. He was not a man who gave his heart lightly, he was not a man who tarried on the surface of emotion. He dived deep, reaching out from the depths of his soul to find solace and intensity in hers.

He pulled her closer and closer, wanting to confiscate and hoard every breath, every sigh, every precious moment. Somewhere in the back of his brain he heard her soft moan, tasted the nectar in his mouth, before it ricocheted through his system like an exotic and powerful opiate. He was a man with no past and an uncertain future, but for the moment he knew he held all he'd ever really need.

"Raeanne," he groaned, tearing his mouth from hers. "Raeanne, Raeanne." His voice was little more than a hoarse whisper and his breathing was labored. Beneath him, he felt the ground list and heel and his heart roared like thunder in his ears. He let her hair fall across him, feeling cool and silky against his heated skin. He buried his face in the warmth of her neck, feeling her soft skin against his lips and her body trembling beneath her bulky clothes. He'd thought he'd known what it was to want her, but he'd never imagined this.

"Rafe."

He heard his name escape from her lips, a breathless plea that drifted in the silence of the snow and the trees. He captured her lips again, his hand finding the zipper of her parka and pulling it open. She was so warm, her waist was so slender and he pulled her to him tight. He wanted her right here—in the snow, in the wilderness. He wanted to tear away all barriers that separated them—clothing, consciousness, opinion, the past. He wanted nothing to stand in the way of making her his own.

Raeanne felt her world careening out of control. She was adrift, beyond her jurisdiction, in over her head. She struggled for composure, wrestled to take command, but being in his arms was more than she could take. There was no foothold to steady her, no firm support to grab on to. He'd overwhelmed her completely and the helplessness she felt terrified her.

He had taken her power with his passion, assumed all command with his desire. He was too strong, he wanted too much and she feared she didn't have enough to give. If he'd wanted to prove his point, he'd done it. If he'd wanted to show her how afraid she was, he had. She was afraid—but not of Wolf Boy. She was afraid of herself and the way he made her feel.

"Rafe," she whispered, pushing away and gasping for air.

Rafe felt the withdrawal and struggled against it. "Don't," he murmured, pulling her back.

"No," she cried, desperate, staggering back a step. "No, I can't."

He let her go, the sound of her voice piercing through the cloud of desire. With the taste of her still on his lips, he saw the fear in her eyes and felt something go dead inside. "Can't, or won't?"

"It doesn't matter," she said in a small voice, a tear spilling down her cheek. "You were wrong. I am afraid, Rafe. I've always been afraid."

She turned and stumbled down the rocks and across the snow to her car. Rafe heard the sound of the engine, watched her steer the car over the rough terrain until she'd disappeared from view. As he watched, he felt a wall of ice slowly close in around him, a frigid barrier keeping him from the warmth he craved.

The fear he'd seen in her eyes haunted him. He'd lived with fear his whole life, seen it enough times in the eyes of friend and foe alike to know it and recognize it. But the terror he'd seen just now had nothing to do with legends and mistakes from the past.

He remembered the feel of her in his arms, savored the taste of her in his mouth. Closing his eyes, he steeled himself against the rush of emotion that gripped him. She had wanted him. He'd felt her body tremble, heard her soft moans of need.

Opening his eyes suddenly, he started down the hill toward his truck at a run. She'd been afraid, all right, but not of him. But something had put that fear in her eyes and he wasn't going to rest until he found out what it was.

"I'm not sure what it is, Daddy," Raeanne lamented, switching the phone to the other ear. "It's just making a mess all over the driveway."

"Could you have run over something?" Raymond Martin asked over the line. "It sounds like you might have cracked the oil pan."

Raeanne remembered how carelessly she'd driven the reservation road back to the highway and the numerous scrapes and crunches she'd heard. "I don't know," she muttered evasively, preferring not to go into detail. "I might have."

"Well," Raymond said slowly, "I'll see what I can do. But you know, with it being Sunday tomorrow and Christmas on Tuesday, it's not likely there's much we can do for the next few days. Why don't I drop the old truck by in the morning? You can use it until we get your car straightened out."

Raeanne thought of bouncing around town in that ancient contraption and felt her head begin to throb. "Let me call around in the morning," she said finally, loving her father for offering, but hating the thought of rattling around in the hellish vehicle. "Maybe I can find a garage open."

She heard her father chuckle over the line. "You forget, honey, this is Whitehorn, not Los Angeles. Everything around here isn't open twenty-four hours a day." He paused a moment to chuckle again. "But I'll talk to you tomorrow. We'll figure out something. Good night, sweetie."

"Good night, Daddy," she mumbled, dropping the phone onto its cradle.

She glanced out the dining room window to the dark driveway where her car was parked. It was too dark to see the huge oil stain that had spread from beneath it, but she knew it was there. It had been foolish to drive so recklessly along the rugged road that led through the reservation, but she hadn't exactly been thinking straight at the time.

Raeanne took a deep breath, thinking of Rafe and the way he'd held her, the way he'd kissed her and the way he'd made her feel. How many years had she fantasized and daydreamed about that happening? How many nights had she lain awake in bed, longing for him to kiss her in that very way?

But all her wishes and dreams hadn't prepared her for the violent reaction she'd had to his touch. He'd stirred feelings in her she'd never known existed, feelings she seemed powerless to control and helpless to stop.

Maybe he'd been right when he told her she should fear him. Because what she had felt when he held her in his arms scared her to death.

With a tired sigh, she turned away from the window, giving her head a small shake in an effort to stop herself from remembering. She wanted desperately to forget, but it didn't do much good. Try as she might, she couldn't forget the feel of his hands on her, his lips hot and urgent and his voice rough with need.

She reached for the package of brightly colored Christmas bows that lay amid the cluttered array of wrappings and ribbons that littered her small dining room table. Pulling a large, shiny red bow from the bag, she finished up the package she'd been wrapping when her father called. When she was done, she added the present to the stack of others she'd completed earlier and, gathering them all up into her arms, she carried them into the living room and arranged them beneath the tree.

She stepped back and admired the festive scene. It looked like something from a Currier and Ives Christmas card—the room lit only by the lights of the tree, reflecting off the ornaments and framed by the brightly wrapped presents scattered below. Still, despite the tree and all its trimmings, it was hard to believe Christmas was in just three days. She felt anything but festive.

She meandered back into the dining room, reaching for a large shopping bag that rested on a press-backed chair. Inside, one lone package remained.

Rafe's present.

Almost reluctantly, Raeanne reached into the bag and pulled out a small black box. Flipping open the top, she stared down at the rugged, all-weather sports watch inside. What had ever possessed her to buy it? It had been an impulsive and stupid thing to do, but it seemed as though she'd been doing a lot of stupid and impulsive things lately. Buying him a present hardly seemed appropriate, given their on-again, off-again friendship, so why had she done it? Why had it pleased her to shop for him and pick out something special?

Glancing down at it, she shook her head. And what was she going to do with it now?

She squeezed her eyes tight, feeling the sting of tears in her eyes and a hopelessness in her heart. She was so confused, so alone. He'd kissed her and awakened in her a passion she hadn't known herself capable of. He'd shown her desire, intensity, but very little else. He'd said nothing to her, made no declaration, given her no real clue as to how he felt.

So why had he kissed her? Because he cared? Because he wanted her? Or because he'd wanted to prove a point, because he'd wanted to make his case and put her in her place? Rafe had a reputation for being cold, but could he be that cold and unfeeling?

And yet how well did she know him? People could change a lot in seven years. Had too much time passed? Had he changed so much that he was a stranger to her now?

She took a deep breath, batting away a tear as it spilled down her cheek. Slamming the lid of the watch's box down hard, she reached for the wrapping paper. She wrapped it quickly, then took it with her into the living room and tossed it carelessly beneath the tree.

"Maybe Dad would like it," she said aloud, the sound of her own voice in the quiet house making her feel even more lonely and discouraged.

The clock above the mantel chimed the half hour—nine-thirty—and yet she felt as though she'd been up for days. The emotional upheaval of the day had left her drained and she hadn't even given the interview with Nan Avery a thought.

She glanced at her briefcase in the foyer. There was so much work that needed to be done—notes to review, transcripts to go over, questions to prepare—and just thinking about it made her feel worse. She didn't have the energy to look at her notes tonight, to think about Ethan and the trial and the defense she would have to prepare. Thank goodness Judge Matthews had recessed the trial until the day after New Year's. She could use the time and all this could wait at least until the morning. All she wanted now was a hot shower and a warm bed.

The shower felt wonderful and she stood beneath the hot spray, letting its warmth penetrate deep. She dried off, wrapping herself in a bulky robe and blowing her hair dry. By the time she'd slipped the dryer back on its hook beside the sink and flipped the bathroom light off, she could barely keep her eyes open.

She stumbled through the darkness, too tired to bother with the lights. She ambled into the living room, pulling the plug on the Christmas lights, shutting the drapes and closing the blinds. She'd just finished checking the lock on the front door and started back through the house when something had her forgetting about how tired she was and brought every muscle in her body to full alert.

She froze, standing in the darkness and listening to the roar of the silence against her eardrums. Through the dining room windows, she caught a glimpse of movement outside on the drive and her heart made a spectacular leap from her chest to her throat. An icy shiver traveled the length of her spine and she shuddered where she stood.

Someone was out there.

Eight

Life seemed to come back into her petrified body in a burst of action and fury. Raeanne moved through the house, silent and alert. In one smooth motion, she grabbed the cordless phone from the desk and the gun from the drawer.

Her fingers felt cold and clumsy on the buttons of the telephone as she dialed 911. The soft, muted tones that sounded as she punched in the keys were like sirens in the dead silence. Waiting for the first ring seemed to take an eternity and she peeked around the corner, seeing a shadow travel the length of her dining room, around the house, and up her back stairs.

A million scenarios passed through her mind—all violent and frightening. Headlines sprang into her head and she saw her name in print—as the victim of a criminal act.

The flat monotone of the first ring exploded in her ear, and she bolted violently. She tiptoed down the hall, creeping toward the kitchen. She thought of what Rafe had said, about Ethan and the trial, about her job and the questions she'd raised. He'd talked about people being upset, about people wanting justice, about the possibility of someone extracting his own form of revenge.

The second ring came after what seemed like an eternity, just as a tall shadow covered the window of her back door. Raeanne's breath caught in her throat and she held it in a strangled sort of gasp.

A third ring sounded in her ear, but she was only vaguely aware of it. Every nerve, every cell, every ounce of her being, was watching the handle on the back door. With a chilling clarity, she remembered pulling the trash can from under the sink and carrying it to the Dumpster out back. And with a certainty that could come only from a system high on adrenaline, she knew for a fact that she'd forgotten to lock the door.

She forgot about the telephone, and stared down at the gun in her hand. She remembered her brave words to Rafe, boasting about her willingness to use a gun—tough, fearless words from someone who'd never even come close to having to. There wasn't a doubt in her mind that she'd use it if she had to, but she'd never had to before and the thought that she might have to now terrified her.

She watched the knob turn and the door swing open in an aberrant, eerie motion that was slow and prolonged, not like normal action at all. She forgot about the telephone, letting the line go dead and the handset slide unnoticed to the floor. With both hands, she grabbed the Beretta, bringing it up into position to fire, and felt the blood in her veins turn to ice.

The moonlight outside made the night sky bright, and

cast the dark shadow of a stranger across her kitchen floor. He stepped inside, a rush of cold wind following in his wake. He looked up, seeing her standing in the hallway across from him, a gun leveled at his chest.

"Don't be frightened."

At the sound of the gruff whisper in the darkness, Raeanne dropped the gun to her side. "Rafe."

The door slammed behind him, throwing the kitchen into darkness and erasing his shadow from the floor. He moved across the room, drawn by the scent of the woman he'd come for, the absence of light a mere impediment of the moment. He found her in the darkness with unerring ease, reaching down slowly and slipping the gun from her hand.

Raeanne stared up at him, his dark eyes bright, in defiance of the night. He said nothing else, made no confession, offered no excuse. He merely stared down at her, telling her his secrets with his eyes alone.

"I don't want you to be afraid," he whispered again, but he wasn't talking about her fear of an intruder.

But Raeanne wasn't afraid, not any longer and she wouldn't be ever again. He was here and that was all that mattered. Maybe there were things they still needed to talk about, maybe there were words she still needed to hear from him, but all that didn't seem to matter. He'd come to her and for now, in the darkness, that was enough.

She stepped close, letting her arms travel slowly along the quilting of his down vest. Rising on tiptoe, she rested her hands on his shoulders and brought her lips to his in a soft, tender kiss.

"Raeanne," he murmured against her lips, his body reacting violently to the softness of her touch. "Rae-anne, I—"

"No," she said, stopping him with another gentle kiss. "I don't want to talk. Not tonight." She slipped her arms around his neck, pulling him close. "Not tonight."

The feel of her soft body against his was almost more than he could take. He'd come wanting to talk, wanting to clear the air between them once and for all. He'd wanted to ask her why she'd been frightened and to assure her that, despite what he'd said, she had nothing to fear from him. But her hands were on him now, she was touching him and all the rest seemed so unimportant.

He'd seen her car in the drive, but when he was unable to get an answer at the front door, he'd come around to the back of the house in search of her. Seeing her standing in the hallway with a gun leveled at his chest hadn't frightened him nearly as much as the thought that something might have happened to her.

Slowly and deliberately, he put his hands on her hips and pulled her to him tight. Staring into her dark eyes, he let her feel his hard body, let her feel what it was she did to him. Her dark eyes grew wide and filled with emotion, but nowhere in them could he find any fear. He saw only life and challenge and need.

He brought his mouth to hers, the storm within him turning violent from years spent waiting. He pushed her lips apart, kissing her long and deep and feeling himself grow dizzy and weak.

He'd been cold for so long—a lone wolf on the prowl in a desolate winter landscape. But holding her in his arms, feeling her soft body against his, it was as though he'd suddenly found the sun.

His heart pounded and he felt the blood pumping hot through his veins. He could feel her beneath the bulky robe—soft, smooth and bare. A shudder traveled through him. He felt shaky and weak and yet never in his life had he wanted more to be strong.

Raeanne surrendered to the violent storm of his kiss. She didn't flinch, nor did she cower away. She met the furious energy of his embrace with a fervent, urgent need of her own.

She felt the need arise in her, soaring up from that private place where she'd hidden it away. It tore through her now, coursing through her veins like fire through a drought-ravaged forest. When he kissed her earlier, on the Indian reservation, the breadth of her feelings had frightened her. The chemistry between them had been so strong, so potent. It terrified her that he had that kind of power over her.

But she was frightened no more. She knew what she wanted and she wanted it now. If things weren't settled between them, so be it. If he still denied her the words she longed to hear, who needed them? She'd waited her whole life for this man and she would wait no more.

She tore at his vest, sending it tumbling to the floor. She felt strong and confident, ready to face her destiny head-on and not run for cover. She had seen him standing in the darkness, had felt his need reaching out to her and something magical had happened inside her. A fountain had burst to life within her—a wellspring of energy and strength. She'd tapped into the source itself—her power, her instincts, her ability, as a woman. She wasn't afraid, she was delirious. She was in the arms of the man she loved, secure in the knowledge that she could please him, and please herself, as well.

He might not have been able to say the words she'd

longed to hear, but it wasn't important. He needed her—she'd seen it in his eyes, felt it in his touch and tasted it in his mouth. And she needed him, too. For now, the knowledge was enough. There would be time later for words and explanations, for confessions and declarations. Now there was only the man she loved and a need so great between them that nothing else mattered.

Rafe tore at the belt of the robe, wanting to devastate and destroy all barriers that separated him from what he wanted most. He labored with hands made weak by need, ripping and tearing until the constricting sash gave way, falling silently to the floor. This afternoon he'd endured the bulky coats and layers of clothing, but now he would tolerate nothing. He yanked the robe apart, feeling the breath in his lungs stall and his heart forget to beat.

He tore his mouth from hers, leaving her gasping and desperate. The hands that reached for her trembled, but never had he felt more alive. Her skin was like velvet, soft beyond belief. His hands drifted over her—caressing, exploring. Her breasts were full and round, her hips supple and firm. He told himself this had to be a dream, because life for him had never been this good.

But Rafe had stopped believing in dreams long ago. He believed only in what he could see, what he could touch and what he could feel. And at the moment Raeanne was all of that. Her slender body torched his senses, her soft sighs inflamed his soul. She was tangible and real and she belonged to him.

He lifted her to him, burying his face in the sweet valley of her breasts. With hands and mouth, he worshiped and explored. Her body blossomed beneath his touch, her hard nipples inciting and fueling the inferno building in him.

Her soft groans sounding in his ears were a salacious symphony of need and desire.

"I want you," he growled against her heated skin. His tongue tasted the length of her neck, leaving a path of hot, wet kisses in its wake. He'd never felt like this before—so alive, so strong, so needy.

"Rafe."

The sound of his name on her lips had the fire within him flaring. His whole life, she'd been his ideal—unattainable and out of reach. And yet he'd wanted her—Lord, how he had wanted her. The long, torturous nights, the cold, cruel days, he had endured. An empty life. She'd been everything he hoped for and all he knew he could never have.

He knew what it was to face his worst fear, to greet the demon and stare it squarely in the eye. He'd had to stand back and watch while she married his best friend. He'd hated himself for wanting his best friend's wife, but a part of him had hated his friend for taking her away.

But Andy was gone, and she belonged to him now—for the moment—and that would have to be enough. It was more than he'd ever hoped for, more than he deserved.

"Rafe," she moaned again, her body impatient and restless with need. She wrapped her legs around him, the bulky robe that dangled from her shoulders falling to the floor. The feel of the rough denim against her legs had the craving in her spiraling, spinning out of control. His hands on her body were driving her mad and the desperation grew critical. She tore at his flannel shirt, pulling it free of his jeans and sending buttons scattering across the carpeted floor.

Rafe carried her with him, finding the bedroom and staggering to the bed. He pulled off his shredded shirt, tossing it aside, but her urgent hands dragged him back into her arms.

She grabbed for his jeans, yanking them apart. He was ready to explode, the need in him like a beast that grew more potent and more determined with every stroke of her hand. His head spun and his spirit cried out. He needed her more than he needed his next breath.

Raeanne stared up into his dark eyes. How could she have ever thought they were cold and unfeeling? Their shadowy depths burned her now, disclosing more clearly the love in his heart than any words she could ever hear. She was staggered by the strength of him and bolstered by his desire. He was a wolf boy—wild, untamed and savage. And he was hungry for her.

"W-we have to be careful," she murmured, knowing she had to be responsible, even though coherent thought seemed impossible.

"I know, I'll take care of it," Rafe assured her, and he did with speed and efficiency.

Ground zero. It came for them both in a union of mind and body, heart and soul. Rafe forgot about what clothing remained. There was no time left for that. He pushed into her—one mighty thrust that sent her reaching, grabbing, wanting. She was not a virgin. Andy had taken that from her years before. But the force driving her was something she'd never experienced before.

For a moment, Rafe couldn't move. He could only close his eyes and succumb to the rush of feelings bombarding him. He stared down at her, watching the play of emotion across her face. He saw no fear, only hunger and need and it made the craving in him all the more unstable. She fit him tightly, like a glove, her body expanding and accepting his intrusion. He knew, as his body instinctively began to move, that he would never forget this moment. It was carved in his soul, like an etching on a rock. It was pure, it was pristine and it was as close to heaven as he was ever going to get.

"Love me," she murmured, reaching up and wrapping her arms around him tight. "Rafe, please, love me."

"I do," he whispered against her lips, kissing her deeply. He forgot about inhibitions and inabilities. He wasn't thinking about masking feelings or hiding the truth. At that moment, all there was for him was Raeanne and the glorious motions of their bodies together.

With each powerful push of his body, Raeanne felt her hold on the real world falter and slip. She didn't know if she was on the road to madness or bliss and she no longer cared. The need in her had become a holocaust, making her wild and desperate. He was Wolf Boy, but she was the savage.

She moved intuitively, instinctively, journeying closer to that magic place, that elusive spot where misery met ecstasy, hunger met need. The world tilted wildly on its axis, spinning faster and faster and her heart beat erratically in her chest. She let his passion carry her out of herself, over the edge and into the void.

Rafe pulled his mouth from hers, feeling her arms contract and her legs spasm tight. His own body shuddered as he tried valiantly to help her through the labyrinth of pleasure, but it was no use. He couldn't hold on any longer. Her movements, her soft moans of satisfaction and the feel of her beneath him, were like gas to a flame—they ignited him, pushing him beyond the limits, beyond all human constraints. His body exploded, hurling him forward and into the white light of rapture.

* * *

The world took its time returning, and Rafe found that he was in no hurry for its arrival. He drifted back slowly— inch by inch, breath by breath—listening to the steady, even beating of his heart blending with hers. She held him, her arms around his neck anchoring him to her, though they needn't have. He had no intention of going.

His hand languidly stroked her long, silky hair, which spilled out across the bedspread like a burst of light around the sun. Every now and then his body would tremble, quaking testimony to the fury that had shaken him to his core. Outside, the wind howled, cold and bleak, but he'd never felt warmer or more content in his life. If he died right now, he wouldn't complain. He was in Raeanne's arms and he knew he could ask for no more.

Raeanne sighed, closing her eyes and letting the warmth of his hard body surround and protect her. They were still locked together, their bodies entwined in an intimate embrace, but their passion had graduated from conflagration to contentment long ago, and she was satisfied to just hold him. She would have been happy to stay that way forever, but she knew the real world awaited.

She thought of the way he had held her, of his touch and his desire and she felt a stirring inside of her. She knew now that this was why she had come home, why she had returned to Whitehorn after so many years. She'd come back for him. She loved Rafe Rawlings, her wild, untamed Wolf Boy, and she always had.

"You're cold," he murmured against her cheek, feeling her shiver beneath him.

"Not really," she whispered, not wanting the moment to end.

But he was already moving. Lifting himself up, he stood, sliding his jeans to his waist. Reaching for the bed-covers, he placed her between them.

Raeanne laid back against the cool sheets, letting him draw the blankets around her tight. But when he picked up the rest of his clothes, she sprang up.

"Stay," she said, placing a hand over his.

He regarded her in the darkness, the sight of her naked in the bed causing his body to react again. "Are you sure?"

She lifted herself up to her knees, letting the covers fall carelessly away. She let her hands travel up his chest, her flat palms brushing the coarse, dark hair. "Very sure."

His boots, socks and jeans slipped to the floor, followed by his shorts. Lowering her back onto the bed, he drew the covers over them both. Pulling her soft, warm body into his arms, he kissed her. "I'm sure, too."

"Are you awake?"

Rafe cracked a lid. The light streaming in through the miniblinds was blinding, and he quickly closed it again. "No."

"Yes, you are." Raeanne laughed, giving him a playful push with her hand.

Rafe had to smile. She felt so soft and warm beneath the covers and their bodies fit so well together. He'd actually awakened long before she had, but he hadn't wanted to move. It had felt so good just to hold her, to have a few moments to reflect and absorb all that had happened, to go back over it and savor it. He'd felt her body stir, felt her slowly find her way to wakefulness, but still he'd made no move to rise. He'd been too content, too satisfied, too happy.

Contentment. Satisfaction. Happiness. The concepts of

those things didn't strike him as particularly odd, except that he was a man who'd known very little contentment, very little satisfaction, and very little true happiness in his life.

He peeked through slitted lids at her, lying beside him, her hair spilling over his chest. He felt almost giddy. How could things change so dramatically in such a short time? Yesterday morning he'd gotten up and driven to the Norths' ranch, knowing she would be anything but pleased to see him there.

He opened his eyes wider, looking at her beautiful face and bright smile. She hadn't been pleased then, but she looked pleased now.

"See, I was right," she said, cuddling close. "You are awake."

"What time is it?" he asked, stretching lazily before pulling her close and pressing a kiss to a corner of her mouth.

"I don't know." She smiled, kissing him back. "Where's your watch?"

He glanced down at his bare wrist. "Oh," he groaned, remembering the broken band that had sent his old, battered watch flying to lie in a heap on the pavement outside the station house. "I don't have one anymore."

Raeanne lifted herself up onto her elbow and gazed down at him. Smiling broadly, she thought of the present she'd tossed so carelessly under the tree.

"What?" he asked suspiciously, seeing the full smile and dancing eyes.

"You don't have a watch?"

"No," he said, reaching up and caressing her cheek. "Is that a problem?"

She turned her face, pressing a kiss into his palm and smiled.

"What's so funny?"

She just looked down at him and smiled more widely. "Nothing."

His dark eyes narrowed. "Why don't I believe you?"

"I don't know, why don't you?" she asked breezily, laughing. She glanced over to the clock radio beside the bed, and gasped. "My God, I can't believe it. It's after eight. I never sleep this late."

"Well, we haven't exactly been doing a whole lot of *sleeping,*" he said with a wicked smile, pulling her close and letting their bodies brush together. "You have somewhere else you have to be?"

Moving forward, she pushed him into the pillows, settling herself atop him. "No," she murmured, pressing his arms back onto the mattress and brushing a kiss over his lips. "But there is something I have to do."

She kissed him, slipping her tongue between his lips and taking command. She moved over him—slow, sensuous movements that left him breathless and desperate.

He groaned, his hands moving the length of her. "Raeanne, you're…you're driving me crazy."

"Hold on, then," she murmured against his lips. "'Cause you haven't seen anything yet."

She rose up, her hair tumbling past her shoulders, her legs straddling his long, lean body. She found him hard, and ready for her and she lowered herself onto him in one strong, determined motion.

Rafe fought the urge to close his eyes—even though the rush of pleasure flooding his system was almost overwhelming. But he resisted, wanting to see her above him, wanting to imprint the image in his brain. She was strong and majestic as a goddess, skilled and sensual as a courtesan, yet to him she was an angel.

It was a long time before they left the bed, before they stumbled for the bathroom and into the shower. After a shower that left her small bathroom filled with huge clouds of steam, they dried one another off and headed for the kitchen.

Raeanne tightened the sash of her robe, reaching into the refrigerator and pulling out a carton of eggs. Her gaze drifted to Rafe, who was making coffee at the counter and a shiver traveled up her spine. He looked so handsome standing in her kitchen—hair tousled, feet and chest bare, dressed only in jeans. She'd never seen him like this before.

She'd known him most of her life. They had talked and kidded and laughed and argued together. His strong, handsome features were no mystery to her. They were dear and familiar. They had filled her dreams, haunted her consciousness and taken up residence in her heart.

But standing in her kitchen after a long night of love, he looked different to her now—the same, yet different. He had come to her, he had taken her in his arms, he had kissed her and loved her and somehow she knew nothing would ever be the same again—for either of them.

She could hardly believe last night had happened, that he'd actually stayed the night, was actually standing in her kitchen now. And yet it seemed as though her whole life had been moving toward this point.

She cracked the eggs, dropping them into the frying pan and whipping them together. She felt herself smiling—actually, she felt like humming and singing and jumping for joy and dancing around the kitchen, but she wasn't sure what Rafe would make of all that. So, for the time being, a smile would have to do.

It had been there. All this time, all these years, she'd somehow just known this would happen. There was something between them—there always had been and there always would be. It had been there in Mrs. Whitney's classroom and it had been there last night when he took her in his arms. It was in his eyes, in his touch, in every move he made. They belonged together, were a part of each other—now and forever.

She and Rafe together. It seemed impossible, unbelievable and yet it was true. This was what she had wanted since that first day she laid eyes on him. She remembered Winona, and her cryptic words that night at the Hip Hop Café. Winona had talked about resolving old problems and making a clear path to happiness.

She glanced at Rafe and then back to the pan on the stove. There were issues still unresolved between them, their paths remained littered with ghosts from the past. But she was so happy now. There would be time later to tackle all those things. None of it seemed important right now. Being with Rafe felt like the most natural thing in the world—it was where she belonged, where she wanted to be. She'd dreamed of being with Rafe hundreds of times over the years. She'd imagined how it would happen and what would occur. Last night had been nothing like she'd imagined, nothing like she'd dreamed, yet it had been more than she'd ever hoped it would be.

"Yum, smells good," Rafe murmured, reaching around from behind and nuzzling her neck. Carefully bringing his arm around, he held up a mug of coffee. "This is for you."

"Thank you," she said, taking the cup from him and giving it a sip. She turned in his arms, smiling up at him. "Delicious."

He bent down and kissed her, tasting the coffee on her lips. "You're delicious," he murmured, kissing her again.

Raeanne thought of herself as a sensible, responsible person, but Rafe Rawlings had a strange effect on her. She marveled at it. One kiss, and she could forget everything—including the eggs on the stove.

"Wait!" Raeanne screamed after a moment, pushing him away, when she smelled the aroma of burning food. "Oh, no," she moaned, batting away the smoke and looking down at the eggs. "I've ruined them."

"I like blackened food," Rafe murmured, taking the pan from her hand and dropping it in the sink. "But I'm not hungry now, anyway—for eggs, that is." He pulled her close, lifting her off the floor and onto the counter. "You're the only thing I want," he whispered against her lips, pulling the robe apart. "The only thing I'm hungry for."

Raeanne gave in to the maelstrom of emotions that ravaged her. His words, his touch, his very presence, had her wanting him and it was as though she couldn't get enough. Her need for him was enormous, her hunger immense. She wanted him more with each touch, with each kiss. She'd spent years waiting, years doing without and it would be a long time—a very long time—before the hunger would be appeased.

"Rafe," she murmured, her hands moving restlessly over his chest, his arms, his shoulders.

"You're mine now," he whispered, his hard chest heaving with emotion. He pulled her to him, sliding her across the counter until she was wrapped around him. "Mine."

"Yours." Raeanne sighed, giving in to a fate she had prayed would be hers. "Yours."

"Raeanne? You awake? Raeanne?"

Both Rafe and Raeanne jumped at the sound of her name and the pounding on the door. For a moment, neither of them could move. Then the pounding sounded again.

"Hey! You in there? Raeanne? Open up."

"Oh, my God!" Raeanne gasped, pushing Rafe away and snatching her robe together. "It's my dad."

Nine

"Daddy," Raeanne said, her attempt at sounding bright and chipper making her voice higher than usual. "My goodness, what are you doing here?"

"Well, there you are," Raymond Martin said testily, stepping into the kitchen and wiping his feet on the mat. His cheeks were bright from the cold and a stocking cap covered his bald head. "Where the Sam Hill you been, child? I've been pounding out here for ten minutes."

"I'm sorry, Dad." Raeanne cringed, feeling her face flush hot. "I…uh…" She shrugged, gesturing toward the robe wrapped around her. "I was in the shower."

"Whose truck is that parked out front?" Raymond asked, doing a double take after spotting the pan full of burned eggs in the sink. "It sorta looks like the one Rafe Raw—" But Raymond's voice trailed off when he caught a glimpse of movement from the far side of the room.

"Good morning, Mr. Martin," Rafe said, stepping into

the kitchen from the small hall and extending a hand to Raeanne's father.

Raeanne just wanted the floor to open up and swallow her whole. This couldn't be happening. She dared not look at her father and she was half-afraid to look at Rafe. If his shirt was still off, she knew for sure she would die from embarrassment. She tried to reason things out, reminding herself she was an adult—unattached and independent and she had every right to entertain whoever she wanted in her own home, whenever she wanted. She didn't need to make excuses or explanations to anyone for her behavior. She was a free agent, wasn't breaking any laws, wasn't hurting anyone.

But this was her *father!* And he'd practically caught them in the act. If humiliation could be fatal, she was doomed.

"Well, Rafe, that is your truck out front then," Raymond said, taking Rafe's outstretched hand and giving it a hearty shake. "I didn't expect to see you here today."

Raeanne looked up guiltily, relieved to see Rafe in a shirt—despite the fact that it was missing several of its buttons—with the tails neatly tucked in. "He…uh, I…uh, called Rafe this morning to see if he would mind…you know, looking at my car," she blurted out nervously.

Rafe looked at Raeanne, raising his eyebrows slowly and giving her a slow smile.

Raymond Martin looked at his daughter, surprised. "Well, now, why'd you do that? I told you I'd be over to look at it." He shook his head, looking back at Rafe, "You didn't need to drive all the way into town just for that. I could have taken care of it."

"I didn't mind," Rafe said casually, looking back at Raeanne. "Besides, she offered to fix me breakfast."

"Well, I hope you're having better luck with the car than she is with those eggs," Raymond said dryly, pointing to the pan in the sink.

Rafe smiled, watching the color darken even more in Raeanne's cheeks. He knew she, too, was remembering how those eggs had gotten ruined.

Raeanne felt her mouth go dry and nervous perspiration break out along her upper lip. The whole situation was just going from bad to worse.

"So, what do you think it is?" Raymond asked, seemingly unaware of the tensions flying around him.

Rafe turned back to Raymond, giving him a blank stare. "Hmm? What about, sir?"

"The car. What does it look like to you?"

"The car," Rafe repeated, shooting Raeanne a quick glance. "Uh, I'm not sure yet."

"Sounded like a crack in the oil pan to me," Raymond went on, pulling a mug from the dish rack and pouring himself a cup of coffee. "'Course, it could be a seal. You never know with those foreign jobs."

"More like a cracked pan, I think," Rafe said, remembering Raeanne plowing over the rugged reservation road and putting two and two together.

Raeanne watched as the two of them chatted for a while. She was calming down and was able to think straight again. Her father, bless his heart, seemed to suspect nothing and she breathed a little easier. Still, she wished he would go.

"I thought I'd get at it after breakfast," Rafe was saying, pouring himself another cup of coffee and offering some more to Raymond.

"Breakfast, yes," Raymond mused absently, glancing

down at the sink again. He shook his head at Rafe's offer to refill his cup. "No, no. No more for me, thanks. Well, honey," he said, putting his empty cup down on the counter and giving his daughter a peck on the cheek, "sounds like you're in good hands here. I'll just get along home then, let you two get to your…breakfast."

"Thanks for coming by, Daddy," Raeanne managed to say, pulling the robe around her more tightly as she walked her father to the kitchen door.

"Sure you don't want me to leave the old truck?"

"No, honestly," she insisted. "I'm—I'm sure we'll get my car running."

"Okay, then," he said, patting her on the hand. "See you later." Looking over his daughter's shoulder, he raised a hand to Rafe. "Good seeing you again, Rafe. Our best to your mother."

"Mr. Martin," Rafe said politely. "Good seeing you, too."

After promising to telephone later, Raeanne closed the door behind her father, leaning back against it. "Do you think he suspected anything?"

"I wouldn't worry about it," Rafe said, slowly starting across the kitchen toward her.

Raeanne squeezed her eyes tight. "I'm so embarrassed. I'd just never live it down if he knew."

"Never?"

She opened her eyes and grimaced. "Do you think he knew?"

"No," he said, reaching for the sash of the robe, pulling on it until she came to him. "Not unless…"

"Unless what?"

"It's nothing," he said, brushing her lips with his. "Forget about it."

"What?" she insisted, pulling back and looking up at him. "Tell me."

He glanced down, then back up at her, and shrugged.

Raeanne followed his gaze, horrified to see that his feet were bare.

"Oh, no," she groaned.

He began unknotting the belt of her robe. "Your daddy doesn't own a gun, does he?"

Raeanne let him brush her lips with his, thinking maybe being caught with Rafe wasn't so bad after all. "No," she purred against his lips. "But I do."

Even as he kissed her, he smiled.

"Okay, you can open your eyes now."

Raeanne slowly lifted her lids. For a moment, she was confused and disoriented and it took her a minute to realize that the soft brown eyes she was staring down at were not Rafe's. It wasn't until a wet tongue snaked out and left a wet trail across her nose that everything registered.

"A puppy!" she shrieked, lifting the hefty little ball of brown fur from Rafe's arms and into her lap. She looked up at Rafe, her face beaming. "Is she one of Crier's?"

"He." Rafe pointed to a pertinent part of the puppy's anatomy. "And yes, he's the runt."

Raeanne lifted the wiggly little pup up, testing his weight. "He doesn't feel like a runt."

"I think his daddy might have been part wolf."

Raeanne reached up, slipping a free arm around his neck. "Like you?"

"Maybe," he murmured, pulling her close and brushing a kiss across her lips. "But be careful—you know what savages we wolves can be."

Raeanne smiled even as he kissed her. She seemed to

lose all track of time, all semblance of reality, when Rafe kissed her, but the wiggly little dog in her arms was hard to ignore. He squirmed, licking them both.

"What's his name?" she asked, giggling. She sat down on the floor and let the puppy romp across the rug.

"He's yours," Rafe said casually. But there was nothing casual in the way he watched her. He loved her gentle manner with the puppy, her loving nature. "You can call him anything you want."

"Anything?" she asked, looking up at him and slowly raising her brow.

He made a face at her. "Well, as long as it isn't one of those foo-foo California names. You're not going to call one of my dogs Biffy or Buffy or something like that."

Raeanne laughed. "I see. Then how about something studly and macho, like…Joe?" She raised a suggestive eyebrow.

Rafe pretended to think about that, lowering himself to the floor and pulling her close. "I like it," he said, kissing her cheek, her shoulder, her neck. "That way you'll always have a Joe around to protect you."

It had been a glorious day. Raeanne stroked the sleeping puppy beside her on the sofa, thinking she'd never felt more content in her life. She watched as Rafe added a log to the fire, coaxing it to a roaring flame. The small living room glowed golden, the light from the fire causing shadows from the Christmas tree and ornaments to dance wildly over the walls and ceiling.

Of course, they never had gotten around to having breakfast, and somehow Rafe had never gotten out to look at her car, but then, there had been more important things to do. There had been years to catch up on—all the times they'd denied themselves to make up for. After the long morning, and a leisurely lunch, Rafe had managed to get in touch with Arnie Henderson, who serviced the squad cars for the department and he'd promised to send a tow truck over to pick up her car first thing in the morning.

She watched Rafe stoke the fire with the poker, sending flames flying up the flue. They'd been practically inseparable. He'd left only for a short time—which she knew now had been for a quick change of clothes and to pick up the puppy. Apart from that, it had been a day devoted entirely to one another.

They had taken the puppy for a long walk in the snow, built a snowman out back, watched a Bogie-and-Bacall movie on TV and they had made love—as long and as often as they wanted.

Rafe stood and stretched, his tall frame silhouetted in the delicate light from the burning logs. Raeanne watched him, admiring the hard, masculine lines and felt a thrill of excitement travel up her spine. It had been a wonderful day.

Of course, there were still things between them that troubled her. Sooner or later they would have to sit down and talk it all out—Andy, the past, their feelings, the future. But not now. Things were so perfect now, so new and she was reluctant to do or say anything that might spoil it. They were just getting started and she consoled herself with the fact that there would be time later for sorting through the debris and clearing away all the litter from the past. For now, all she could think about was the moment and the man she loved.

"Warm enough?" he asked, sliding onto the sofa and gathering her up in his arms.

"Now I am," she murmured, feeling as contented and relaxed as the puppy on her lap.

The mantel clock above the fire chimed the hour and she turned to read its dial. Nine o'clock.

"I should be getting home," Rafe said, brushing an errant strand of hair from across her face and feeling her body tense beside him.

"Oh, I thought—" she began, every ounce of warmth leaving her body. She suddenly felt very foolish. She'd been so happy, so satisfied being with him, she'd just assumed he felt the same way.

"What is it?"

She shrugged, looking away so that her feelings wouldn't betray her. "I thought maybe…"

"Yes?"

She looked up at him. The feelings were there, she couldn't hide them. "That you'd stay."

The emotion in her eyes had his heart quaking in his chest. He wanted to stay—forever, if she'd let him—but it had been important to them both to know there was an option. "Are you asking?"

"Yes," she whispered.

He pulled her beneath him, kissing her. "Then I'm staying."

"Did he?"

Rafe put the sleepy puppy back in the blanket-lined box beside the bed, then crawled beneath the covers beside her. "Finally. But I think I've got frostbite."

Raeanne gasped when she felt his cold hands on her. "You're freezing."

"But it doesn't take me long to warm up," he murmured, pulling her close.

"Stop!" she shrieked, but the cold didn't really bother her. She loved the feel of their bodies together. "Stop or I'll scream and wake the dog."

Rafe glanced down at the box and shook his head. "No, I've convinced him it's time for him to sleep."

Raeanne gave him a deliberate look. "More of your strange powers?"

He wiggled his eyebrows up and down. "Watch it, or I'll turn my wild, feral ways on you."

"I think you already have," she murmured, brushing his mouth with a kiss. He started to pull her to him for another kiss, but she shook her head, pushing him away. "No, no. We were talking about the case."

"Ah, yes, the case." Rafe sighed, falling back against the pillows. "You were about to tell me what makes you so all-fired sure that there was something deep and dark between Walker and Avery."

"Not deep and dark," Raeanne protested, picking up the conversation where they'd left it before the puppy interrupted with its whining. "Just something else."

"What makes you think so?"

She shrugged. "A feeling."

It was late, sometime after two, but neither of them was sleepy. For the better part of the past hour, they'd been talking—lying in the bed, whispering in the darkness, like kids at a slumber party. They'd talked mostly about casual things—movies and sports and people they knew. But then the conversation had taken a turn and they'd begun discussing the trial in which they worked on opposite sides.

"A feeling?"

"Yeah," she said, hearing the skepticism in his voice. "I do get them sometimes, you know."

"Oh, yeah," he said with a deep, satisfied breath. He reached up and stroked her cheek with the back of his finger, letting the finger slide to the tip of her breast. "I...know."

"Now stop that," she chided him, pushing his hand away. "I'm serious. I can't believe you're satisfied with this...*flimsy* story of cattle rustling. I've gotten to know Ethan Walker pretty well and the guy's just not a killer."

"The guys's a hothead," Rafe reflected, his mind jealously imagining the two of them together in the small interview room at the jail. "Even as a teenager, he was big, and tough, and was known to have one hell of a temper."

"A lot of people have bad tempers," she said pointedly, giving him a look. "If you know what I mean."

"You're so subtle, but I think I get your drift," he said dryly. "But regardless of why, Walker hated Avery, you can't deny that."

"I don't," she said, raising herself higher on her elbow. "In fact, I'll go so far as to admit that he *still* hates Avery, which only proves to me that Ethan—like just about everyone else in this town, including his wife—assumed Avery was alive all these years." She thought a moment, absently shaking her head. "And it would take more than being accused of cattle rustling to keep those feelings alive for almost thirty years."

"Okay," Rafe conceded, believing her wrong, but not wanting to argue the point. "So tell me what Nan Avery said that made you think you're on the right track."

"You heard her yourself," Raeanne said, reaching out and pushing his long hair away from his forehead. "She said she remembered Charlie saying he wanted to put Ethan in his place."

"And you think that helps your case?"

"No," she admitted, letting her finger drift down his cheek and around his chin. "But it sounds like Avery just might have had it in for Ethan, rather than the other way around."

"How do you figure?"

She smiled smugly, settling against him. "Do you remember how Nan started getting really uncomfortable toward the end there?"

"Yeah. What about it?"

"Do you remember what we'd been taking about?"

"Yeah, you started poking your nose into her relationship with her husband," he said, rising up and placing a kiss on her nose. "Something you had no business doing."

"Oh?" she queried. "Not even when it might pertain to my case?"

"What could Charlie Avery's relationship with his wife have to do with helping your client?"

"You remember all those old rumors—about Avery and the Baxter girl. Before Charlie's bones were found, just about everyone in Whitehorn assumed he'd run off with her."

"Those were just a bunch of old rumors," he said. "Something Lily Mae Wheeler and her old-biddy friends liked gossiping about—like babies being raised by wolves and things like that."

"Maybe," Raeanne conceded, detecting the anger in his voice. He, of all people, knew how ugly rumors could be. "But it was only after it had been determined that Avery had been dead all this time that anyone began to think anything different." She lowered her head to his shoulder, staring out into the darkness. "Nan admitted it herself that Charlie drank, he stayed out nights. I don't know how all those old rumors got started, but you can bet things between the Averys were far from perfect."

"Okay, let's say you're right. Charlie Avery was a real bastard—drank, chased women, abused his wife, kicked puppies and stole candy from babies—whatever! I still don't see how this proves Ethan Walker didn't kill him."

Raeanne took a deep breath. He was right. None of that proved anything—least of all Ethan's innocence. But that wasn't the point. Despite the fact that she believed he was innocent, it wasn't her job to prove it. All she wanted was to place enough doubt in the minds of the jury to make it impossible for them to convict Ethan Walker. To make them think twice about Charlie Avery—about the kind of man he was, the kind of husband and father he'd been.

"It doesn't," she admitted on a long sigh.

"So how come you're so sure you're right?"

She raised up on her elbow again and looked down at him. "A feeling."

He smiled. "So we're back to that again, huh?"

"What's the matter, you don't trust your feelings?" Even though her tone was playful, she felt the slight tension in his body.

"I trust my feelings," Rafe said, his voice devoid of any emotion. "It's just everyone else's I have a problem with."

"That sounds so jaded," she said, lowering her head to his shoulder again. "Is that the cop talking, or Wolf Boy?"

He smiled in the darkness. "Maybe a little of both. But if I'm jaded, you have to admit, I've got cause. Think about those stories about me—feral child, nursed by a she-wolf and raised in the wild."

She remembered, and her heart twisted painfully. "People tease when they don't understand."

"Oh, was that it? They didn't understand?" he asked cynically, his smile fading in the darkness. "*I'm* the one who doesn't understand. How do you understand a mother who leaves her baby in the woods—who just tosses him away like so much trash, who walks away and never looks back? Even a dog doesn't do that, no matter how small the runt, or how sick."

Raeanne heard the emotion in his voice and squeezed her eyes tight. "You don't know that's what happened."

"You're right," he acknowledged, drawing in a deep breath. "I don't know. I don't know any of it—I don't know exactly when I was born, I don't know exactly where. I don't know if I have a brother, or a sister, why I was born...or why I was left behind." He exhaled, letting the breath out in a long, labored sigh. "What was it about me that she didn't want?"

"It wasn't you at all," Raeanne insisted.

"No? How can you be so sure?"

"I can be sure because you were an innocent little baby, that's why," she went on passionately. "You'd done nothing. Being abandoned isn't even about you. It's about her."

"Maybe," he conceded quietly, after a moment. "I thought about that. Maybe she was young, alone, maybe her husband had left her, maybe she'd been raped—who knows? The point is, I don't know. I don't know any of it." He turned to her in the darkness. "Do you have any idea what that's like? Do you know what it's like to look back and see nothing?" He laughed in the darkness. It was a sad, solemn sound that bore no resemblance to humor. "I almost wish sometimes those stories about me were true. A pack of wolves might sound strange, but it's better than having nothing, better than all the questions."

"There are a lot of questions," she admitted. "But there is also Emma, and the wonderful life you've had with her. She loves you—as much as if she'd given birth to you. And you love her, too, Rafe. In the end, that's all that matters."

Rafe shrugged. "You're right, I know. It's just… when you've been tossed away once, I guess you start expecting it to happen again." He reached out, stroking the silky length of her hair. "I guess that's why I get a little suspicious of people's motives."

The moonlight coming through the miniblinds made crazy patterns on the ceiling, and Raeanne watched them, thinking of what had happened between them at the reservation. "Are you suspicious of me?"

Rafe moved, pulling her beneath him and staring down at her. "Should I be?"

Raeanne felt a flame in her belly flare. She slipped her arms up and encircled his neck. "What ulterior motive would I have for wanting you here—like this?"

He stared down at her for a long moment, his face pale in the moonlight. "Why do you want me here?"

She reveled in the strength of his arms, his shoulders, his chest, and felt the flame within flare higher. "You don't know?"

"I don't like guessing games."

She stared up at him, his expression hidden by shadows. "Is that what this is to you? A game?"

"Now who's sounding suspicious?"

"Maybe I'm just scared."

"Did Andy scare you?"

She closed her eyes. She didn't want to think about her dead husband now, not when she was in the arms of the man whose love she'd wanted even when she was another man's wife. "Sometimes, when he was drinking."

"Did he ever…hurt you?"

Raeanne thought of the times when she'd run from her husband, from his rages and violent temper. She was ashamed when she remembered how she'd allowed his verbal abuse to continue, too embarrassed to admit she hadn't had the courage to leave. "Just in the things that he said."

Rafe gathered her close, hating the friend he'd entrusted with the woman he loved. "I never knew."

"Andy was the one person you were never suspicious of."

"I know," Rafe whispered, slipping her legs apart and settling between them. "But maybe he should have been suspicious of me."

She looked up at him in the darkness, surprised. "Why?"

"Because I wanted his wife."

Rafe pushed into her, and Raeanne felt her world spin out of control. "She wanted you, too."

"I better get going."

Raeanne watched Rafe as he paced restlessly back and forth across the living room floor, and her grip tightened nervously around her coffee mug. She knew he had to leave, they'd talked about it last night. It was Christmas Eve, and they both had family obligations—she with her family, he with his. But they'd barely finished their morning coffee. They had hours before those commitments were to begin.

"So soon?" she asked, trying with some difficulty to keep her tone light. "It's early yet."

"It's going to start snowing soon," he said, walking to the window and glancing up at the storm clouds moving across the sky. "And I have to check in at the station before heading out to my mother's."

Raeanne's heart sank. He wanted to leave—in fact, he could hardly wait. What had happened? Last night had been so special, they'd been so close, had shared so much. But he'd been quiet and withdrawn since they'd gotten up. What had changed?

"I—I still don't understand why you have to be the one to work tomorrow," she said, stammering just slightly in her effort to keep the worry out of her voice. "I mean, it's Christmas. You're a detective. Don't you have seniority or something? Surely there's a rookie or someone who could work that shift?"

Rafe shrugged, returning his coffee mug to the low table in front of the sofa and reaching for his jacket. "Most everyone else is married," he said simply. "If I work, it frees up one of them to be with their families."

Raeanne set her mug down beside his, it's bitter flavor suddenly making her stomach feel uneasy. "Why didn't you?"

Rafe straightened up and looked at her. "Why didn't I what?"

"Marry?" She looked up at him, but couldn't quite make eye contact. "Surely there must have been opportunities?"

The hand on his jacket hesitated only momentarily, but it was enough for her to notice.

"Just not the type, I guess," he shrugged after a moment, lifting his jacket off the back of the chair.

She quickly looked away, blinking to force back the sting of tears. Why was she acting like such a fool? What was she getting so emotional about? They'd had a wonderful few days together, why did she insist on making more of it than it was? What had she expected him to say—that he'd never married because he always wanted her? That he'd pined away waiting for her all these years?

But as ridiculous as it seemed, that's exactly what she'd wanted, and last night she'd begun to believe it might actually be true.

"Maybe you just never found the right person," she said, busying herself by picking up the cups and napkins.

He looked across the room to her. If he could just tell her what he was feeling, tell her how clumsy and alone he felt. He'd opened up to her last night, poured out his heart, telling her things he'd never told anyone else—things about his past, about his abandonment. He wasn't used to sharing his private life with anyone, and remembering the things he'd said, the secrets he'd revealed, made him awkward and uncomfortable. He'd taken a lot for granted last night—like the fact that she might love him. Now he truly doubted that was so. He was kidding himself to think that taking her to bed had changed things.

"Maybe I never will," he said in a cold, flat voice.

Raeanne searched his face. A cold feeling spread through her, like icy flood waters from a frozen stream. Nothing had changed. He didn't love her, and he never would. If he'd had any feelings for her, she'd given him every opportunity to say so, but all he wanted was out—to run away—to put as much distance between them as he could.

"Look," he said, shrugging into his coat and heading for the door. "I'll…uh…I'll call you."

Raeanne rose slowly to her feet, turning to face him. "Just tell me one thing, Rafe."

He stopped in the small foyer and turned back to her. "What?"

"Why did you do it?"

He regarded her for a moment. "Why did I do what?"

"You know exactly what I'm talking about," she said, the emotion spilling out in her voice. She wasn't sad any longer, she was angry. How dare he do this to her again, how dare he withdraw and leave her? "I'm talking about last night, and the night before that." She lowered her head, taking a deep breath. "Why now? Why after all these years?"

"I thought it was something we both wanted."

She looked up. "Was it? Or was it just you satisfying an old curiosity?"

He took a step closer, his dark eyes narrowing. "Is that what you think?"

"What else am I supposed to think?" she demanded. "Well, I guess you got what you came for anyway, right?"

"What the hell is that supposed to mean?" he demanded, defensive now.

"You're smart, you figure it out."

He stalked across the room, stopping just in front of her. "Well, I figure maybe I wasn't the only one who was curious."

Raeanne stared up at him, hardly believing this was the same man who only a few short hours before had made her feel like the most important person in his life. Is that all she was to him—a curiosity? The one who'd gotten away? Didn't he know that she loved him, couldn't he tell?

"Well, you said you always wanted Andy's wife," she said in a cold, harsh voice. "Now you've had her. I think it's time for you to leave."

Rafe's jaw clenched tightly, his dark eyes piercing

through squinted lids. He turned and stalked back across the room, angrily yanking the door open.

"And don't bother coming back," she said as she followed him through the small foyer.

"Don't worry," he said, stopping on the porch and looking back at her. "I won't."

Raeanne closed the door behind him, turning her back so she didn't have to see his image through the glass. She walked back into the living room, straightening the magazines on the table and collecting their empty coffee cups. She stopped when she heard the sound of his truck starting up out front, but only for a moment. She'd made a mistake, misrepresented the situation, but she knew the truth now. He was gone, and she'd get over it.

It was strange, she thought as she headed for the kitchen and placed the dirty dishes in the sink. She'd come back to Whitehorn to resolve her feelings for Rafe, once and for all. And she'd done that. It was over between them, it had ended—not with a bang, but a whimper. But she didn't feel like breaking down, she didn't feel like crying, or yelling, or screaming. She just didn't…feel.

Was this what it was like, she wondered as she tidied up her small kitchen. Was this what it was like to be a wolf boy—no tears, no emotion, no regrets? Was this what it was like to have no feelings at all?

Grabbing a large shopping bag, she walked back into the living room, the puppy following playfully, nipping at her heels. She began collecting the Christmas presents from around the tree, and placing them in the bag. She would have to leave for her parents' house in a few hours to help her mother prepare for the gathering of relatives and friends. She'd take the puppy with her, her parents would love him.

She stacked the presents carefully into the bag, her mind busy with what she would wear—which sweater would go with which pair of slacks. Suddenly she realized she held the package she'd wrapped for Rafe, the watch she wrapped and placed under the tree.

She didn't even feel the shopping bag slip from her hands. She wasn't even aware of the loud thud it had made when it dropped to the carpeted floor and spilled the packages at her feet. All she remembered was reality crashing down on her, and feeling coming back in a rush.

She moved toward the sofa, stumbling over packages and bumping into the coffee table. Dropping down onto the cushions, she reached for the watch. He didn't love her, he never had. She'd been a curiosity to him, the one that had gotten away. But he'd gotten what he wanted and now he was gone.

She wasn't aware of her tears until they spilled down onto the package, blurring the colors and the crinkling the paper. Rafe was gone. It was over. And she'd never felt more alone in her life.

Ten

"You think it's the same guy?"

Rafe stepped out of the elevator and shrugged. "Could be. Description fits, age is about right."

The lines across Harlan's florid forehead deepened. "Your friend give you any reason for the alias?"

"Not really. As far as we know, there are no outstanding warrants. He's not wanted for anything."

Harlan massaged the bridge of his nose thoughtfully. "I don't know. I suppose it wouldn't hurt to talk to him. See what he knows."

Rafe cocked his head to one side, giving Harlan a deliberate look. "I thought you were the one who wanted to leave no stone unturned."

Harlan laughed, making a face. "I know, I know. But that was before we rested our case. Now I'd hate to upset the apple cart."

Rafe almost smiled at the lawyer's nervousness—almost. "Want me to bring him in?"

Harlan nodded to several spectators standing in the corridor and reached for the courtroom door. "I suppose you better."

"Good morning, gentlemen," Winona said, reaching the door just as they did.

"Miss Cobbs," Harlan said graciously, opening the door and stepping back to allow her to pass. "Lovely to see you, as always."

"What's the matter, Harlan? You look worried, for a man who's convinced he's got a winning case."

"Is that wishful thinking, dear Winona, or are you treating us to more of your second sight?" Harlan asked with a smile that threatened to crack.

"Just an observation," Winona smiled. She turned to Rafe. "So, Rafe, it's been ages since we've talked. How were your holidays?"

"Very pleasant, Winona," Rafe answered with a polite nod. "And yours?"

He heard as she rattled on about an aluminum tree and a broken string of lights, but he didn't hear much of what she said. Winona Cobbs made him uncomfortable. He wasn't sure exactly how much he bought about all the talk of her "special talents," but he had to admit the old woman made him uneasy. Psychic abilities or no psychic abilities, that smug smile of hers always gave him the uncomfortable feeling she knew more than she was saying.

"Well, I better find myself a seat," Winona said after she finished. She stepped into the courtroom, then stopped and turned around. "Oh, Rafe," she said, snapping her fingers. "Do you have the time?"

Rafe immediately thought of Raeanne and how she'd asked him about his watch. The hair at the back of his neck prickled. "Uh, no. Sorry Winona, I don't."

"It's 8:19," Harlan chimed in, pointing straight up, to the wall clock just above the courtroom door.

Winona glanced up at the clock, and then back to Rafe and smiled—the very smile that made him so uncomfortable. "Thanks."

"Old bat," Harlan mumbled as they watched her amble down the center aisle and into a row of seats. He glanced up at Rafe. "Just what I need on a Monday morning—a close encounter with the spirit world. What was all that about the time?"

"Beats me," Rafe lied, unable to shake the uneasy feeling. "But she always did give me the willies."

"I know what you mean," Harlan agreed, starting down the aisle. "But, getting back to what we were talking about, why don't you give your friend up in Wolf Point another call? Tell him to pick up our fellow, so we can have a little talk with him."

"Will do," Rafe said. He followed Harlan through the gate to the counsel table, but then, reaching for his chair, he glanced back—just in time to see Raeanne walk into the courtroom.

It wasn't the first time he'd seen her in the nine days since she'd ordered him out of her house and out of her life, but it didn't seem to get any easier. The trial had resumed the day after New Year's, and for three agonizing days last week he'd had to sit opposite her in the courtroom and watch her work.

If she was bothered at all by any of what had happened between them, she certainly hadn't shown it. She'd been as cool and in control as ever, hovering over her client and determinedly protecting his rights.

He had noticed one difference, however. Before they had…

He stopped and scowled. Before they'd what? Made love? In light of what had happened, *love* hardly seemed the right word to describe what had gone on between them. She didn't love him. She'd come right out and told him she felt sorry for him. So whatever it was that had gone on between them, love hadn't been a part of it.

But, regardless of that, before they…*were together,* she at least had acknowledged him—he'd either been her friend or her foe, her ally or her adversary. Now, on those rare occasions when she did turn those velvety brown eyes toward him, they simply stared right through him as if he weren't even there.

Rafe felt a painful tightening in his chest. He couldn't deny it hurt to be relegated to nothing in her eyes. He knew he should feel relieved. At least it was over now— finally. He'd finally scratched the itch, finally caught the one who'd gotten away. Now if he could just find a way to forget and move on…

He watched her as she slipped into her seat and opened her briefcase. He remembered holding her, waking up with her in his arms. He remembered the feel of her body, the touch of her skin, the soft sound of her moans.

Rafe closed his eyes against the sudden rush of emotion. He reached for his chair, pulling it from the table and quickly sitting down. He felt winded and a little dizzy, as if he'd just taken one to the stomach. He was Rafe "Wolf Boy" Rawlings, he reminded himself, and Wolf Boy needed no one.

So why did every cell in his body feel hungry? Why did every nerve, every muscle, crave her touch and ache for her magic?

Judge Matthews's gavel came down swiftly. The sudden crash had Rafe's head jerking up, and his thoughts scattering.

"As the jury will recall, the prosecution rested its case Friday afternoon. Defense counsel, are you ready to begin?"

Rafe turned his head, watching as Raeanne came swiftly to her feet.

"We are, Your Honor."

Raeanne put down the transcript, the long, continuous folds of paper spilling off her lap, across the sofa and onto the carpeted floor. She rubbed her tired eyes. They were itchy and red from the long hours of reading, but she couldn't afford to stop. With the prosecution's case over, the ball was in her court now, and she couldn't afford to lob it.

She reached down, stroking the sleeping puppy nestled beside her. She envied his peaceful rest and seemingly stress-free existence. What she wouldn't give for a little of that simplicity right now.

Raeanne thought of the case she would present to the jury—such as it was. She didn't have much to work with— a few experts to testify about times and dates, several witnesses to testify that they'd seen both Charlie Avery and Ethan Walker arguing with other people, and a few more witnesses to testify to Ethan's character.

She was still pondering the possibility of putting Ethan on the stand, unable to come to a decision yet. Over the weeks, he'd mellowed some, but not nearly enough to make her comfortable putting him before the jury. Attitude never played well with juries, and Ethan had a big one. And enough attitude could just lose this one for them.

She glanced down at the transcript, knowing she should review it again. Her case wasn't much, and she couldn't afford to be sloppy. Missing something would be a mistake.

A mistake. She put her pen down, resting it in her lap. The only mistake she'd made so far was fooling herself into thinking Rafe Rawlings might actually have some feelings, that he might actually admit to being human like everyone else. She thought of him in the courtroom today. She hadn't had to look at him to know he was watching her.

She'd been grateful for the break in the trial Judge Matthews had called for the holidays—for more than just professional reasons. While it had been good to have the additional time to review and prepare her case, what she'd really needed was time to pull herself together after Rafe stormed out of her life.

Christmas had been awful, and even though she'd tried her best to put on a brave front before her parents, they had immediately sensed something was wrong. She was thankful they hadn't pushed, and had spared her the agony of poring over everything again. Somehow she'd gotten through the holiday festivities and the family parties, and the visiting relatives, the presents and the meals, but it hadn't been easy. She'd passed through them in a numb, unfeeling sort of haze.

She picked up the transcript once more, making an attempt to gather it into a containable stack. The irony was that ultimately the thing that been keeping her going through the past nine days was this damn trial. It had helped to occupy her mind. She'd thrown herself into it completely, working obsessively day and night, writing motions, citing cases, and researching precedents—anything and everything to keep busy and stop thinking about Rafe.

Some of the time it worked, but most of the time it didn't. There were those moments when she became absorbed, when she became wrapped up in what she was doing and forgot for a while, but unfortunately that didn't happen often. Most of the time he was right there, on the outskirts of her consciousness—haunting and hurting.

Still, as difficult as the days had been, the nights had been much worse. In the darkness of her bed, she'd been alone, with nothing but her thoughts—and they all were filled with Rafe.

Raeanne shook her head, trying to concentrate on the transcript in front of her. There would be time later to dredge all this up, long hours in the night to think of Rafe and play back in her mind, chapter and verse, all the mistakes she had made.

She reached for her coffee cup, surprised to find it empty. She stared down at the mug, considering for a moment whether she needed more caffeine. Glancing up at the mantel clock, she shook her head slowly and decided to make another pot. It was only a little after eight, and already she was having trouble concentrating. She needed something to perk her up.

She'd just gotten to her feet and started for the kitchen when the telephone rang.

"Hello?"

"Raeanne?"

For a moment she could do nothing, just stand there and

listen to the roar in her ears grow louder and more fierce. She felt breathless and faint, and visions sprang to life in her head—moonlight, darkness, dark eyes, hard bodies and twisted sheets.

"Are you there? Raeanne?"

"Uh—y-yes, I'm here."

Rafe closed his eyes at the sound of her voice. It was barely above a whisper, and he pulled the phone close in an effort to block out the noise from the squad room. "I've got someone down here. I think...I think you might want to talk to him."

Raeanne took a deep breath, the sound of his voice on the line feeling like a hot dagger in her heart. She thought for a moment. "Who is it?"

"Well, twenty-seven years ago he was Charlie Avery's best friend."

Raeanne set her coffee cup down. "Oh, yeah?"

"Yeah," Rafe said. "And he has a lot to say about why he hated Walker so much."

"Where are you, at the jail?"

"No, the police station." Rafe rubbed at the pressure building at his temples. "My office."

"I'll be right there," she said, knowing from the sound of his voice it was serious.

"Uh—Raeanne?"

She stopped, holding her breath. "Yes?"

"Uh..." Rafe closed his eyes and cursed under his breath. A million things swelled in his heart, things he wanted to tell her, things he wanted to say. But he swallowed them. "It's dark. Be careful."

Raeanne heard the line go dead and let her breath out in a long sigh. Dropping the receiver onto its cradle, she

headed for the foyer. Finding her boots on the rail of the
hall stand, she carried them back to the sofa.

What was she doing? she thought as she laced them
up. Why was she going? She hadn't even asked him what
this was about.

She thought of his short, no-nonsense words, the sound
of his voice. She knew one thing for certain. Rafe
Rawlings might be a cold, unfeeling bastard, but he was
a damn good cop. If he said it was important, she knew
it must be important.

Automatically reaching for her briefcase, she pulled
out her keys and headed for the door. At least it better be
important, she thought as she leapt down the porch steps.
Because seeing Rafe would cost her.

Rafe stared down at the telephone on the desk. He
closed his eyes, bracing himself against the painful throbbing at his temples. Suddenly he turned and yanked open
a side drawer, reaching inside for a bottle of over-the-
counter pain relievers. Struggling with the child-protective
cap, he snapped off the cap and popped two tablets into his
mouth. The caustic taste of the pills was bitter, but oddly
satisfying. It matched his mood, which was pretty bitter,
too.

He closed his eyes again, rubbing his temples, and heard
the sound of her voice in his head. She'd be walking in here
in a little while and he didn't want to think about how hard
that was going to be on him. But he was going to have to
find a way to deal with it.

He took a deep breath, pushing himself away from the
desk and crossing the noisy squad room to the window. He
stared out into the darkness, where the streetlights illumi-

nated the snowy walks and wet streets. There were no Christmas lights, no holiday decorations adorning the lampposts and storefronts any longer. That was all over with now.

He thought of the miserable holidays he'd spent—the lonely, empty days and the long, endless nights. There had been friends, and family, and traditions to follow, but he'd felt a part of none of it. He'd just wanted to be left alone, to be with his dogs, to help Crier with her pups and to hide away from the rest of the world, lick his wounds and deal with the pain as best he could.

But his best hadn't been very good. It still hurt, and he suspected it always would. He'd spent a lifetime on the outside looking in, wanting a woman he'd convinced himself he could never have. He'd endured the pain, standing aside while she made a life for herself—first with his best friend and then with a career. But as difficult as those years on the sidelines of her life had been, they were nothing compared to what he'd endured in the past nine days.

From the window, he watched a pickup slide through a red light, and a squad car take off after it, sirens blaring. He watched the warning lights on the squad car flash and turn, thinking of all the warning lights he'd ignored.

For the past seven years he'd convinced himself that if he could just be with her, if he could just satisfy his curiosity about her once and for all, he'd finally get over her. But now he realized how naive that thinking had been. Being with her had nothing to do with curiosity, with scratching an itch. He just wished he'd realized that before he went to her house that night eleven days ago. All the warning signs had been there, but he'd ignored every one. He'd been thinking with his heart and not with his head and now he was paying the price.

REBECCA DANIELS   179

He ran a hand through his hair and walked back to his desk. She would be arriving soon, and he had to try and prepare himself for that. He hoped like hell he knew what he was doing. Harlan was going to hit the roof when he found out, but he'd deal with that when he had to. He'd done what he had to do, what he knew was right. But that wouldn't make seeing her any easier.

"O'Brien?"

"Right. Except the last year or so he's been using the name Bryant. That's why it took us so long to locate him."

Raeanne looked through the glass door at the ruddy-faced, weather-worn cowboy sitting behind the desk. "And he worked for the Kincaids?"

"For Avery, to be exact," Rafe filled in. "He and Charlie were pretty good buddies, from what I understand. After Charlie left, Kincaid fired him. He's bummed around here and there. Been working up near Wolf Point the last few years."

Raeanne turned the information over in her mind. "Harlan been down to talk to him yet?"

Rafe hesitated a minute before answering. "No."

Raeanne looked up at him. His handsome profile made it almost too painful. "Why'd you call me?"

He slowly turned and looked down at her. "Talk to him. I think you'll understand."

Raeanne felt a swell of emotion in her throat, and a little of the steadiness seemed to leave her legs. "Well," she said after a moment. "Let's do it, then."

Rafe opened the door, stepping aside to allow her to pass. "Rusty. There's somebody I want you to meet."

The vile odor of stale beer and sweat assaulted Raeanne's senses the moment she stepped into the room, but she ignored it. She'd interviewed too many clients in smelly holding cells and stinky lockups to be shocked. Still, it was hardly something one became accustomed to.

According to his expired driver's license, Rusty O'Brien, a.k.a. Rusty Bryant, was only fifty-three, but hard living, and hard drinking, had made him appear years older. His long hair was gray and matted and a florid complexion peeked through a grizzled beard and a tobacco-stained mustache. When he spotted Raeanne, his tired, watery eyes opened wide.

"Hi, Rusty," Raeanne said, offering him her hand with the faint hope that he wouldn't take it.

"Well, will you get a load of this…" Rusty said, his smile revealing several teeth missing. He reached out reverently and shook Raeanne's hand. "If I'da known they had such pretty-lookin' lady police back here in Whitehorn, I'da never left."

"Rusty, this is Raeanne Martin," Rafe said, removing Rusty's hold on Raeanne's hand. "She's a lawyer."

Rusty glared up at him. "Hey, I thought you said I wasn't under arrest."

"Oh, you're not," Rafe assured him. "Miss Martin represents Ethan Walker. Remember, I told you about him?"

Rusty sat back in his chair, nodding his head. "Yup. Accused of killing poor Charlie."

"Detective Rawlings tells me you knew Charlie Avery pretty well," Raeanne asked, pulling up a chair from the other side of the desk.

"Sure did," Rusty said, nodding again. "Me and Charlie, we was just like that." He held up two grubby-looking fingers, pressing them close.

"I see," Raeanne said, glancing up at Rafe, then back to Rusty. "What about my client, Ethan Walker? Did you know him, too?"

Rusty shrugged. "Like I told the officer here, I knew of him."

"Because of Charlie?"

"Yeah, because of Charlie."

"Did you and Ethan get along?"

"Me and the kid?" Rusty asked, thinking. "I don't know. As I remember, he was kind of cocky for my tastes. One of those big, hotheaded, pain-in-the-butt kids, if you know what I mean."

Raeanne smiled. "Yeah, I think I do."

"But he and Charlie..." Rusty hooted, showing his toothless grin. "Boy I tell ya, those two had it in for one another—big-time."

Raeanne glanced up at Rafe again, and he urged her on with a nod of the head. She looked back at Rusty and smiled. "Did you know that cattle was being rustled from the Kincaid's ranch?"

"Yeah, I remember." Rusty snorted. "Old man Kincaid was pissed. He crawled all over Charlie's ass—" He stopped, giving her a sheepish grin. "Pardon the language, ma'am. I guess I've spent too much time with foulmouthed cowboys to know how to speak to a lady like you."

"It's okay, Rusty," Raeanne said, dismissing his concern. "You were telling me about Mr. Kincaid."

"Oh, yeah, right." Rusty nodded. "Well, as I was saying. Old man Kincaid was...pretty mad. He told Charlie he better find out who was doing it, or he'd be out of a job."

"So he put a lot of pressure on Charlie?"

Rusty nodded again. "Yeah, you could say that."

Raeanne thought for a moment. "Did you ever see Charlie and Ethan Walker fight?"

"Hell, yes, I did." Rusty snorted again, running a hand across his scratchy beard. "Me and half the town. Those two had a couple real wingdings, as I remember."

"And that was because of the rustling, of course, right?"

Rusty's hand stopped, and he cocked his head to one side. "The rustlin'?"

"The Kincaid cattle," Raeanne said. "Charlie accused the Walkers of stealing the cattle."

"That?" Rusty snorted, his shoulders shaking with a silent chuckle. "That was just what Charlie told old man Kincaid to get him off his back."

Raeanne's gaze shot to Rafe, and he gave her a knowing shrug in response. Taking a deep breath, she turned back to Rusty. "Are you saying that Charlie and Ethan never fought over stolen cattle?"

"Well, I suppose they coulda, but I never seen 'em," Rusty said thoughtfully. He looked up at Rafe, giving him a toothless grin and a wink. "There's only one thing that gets two young bucks as hot as they was, and it sure as hell ain't no bull."

Raeanne felt her heart lurch in her chest. "What did they fight about, then?"

Rusty looked across the table at her, the deep, weathered lines around his mouth and eyes deepening. "A woman."

Raeanne sat back in her chair, and glanced up at Rafe. She felt oddly winded, and a little dazed. A woman. Somehow, she had just known that had to be it. It was the only thing that made sense. The animosity between Avery and Ethan had been too deep, too...passionate to be explained away by a few head of cattle.

"Do you know who it was?" she asked after a moment.

"No," Rusty said, shaking his head. "But I know she was young." Rusty laughed. It was a funny, wizened-sounding laugh that ended in a cough. "And she had old Charlie in a state, I can tell you that."

"And Ethan Walker?"

Rusty laughed again. "When Charlie found out his little filly had been seeing some young buck, well…he got mad, I'll tell you. *Really* mad."

Raeanne leaned forward in the chair again, resting her elbows on the desk. For years it had been suspected that Charlie Avery had run off and deserted his wife and family for another woman. But once Avery's remains were found and identified, it had been as if all those old rumors had been forgotten.

"Did you know that Charlie Avery was married?" she asked after a moment. "Did you know he had a family?"

Rusty looked across at her and made a face. "'Course I did. Me and Charlie, we were like this." He raised his fingers again, demonstrating their closeness.

"Do you know if his wife knew about this other woman?"

Rusty's face sobered. "Now, that I don't rightly know. Charlie and me…well, we were good buddies all right, like I said. Worked together, drank together, you know? But…well, we didn't go stickin' our noses into each other's personal business, if you know what I mean." Rusty looked up at Rafe again and shrugged apologetically. "But Nan now, she always sounded like a real nice woman to me. A real lady."

"And you say you have no idea who this other woman was?" Raeanne went on, her mind racing. She thought back to the evidence found at the scene—Ethan's class ring, and the matching compact and lipstick.

Rusty looked back at her and shook his head. "Nope. Charlie was real tight-mouthed about it, except…"

"Except?" Raeanne said when his voice trailed off.

"Oh! Well…except," Rusty repeated thoughtfully. "I kinda think ol' Charlie was…well, I think he was almost…*proud* of it, you know? He wouldn't tell me who he was seeing, but he still wanted me to know about it, if you know what I mean. Like he wanted to…"

"Boast about it?" Rafe suggested when Rusty's words faded again.

"Yeah, that's it," Rusty said, snapping his crooked fingers together and nodding his head. "Yeah, boast. That's it, that's what he did."

Rafe turned to Raeanne, who sat looking up at him. "You have any more questions?"

Yeah, she thought to herself, she had a million of them—for Ethan. She was convinced he'd been keeping something from her—something or someone he wanted to protect. Could it be this woman? And was it the same woman who had lost the compact and lipstick at the sight of the murder? She glanced back at Rusty, and shook her head.

"Thanks, Rusty," she said, coming slowly to her feet. She reached across the desk, offering him her hand. "I appreciate you talking to me."

"Oh, it was my pleasure, little lady," Rusty said, standing quickly and taking her hand. He gave her a stiff, courtly bow. "My pleasure indeed."

Rafe followed her out of the small office and into the corridor. "Well, what do you think?"

Raeanne took a deep breath, her mind reeling with possibilities. "I'm not sure what to think."

He turned and followed her as she started down the corridor toward the door. "At least you were right about the cattle rustling."

"I guess I was," she muttered, staring down at the worn linoleum floor and trying not to think about the night in her bed, when they'd talked in the dark.

"The other stuff, though." He sighed, looking down into her large, dark eyes. "About the woman. Sort of adds fuel to the fire, doesn't it?"

"Yeah," Raeanne mumbled glumly. "And the last thing we needed was more motive."

Eleven

"Why did you do it?"

Rafe's head snapped around, his gaze colliding with Raeanne's dark, questioning eyes. His heart lurched suddenly, and the warmth drained slowly from his body. She'd taken him by surprise, voicing the question he'd been asking himself a million times in the past nine days. Why had he stormed out of her house? Why hadn't he given her a chance? Why had he thrown out obstacles and created problems? Why had he walked out on his only chance at happiness?

The nights he spent with Raeanne had been the best in his life, been better than any he'd ever hoped he'd have. So why had he been so afraid?

He knew why. He knew why, and it tore him up inside. He loved her—it was as simple as that. Rafe Rawlings loved Raeanne Martin, and he wanted desperately for her to love him back. He'd spent years wondering, a lifetime waiting, but when it came right down to it, he realized he didn't have the courage to face the answer. And so he'd chosen the coward's way out. He'd walked away, choosing to live the rest of his life in a void, not knowing, rather than risk a truth that would make living unbearable.

"Tell me," Raeanne demanded. "Why did you call me? Why did you let me talk to him?"

Rafe closed his eyes, drawing in a deep breath. What an ass he was—jumping the gun and jumping to conclusions. She didn't want to know about them, wasn't concerned about what had happened—or why. She'd already put their…their episode to rest. Why couldn't he?

"I thought you should know," he said simply. "It's more ammunition Harlan will use against Walker to strengthen his case."

Raeanne looked up at him. It did look as if Ethan had even more reason to want Avery dead. But her instincts told her there was more to the story, something that might actually help their case instead of hurt it. "Well, I guess I'll just have to find some way to see that it doesn't."

"That might be hard to do."

She shrugged. "All it really shows is that there was a woman involved in all of this. It still doesn't prove that Ethan killed Avery."

He regarded her for a moment. Her determination amazed him, and, grudgingly, he was impressed. Her case had just been dealt a powerful blow, and yet she was going down fighting. "It gives him a powerful motive to want the guy dead."

"Does Harlan know?"

"About Rusty? Of course."

"No, I mean about tonight. About me."

Rafe pushed the door open and followed her outside. "Not exactly."

Raeanne supposed it wasn't unusual that he walk her to the car, but still it made her uneasy. It was a courtesy, a friendly gesture, but she hardly considered them friends any longer. It made her uncomfortable. Dealing with him in the sterile, well-lit environment of the police station was one thing, but in the quiet darkness of the deserted parking lot, it was another entirely. It was obvious he wasn't anxious to spend any more time with her than necessary, so why had he followed her out?

The night was cold, and a chill ran through her. She shivered, pulling her jacket tight. The parking lot was empty, and their footsteps sounded loud and forlorn on the pavement.

"Not exactly?" she asked, glancing back at him. "What is that supposed to mean?"

"It means he knows we've brought him in, it means he knows we've talked to him," he explained, flipping the collar up on his corduroy sports coat and slipping his hands into his pockets.

"He just doesn't know you've contacted me, right?"

He looked down at her and shrugged nonchalantly, his breath showing white when he talked. "You seem to have all the answers. Why are you asking me?"

She stopped at her car and turned to him. "This could be bad for you. Harlan's going to kick."

"I can handle Harlan," he said. He just wasn't sure he could handle the soft, sad look in her eyes.

She looked away quickly. His dark gaze was too penetrating, too probing, and she was afraid she would reveal too much—too much about the tears she'd cried and the long nights she'd spent awake and alone. She reached into her pocket and fished out her keys. Turning the lock, she pulled the door open and tossed her briefcase onto the seat. But before she could get in, he stopped her with a hand on her arm.

"Wait," he murmured, as the car door swung closed. Alone with her, he felt a tremor reverberate through him. Inadvertently he tightened his hand on her arm and pulled her a step closer.

"Yes," she whispered, a pressure swelling in her throat. It was there again, in his eyes—the emotion, the awareness. She could see it as plainly as she'd seen the truth through all the lies that had been told about him. But she didn't trust her feelings anymore.

"How's…uh, how's the car running?" he asked, his hand still on her arm.

"F-fine," Raeanne stammered, nervously clearing her throat. "Arnie did a good job."

"Good," he said absently. He looked down at her, feeling an urgency and an ache spreading throughout his body. It would be so easy to pull her into his arms, so easy to smother her with kisses and overwhelm her with passion. He could make her melt in his arms, could make her sigh with contentment and go weak with need. What did it matter whether she loved him or not? What did he care if she pitied or prized him? Why couldn't he just take what she offered, hold her as long as she'd let him and accept what pleasure he could?

Because he was a coward. Because living without her was easier and safer—it required no chances and resulted in no losses. If it hurt, what did it matter? He'd borne the pain of his love for so long, he wasn't sure he would recognize anything else.

Still, for a moment, in the cold desolation of the empty parking lot, he let himself imagine. For a moment, he let himself dream. He granted himself an instant of recollection, a flash of remembrance of the touch and the taste of her and the feel of her beneath him, in his arms.

"Rafe?" she whispered, the hard, rigid expression on his face sending another chill down her spine.

"I'm sorry," he said, giving his head a shake and dropping the hold on her arm. He stepped back a pace, feeling oddly dazed and annoyed. It had been stupid to touch her, stupid to remember the two of them together. He was too raw, too vulnerable. It would be too easy to slip, to let down his guard, to say too much. "I—uh, I just wanted to ask about the dog."

A cold realization hit her hard, causing her breath to catch in her throat and the blood to turn to ice in her veins. "Do you want him back?" she asked suddenly, defensive and defiant. "Is that why you followed me out here?"

The anger felt good, and Rafe let it course freely through his system. It gave him a good, safe haven to channel all the emotions churning around inside of him, and focus them sharply. "You don't want him?"

"Not if it's going to make you uncomfortable," she snapped, her voice raising a notch. "He belonged to you. If you want him back, just say so."

"I'm not the one who's uncomfortable," he said angrily. "Of course I should have asked if having a mutt would bother you. Maybe what you really want is a pedigree."

"What?" She was yelling by now. "Don't try and put this thing off on me! If you want him, take him!"

"I gave him to you," he said, raising his voice to match the level of hers. "I don't want him."

"Well, I don't want him either!" she screamed, her hands on her hips.

"Look," he said, his voice hoarse and unsteady, "I don't want to argue."

"Neither do I," she admitted in a tight voice.

"I was just curious how you and the puppy were getting along, that's all." He stopped for a moment, struggling. "I…want you to have him."

Raeanne looked away quickly. She felt silly now. She'd been edgy and awkward, being with him alone in the dark and it had caused her to overreact.

"We're fine," she said clumsily, wanting nothing more than to just forget all about this ridiculous conversation. "Actually, we're…we're becoming pretty good friends."

Rafe cursed himself under his breath, choosing the harshest, cruelest words could think of. He sensed her discomfort, and it only made him feel worse. It had been stupid to say what he had about a pedigree. He'd sounded pathetic and petty, and revealed far too much.

"That's good," he murmured uneasily. His throat felt dry and tight, and he cleared it. "He'll be a good watchdog."

"Well, right now I'd just settle for housebroken."

Rafe closed his eyes, remembering the night he'd nearly frozen outside her house, waiting for the puppy to take care of business. He hadn't really minded. Running back inside and slipping into bed beside her had made it worth it. Her warm, beautiful body had made him forget about the cold night, had made him forget about all the cold nights he'd ever spent alone and unhappy.

The sudden stab of longing was almost overwhelming, and it left him reeling. It was so quiet, so still. There wasn't a sound to disturb the silence—not a car, not a dog, not even any noise from the station behind them. It was as if the world had suddenly paused, as though everyone waited and held their breath.

He took a step closer, his hands reaching out to pull her to him.

"No," Raeanne whispered, but even to her own ears her voice sounded faint and far away. She was mesmerized by his eyes, by the look on his face. She remembered the hypnotic power he'd had over the wolves, how he'd spoken to them with his eyes alone and wondered if he was performing the same magic on her. "No, Rafe, don't."

But he ignored her plea, he ignored her pitiful struggle, and the fear in her eyes. He pulled her close, bringing his lips close to hers.

"I can't stop thinking about you," he whispered against her mouth. The hand at her waist trailed down to her bottom, pressing her into him.

Raeanne gasped, feeling him hard against her. She wanted to run, to hide, to scream in terror, but she could do none of that. Her legs were weak, her arms felt useless, and the hunger in her was so strong it threatened to block out all reason.

"I think about you—about us," he murmured, his voice rough and strained with need. He moved against her, feeling her body tremble and the breath catch in her throat. "About holding you, and touching you." He brushed her lips with a kiss, his voice becoming a whisper. "About being inside you."

"No, no," Raeanne begged, but the words came out more like a whimper.

"Yes, Raeanne," he groaned, pressing his mouth to hers. He pushed her lips apart, letting his tongue taste and explore. She tasted heady and rich, and he felt as though he'd been hungry forever. He forgot about the frosty winter air, forgot the other officers who could see them from the windows. He forgot they were in a parking lot, that there had been hard feelings and harsh words between them. He forgot who he was and that she could never be his.

Raeanne resisted, but her struggles were feeble. She knew she had to stop him, knew this whole thing had to cease, but she couldn't seem to make herself move toward that end. His need was so great and his mouth so fierce on hers, that she was swept up and pulled along. The path between them was scattered with hazards and risks. They had to steer clear of trust, avoid all honesty. Nothing had been settled, nothing clarified. Issues remained uncertain, conditions unstable.

And yet she couldn't deny the passion. It was there between them, it was real, and it was strong. She wanted to walk away, wanted to get on with her life—it was something she needed to, something she had to. But with his hands on her, with his body so close and his kisses so urgent, it seemed impossible.

Was it so wrong to want him? She'd lived her whole life loving him. Was it such a sin to want his touch, to want his kiss, to want his passion, when there was so much left unsettled between them?

"Raeanne," he murmured against her lips. "I want you. I want you so much."

He wanted her. She hadn't needed to hear the words to know it was true. He wanted her—her lips, her arms, her body. He wanted her here, now, while passion was high and desire threatened to spin out of control. He wanted her…but not her love.

She wished she could just accept that, wished she could be happy with what he offered and learn to live without the rest. But she couldn't. She couldn't take the hurt, couldn't accept him running away every time they started to get close. She not only wanted his love—she needed it. And without it, all the desire, all the passion, just wasn't enough.

With what strength she had left, she pushed out of his arms. "No," she gasped, shaking her head.

"I want you," he whispered again, ignoring her protests and reaching for her again.

"No!" she said again, stronger and louder. She knew he'd heard her, knew he understood this time, for his whole body went rigid. She took a deep breath and looked up into his eyes. "I don't want this."

Rafe felt a chill travel through him, a squall storming through his system, bringing him back to earth, back to reality. He steeled himself against the upheaval, willing his breathing to slow and his heart to return to normal.

"No," he said, resigned, dropping his hands to his side. "I know you don't."

He didn't stop her when she pulled the car door open again and slid in behind the wheel. He didn't want to. He wanted her to go. He didn't want to see her, didn't want to think about her, didn't want to be reminded of what a fool he'd made of himself.

He stood in the deserted parking lot long after her car had sped past and its taillights had disappeared into the night. The wind gusted around him, cutting through his corduroy sport coat and buffeting his hair into his face.

The frigid winter cold felt harsh and biting against his skin, but he made no move to go inside. Its iciness suited his mood. He needed something brutal and unmerciful to make him forget about how warm she had felt, how hot her breath had been against his cheek and how feverish the taste of her had made him.

He wasn't sure he could sink any lower. He knew she didn't love him and yet there he'd been—clutching at her, willing to grab at any crumbs she would give him.

"Hey, Rawlings."

Rafe turned around at the sound of the voice. A uniformed officer stood in the open doorway of the station, peering through the darkness. "Yeah?"

"Collins on the horn for you. Line two."

"Got it," Rafe said, starting slowly back across the lot. He wasn't exactly looking forward to the call. Harlan was going to hit the roof, but there wasn't much he could do about it now.

He heard his mother's voice in his head. Emma had always told him, *A man has to do what a man has to do.* And that was exactly what he'd done. He'd given Raeanne the information, let her interview Rusty O'Brien, because he knew he had to. Her instincts had been right and she'd deserved to know. If it blew their case out of the water, then so be it. But explaining that to Harlan was going to be a little difficult.

He glanced back for a moment, down the street where her car had sped and disappeared. He'd called her because he had to, but touching her had been way out of line. Touching her had been a mistake, a mistake that would probably haunt him for the rest of his life.

"Your Honor, I object." Harlan hauled himself up and out of his chair with a speed that seemed to defy his portly frame. "This is highly irregular."

"It's highly regular, Mr. Collins," Judge Matthews pointed out in a patient voice. "Objection overruled."

"But this witness has no relevant testimony to offer," Harlan continued, his mustache twitching from side to side as he spoke. "I'd ask for an offer of proof."

"Mr. Collins is well aware of what this witness is testifying to," Raeanne said. "This is just an attempt by the prosecution to delay."

"Which is something I will not tolerate in my courtroom," Clarence Matthews decreed, turning and signaling to the bailiff. "Please ask the jury to return."

Raeanne forced herself not to react, schooling her features and demeanor to remain passive, but inside she was a bundle of raw nerves. She nonchalantly slipped her hands beneath the table, rubbing her sweaty palms on her wool skirt.

So far, so good, she told herself as she watched the jury shuffle back into the box. *Just slow and easy. Slow…* She took a deep breath and attempted to calm her racing heart by sheer willpower. Inhale. Exhale. *…and easy.*

Judge Matthews turned to his clerk and nodded.

"The court calls Russell 'Rusty' O'Brien," the court clerk announced in a colorless monotone.

Raeanne's heart raced, despite her best efforts. She watched as the bailiff escorted Rusty through the doors of the courtroom and down the center aisle. He looked jittery, and his watery eyes darted nervously around the courtroom. The plaid shirt he wore looked new and so did his jeans and the long strands of his wiry gray hair were plastered down slick against his head.

Slow and easy, Raeanne reminded herself, watching him with a careful eye. She had a lot riding on his testimony and she hoped like hell he hadn't decided to take a little "nip" to calm his nerves this morning.

Nerves. She knew all about them. It had been a grueling two weeks since she'd first interviewed Rusty at the police station and she felt every long, exhausting minute of it in her taut, tense muscles as she watched him climb behind the bench and take the witness stand. She'd reworked and reorganized her entire case after that interview, carefully analyzing and evaluating to settle on the most tactically appropriate time to introduce his testimony.

And now the time had come. Of course, Harlan had fought her, as she'd expected him to, requesting that the judge not allow Rusty to testify. But Judge Matthews had ruled against him and now it was all on her. If everything went the way she hoped, Ethan had a good chance of walking out of here a free man, but if not…

Well, she wasn't going to think about that now.

She glanced across the courtroom to find Rafe's dark eyes watching her. She felt her heart speed up even more and quickly looked away. She'd almost been grateful for the intense demands and punishing work load of the past couple of weeks. At least they had kept her from thinking about him and about what had happened in the police parking lot that night.

She thought about the way he'd held her, how he'd kissed her and how much he had wanted her. It would have been so easy to just give in, to embark on an affair. She almost wanted him that much—almost.

She closed her eyes tight, feeling an unpleasant strangling sensation in the back of her throat. She wasn't going to think about that now, either.

"Do you swear to tell the truth, the whole truth, and nothing but the truth?" the clerk asked, swearing Rusty in.

"I—I do," Rusty said solemnly, nodding his head. "I certainly do."

Rafe had discovered after nearly eight weeks in a courtroom that he loved to watch Raeanne in action. He liked the confidence, the solid command, the style, she possessed. For some absurd and totally irrational reason, he took pride in watching her, as though they were a part of one another's lives and shared in each other's triumphs and failures.

He felt his head throbbing painfully at the temples. What a fool he was. There was nothing between them— no special feelings, no special ties, nothing! And two weeks ago, in that parking lot, she'd managed to convince him a physical attraction wasn't enough. She simply no longer wanted any part of him.

And yet he was finding he couldn't quite let go of her. She'd been with him too long—in his heart and in his head. She was a part of him—like a wish, or a dream— and something inside just wouldn't let go.

He watched her as she questioned Rusty on the stand, noting the skillful way she focused on his answers, the artful manner in which she pulled from him what she wanted the jury to hear. She directed her entire being to that purpose, using mind, body, heart and soul.

He glanced at the faces of the jury—twelve men and women who were completely captivated by the drama she masterfully unfolded before them. He was the one who was suppose to have special powers. He was Wolf Boy and Wolf Boy conversed with the animals, Wolf Boy communed with nature, Wolf Boy was in tune with the earth and the skies. What a joke.

He watched her as she listened to Rusty, watched her weigh and evaluate every word he said. She was the one who was special. She was the one with the power. He was simply a man—a man who dreamed the impossible, a man who needed the woman he loved, a man who had to learn to live without her.

"What the hell is she doing?" Harlan asked, leaning over and whispering in his ear.

"I think it's called kicking our asses."

Harlan shot him a look that let him know he was responsible if that was indeed the case, then rose to his feet. "Objection. Judge, she's leading the witness."

"Objection overruled," Matthews said, tapping his gavel once, lightly. "Continue."

Raeanne waited until Harlan had sat down again, her eyes briefly holding Rafe's, before she turned around and started again. "So, Mr. O'Brien, essentially what you're saying is there is no foundation for the charge Avery made against the Walkers, is that right?"

"Right," Rusty said, nodding. "Charlie made it up. The whole thing."

A low rumble moved through the courtroom as the information was absorbed by those who were listening. Judge Matthews rapped his gavel several times in protest against the disturbance. "Order in the courtroom. Order!"

Raeanne took her time walking back to the counsel table, waiting for the right moment. When she thought it had come, she glanced purposefully at the prosecutor's table. Unfortunately, though, instead of Harlan's shrewd eyes, her gaze locked onto Rafe's and faltered for a moment.

She couldn't let herself be distracted, couldn't let her concentration be broken. There was too much at stake, too much was riding on this, for her to drop the ball now. But Rafe Rawlings did distract her. She couldn't concentrate when she looked at him.

So, taking a deep breath, she forced her gaze away, turning to Harlan and smiling, just as she'd planned. "Your witness, Counselor."

There was a moment when she thought Harlan might not have heard what she'd said, for he stared up at her with a startled, confused expression. It was obvious she'd taken him by surprise and she couldn't help feeling just a little smug. After getting kicked around in the courtroom for weeks on end, it felt good to be the one in control for a change.

Slow and easy, she reminded herself as she sat down and turned her eyes to the bench. Beside her, she heard Harlan scrambling through papers and files. He had no doubt been expecting the worst from Rusty's testimony, assuming everything would come out about Charlie's involvement with another woman. The fact that she hadn't asked Rusty about any of that had thrown the prosecutor an obvious curve.

"Are you ready on cross?" Judge Matthews asked testily.

"Yes, Your Honor," Harlan said after a moment. "Ready."

Raeanne watched and listened carefully as Harlan cross-examined Rusty on superficial details and tidbits of information. He questioned Rusty in detail about the cattle rustling, but stopped him when it looked as though he were about to say something about Avery's drinking or infidelity.

As Rusty talked, Harlan looked back at her and smiled. Raeanne smiled back, thinking Harlan probably thought he'd really gotten away with something. But that was just fine with her. He was never more vulnerable than when he was playing the flashy, flamboyant lawyer. He got cocky then and sloppy and that only made it better for her. She wanted him to get good and comfortable, wanted him to think she'd made a critical error, or blown an opportunity. He'd know soon enough what she had in mind. Then they'd see who was smiling.

She glanced across the courtroom at Rafe, whose dark eyes were watching the testimony carefully. Any good feelings she'd had from outmaneuvering Harlan faded at the sight of his handsome profile.

Was it always going to be like this? Was everything else going to take second place because she didn't have him in her life?

Twelve

"I've decided," Ethan said, walking restlessly to the window and peering through the dusty venetian blinds into the reception area. "I'm not going to."

Raeanne closed her eyes and slowly lowered the file she was holding to the table. It was late, and they'd been talking for hours. She'd told him about Rusty, about what she'd learned about Avery and about the woman involved with them both. What she needed from him was answers, not for him to close down. "What do you mean, you're not going to?"

"I mean I've decided not to testify," he said, with his back still to her. "It's my choice, and I've decided I don't want to."

"Wrong," Raeanne said, rising slowly to her feet and jamming the file into her stuffed briefcase. "We've gone through this, it's already been decided. You're going to testify."

Ethan spun around. When he was mad, he could be formidable and he was furious now. "Like hell! Don't forget, you work for me. It's my decision, and I'm not going to do it."

Raeanne pinched the bridge of her nose, trying without much success to relieve some of the pressure building there. "Look," she said reasonably, taking a deep breath. "I thought we'd gotten past that 'Me Tarzan, you Jane' routine a long time ago."

She walked across the small room to where he stood glowering down at her. She knew him better now and the anger in his eyes no longer concerned her. It did no good to argue with him, it only made him dig his heels in deeper. Her only hope was to reason with him. Ethan Walker might be a hothead, he might be a loner with a reputation for being difficult, but he was smart. And one way or another, she was going to have to make him understand.

"We're down to the wire here, Ethan. This is it," she said. "We're at the one-yard line, and the ball's been snapped. I have got to find a way to put a doubt in that jury's mind, I've got to find some way to cloud the issue, to put a question in their mind as to who really did kill Charlie Avery."

"But what about the blow to the head?" Ethan insisted. "Tracy Hensley all but said it would be impossible for someone my size to have done it."

"That's a start," Raeanne acknowledged. "But we need more. I need for you to get up on that stand and let the jury see you couldn't have done it. I need for you to tell me everything—about Avery, and about the woman Rusty told me about."

Ethan looked down at the delicate hands that gripped his work-worn ones. "I—I'm not sure I can do that."

Raeanne had gotten to know Ethan well enough in the

past couple of months to know that had been a difficult confession for him to make. He was a man who had always done what he had to do, who had always relied on his own strength, his own abilities, to maintain control. But since this whole nightmare began, he'd been in control of nothing. It hadn't been easy for him to sit back, to take to the sidelines, to step aside and trust his fate to her and a justice system that had shown him nothing but accusations and indifference.

She thought of Rafe—of his tough exterior, his suspicious nature and his distrust of others. They were really very much alike—Rafe and Ethan—even though she doubted either would ever be able to see it. Maybe that was why they didn't get along, why they didn't trust one another. They were both men who were used to being in control and who didn't like relying on others.

Rafe would never rely on her, she knew that now. Maybe he was incapable of it, maybe it just wasn't in his nature to do so—it didn't matter. She knew it now and she would have to find a way to move on. What was important now was that Ethan rely on her, that he trust her to know what was best for him.

"Tell me, Ethan—now," she insisted. "You have to tell me everything."

"There's nothing to tell. There was a girl, we dated a few times, that's all."

"And you found out she was seeing Avery, as well?"

Ethan lowered his gaze to the table. "Yes."

"Did this bother you?"

"What do you think?" he snapped, glaring up at her.

"I think that's a pretty good motive for wanting to kill someone."

His eyes narrowed. "Is that what you think?"

"I think you're keeping something from me."

"I've told you everything you need to know."

"Oh, I see," Raeanne said, holding up a finger. "You're the one deciding what I need to know and what I don't, is that it?"

Ethan dropped his gaze back to the table. "I've got nothing else to say."

Raeanne struggled to control her frustration. "Well, I've got plenty. The way I see it, you gave that girl your class ring, didn't you? That's how it got up there with Charlie."

"I told you, I don't know how it got up there," Ethan insisted, pounding his fist on the table.

"You gave it to her and she left you and went to Charlie," she went on, undeterred by his display of anger. "It was probably her lipstick and compact that was found, right?"

"You seem to have all the answers."

"Who was she, Ethan?" she demanded.

"That's not important."

"Was it...Lexine Baxter?"

Ethan pushed back from the table with such force the chair fell back against the floor. "I don't want to talk about this anymore."

"But we are going to talk Ethan," Raeanne said calmly, walking around the table and righting the chair. "We're going to talk right now."

"Want me to freshen that for you?"

Rafe glanced down at the drink he'd been nursing for well over an hour. "No thanks Pete, this is fine."

Pete Riddick shrugged, and reached for another glass to dry.

It was almost closing time and the Sundowner Saloon was nearly deserted. A slow country tune played on the jukebox, sounding sad and mournful and the big-screen TV in the corner stood dark and silent. A small group filled a far booth, their occasional outbursts of laughter the only thing that disturbed the tranquil atmosphere. But that was fine with Rafe. The quiet, lonely darkness suited him.

Pete shrugged. "Not on duty tonight, I take it?"

Rafe shook his head slowly. "Not tonight."

Pete arranged the clean glasses in an even row above the bar. "You know they got me the other night."

Rafe looked up from his drink. "Got you?"

"Yeah," Pete said, wiping his hands on the towel. "Damn kids. Spray-painted the whole side of my place. Left a big mess, I'll tell ya. Brother, what I'd give to get my hands on those damn hooligan punks."

"Taggers."

Pete slung the towel over his shoulder. "What was that?"

"Taggers," Rafe repeated, taking another sip of the drink. "That's what they call themselves now—taggers."

Pete snorted. "They're still punks, as far as I'm concerned."

"Yeah, well…" Rafe mumbled.

"How's the trial going?" Pete asked conversationally, refilling a bowl with beer nuts and returning it to the bar. "The *Journal* says it'll be going to the jury pretty soon."

Rafe nodded, reaching for a handful of nuts and popping them into his mouth. "Pretty soon."

"So, you think they'll do it?" Pete asked, resting his elbows on the bar. "Think they'll convict him?"

Rafe shrugged. "Don't know."

Pete shook his head and sighed. "Ethan Walker, that was a shocker, I don't mind sayin' it. I mean, he was always kind of a troublemaker, I'll admit it, but I gotta tell ya, I wouldn't have pegged him as a killer. And I'm usually pretty good at that kinda thing." He pushed himself away from the bar and shook his head again. "Nope, never in a million years," he said as he turned and headed down the bar with a broom in his hand. "Not Walker, not a killer."

"No," Rafe muttered darkly, finally finishing the rest of his drink. He watched as Pete rounded the end of the bar and began sweeping up around the empty booths. "Walker's just a prince of a guy."

Rafe considered another drink, then decided against it. There wasn't enough whiskey in Pete's well-stocked bar to help him forget the woman he wanted to forget.

He thought back to the nights he'd spent with Raeanne—in her bed and in her arms. He remembered the long hours of lovemaking, the times they'd spent just talking or laughing, of the ease and good feeling between them. Those few short days he'd spent with her were like no others he'd ever spent in his life. He'd been happy, relaxed and content. He'd forgotten about Wolf Boy and the legends that had followed him from childhood. He'd forgotten about the blank slate he carried with him and all the questions he had about his past. With her he'd felt whole, he'd felt complete and he knew he'd never feel that way again.

This wasn't the first time he'd been relegated to the sidelines of her life. He'd spent most of his life there. He would have thought he'd be used to it by now. But it was different this time and that bothered him. He'd spent years watching her, but watching her then had been very different from watching her now. Before, he hadn't known her, hadn't held or caressed her, hadn't felt her special magic in his heart.

But now he had. He knew with painful clarity exactly what it was he was missing and it tore him up inside to know she was lost to him for good.

"Hi."

Rafe looked up as the tall blonde from the group in the booth approached the bar. Rafe raised his glass, and gave her a silent nod.

"You drinking to celebrate, or drinking to forget?" she asked, signaling to Pete to refill the empty mugs she carried.

Rafe wished he *could* forget. "Just drinking."

As Pete refilled the mugs at the tap, she strolled down the bar, moving closer. "I know you, don't I?" she asked, squinting at Rafe. "You're that wolf boy, aren't you?"

Rafe set his glass down and looked at her. She was young, maybe too young to be ordering beer in a bar, but he didn't feel like being a cop tonight. She was pretty, despite the thick makeup that caked her face, and still young enough not to show the signs of a life filled with too many late nights in too many bars.

"Yeah," he answered in a low voice. "That's me. Wolf Boy—in the flesh."

Her smiled broadened, showing off a row of straight, even teeth. "They say you were raised in the woods."

"Did they also tell you I can talk to the wolves and cast spells on people?"

Her eyes widened. She obviously was not entirely sure if he was serious. "Wow! No, but I heard you could make a person do what you wanted just by looking at them."

Not bad, Rafe thought hearing this newest twist. The stories about him seemed to go farther and farther and get better and better, with each generation. He looked up at her and smiled. "Then you better be careful."

"Oh?" she asked, giving him a coquettish smile. "What would you make me do?"

Rafe regarded her for a moment. He felt depressed and alone and there was something about her standing there in the dark, deserted saloon that seemed so poignant and sad. Montana was filled with women like her—girls who went from bar to bar, cowboy to cowboy, town to town. He knew all he would have to do was offer and she'd be his.

He thought of Raeanne and the offer he'd made to her in the darkness of a parking lot. But what he'd offered, she hadn't accepted and she would never be his.

"Your beers are ready," he said, nodding to the end of the bar.

"Oh," she said, her smile breaking into a full grin. "Okay. If you're not busy, come by and join me and my friends." She lifted a hand, giving him a little wave. "Bye, Wolf Boy."

Rafe nodded, watching her as she walked away. It would have been so easy. He could have her back in his truck and back to his small apartment above the dry cleaner's in a matter of minutes. She would open her arms to Wolf Boy, she would want him because she believed him to be half man, half magic. There would be no pity in her eyes, no look of sympathy, no charity for a stray. It would have been so easy—so easy.

So why hadn't he? Why hadn't he taken her to bed, why hadn't he used her round breasts and slender legs to purge all the memories, all the nightmares, from his head?

He thought of Raeanne again and slammed his fist down hard on the bar. His glass jumped and turned over, rolling toward the edge.

"Hey, go easy on the furniture, will ya?" Pete said, reaching out and catching the glass before it hit the floor. He sat it down and returned to his sweeping.

"Sorry," Rafe mumbled, stepping down off the stool and tossing some money on the bar.

"You okay?" Pete asked carefully. He leaned the broom against the table he'd been sweeping under and took a cautious step forward. "You don't look so good. Want me to call someone for you?"

Someone, Rafe repeated to himself. There was only one person he wanted, only one person who could really make him feel happy and like living again.

But he had to forget about all that. The woman he wanted would never be his and he couldn't flood his system with enough alcohol, or surround himself with enough women to make him forget that. It was something he just had to accept and something he had to learn to live with.

"No," he called back to Pete, whom he'd left standing at the bar. "There's no one."

Raeanne rushed across the parking lot, carefully jumping slushy puddles and muddy patches. The snow was deep, still covering everything, but it hadn't stormed for days, and Raeanne was convinced the wind felt warmer. There was definitely a chill in the air, but after the long, difficult winter, the milder temperatures felt like an outright declaration that spring was on its way and that was enough to give her spirits a boost. Today was going to be a big day and she needed all the help she could get.

She rounded the corner of the lot and stepped onto the sidewalk, surprised to see several squad cars and a small crowd gathered at the entrance to her office building. The puppy in her arms barked with excitement and Raeanne quickly soothed him.

"Shh, calm down," she said quickly, quieting him with a mollifying pat on the head. "It's okay. It's all right."

But as she walked closer, she saw what it was that was drawing all the attention. Broken glass littered the walk, and ugly black streaks of paint marred the sedate gray stones along the entrance to the Blue Lake County administration building.

"Taggers."

Raeanne jumped at the sound of Cinda's voice behind her. "It's awful. What a mess."

"Looks like they might have caught them, too," Cinda said, nodding toward three young men looking quiet and downcast as they stood near the squad cars. "I don't know, but I think I recognize that tall one. I think I represented him on a juvenile charge."

Raeanne surveyed the damage and shook her head. "Looks like you might be again."

"What are you doing in so early?" Cinda asked, reaching over and giving the puppy a scratch behind the ear. "It's not even seven-thirty."

Raeanne gave her a deliberate look. "I could ask you the same thing."

Cinda smiled, knowing her reputation around the office and the courts for being chronically late. She opened her coat to reveal a sweat suit and running shoes. "I'm running the stairs."

"Running the stairs," Raeanne repeated, rolling her eyes. "Since when have you been a health nut?"

Cinda scowled. "Since I pulled out a pair of Bermuda

shorts I wore last year and couldn't get them zipped up."
She looked at Raeanne. "So now you know my excuse.
What's yours?"

Raeanne drew in a deep breath. "Ethan Walker takes the
stand today. I just want to check things—make sure everything goes as smoothly as it possibly can."

"Sounds like you're almost ready to go to the jury. Expecting to close today?"

Raeanne shrugged. "That depends on how long
Harlan's cross takes, but I think it looks good. I don't think
Harlan is going to want the jury to hear what Ethan has to
say more than once."

Cinda sank her hands deep into the pockets of her coat.
"It's been a long trial."

"Too long," Raeanne said with a tired sigh.

Cinda studied her carefully. "This really is getting to
you, isn't it?"

Raeanne shrugged again, not feeling comfortable with
the concern. "I'm okay. I'm just anxious to have it over."

Cinda nodded, but still looked skeptical. "Client still
giving you trouble?"

"Ethan?" Raeanne shook her head. "No—his bark is much
worse than his bite. We've developed an understanding."

Cinda considered this. "Sounds like you've gotten to
know him pretty well."

Raeanne smiled bleakly. "Yeah, there's something
about a murder trial that does that to you."

When they both laughed, the puppy barked again.

"Hey, puppy, what are you barking at?" Cinda asked,
grabbing one of the dog's paws and giving it a playful
tickle. "You're a cute little fella, you know that?" She
glanced up at Raeanne. "When did you get a dog?"

Raeanne felt herself tighten. "Oh, uh, a…friend gave him to me."

"A present?" Cinda asked, looking up at her.

Raeanne shook her head. Cinda was suspicious enough about Rafe. There was no sense giving her any more ammunition.

"What's his name?"

"Joe." Raeanne gazed down at the wiggly little dog in her arms and let him lick her chin.

Cinda looked around quickly, lowering her voice. "You're taking him to work?"

"Well—" Raeanne looked guilty "—he gets so lonesome shut up in the house alone all day."

"Oh, brother," Cinda said, rolling her eyes heavenward. "A nervous mother."

"I'm not nervous," Raeanne protested, but she couldn't help smiling. "I just worry about him."

"You know," Cinda said dryly, "I think there's a county ordinance or something about animals in the building."

"I don't care. It's just this once," Raeanne said, giving the pup another little hug. "I'll sneak him in early and shut him up in my office while I'm in court. No one has to know. And I can at least see him at lunch, maybe take him for a walk or something."

Cinda gave a conspiratorial look around, and leaned in close. "It's just a dog, Raeanne," she said in a stage whisper. "You realize that, don't you?"

Raeanne laughed. Cinda was right, of course. The pup was "just a dog." But she adored the little guy and the fact that he'd been one of Rafe's dogs…well, she couldn't deny that made a difference. "Yes, I realize that."

Cinda looked at her and shook her head in wonder. "This trial better end soon. You're going off the deep end."

"Is the public defender offering curbside service now?"

Both women turned at the sound of the deep male voice behind them, and the puppy barked excitedly.

"Actually, Detective Rawlings," Cinda said in an official voice, "there isn't enough business coming across our desks, so we thought we'd come down here and see what we could drum up."

"I see," Rafe said, his gaze shifting to the crime scene before them. "Looks like you got lucky."

"It's a mess, all right," Cinda said, turning back and giving Rafe a deliberate look. "Where's there a cop when you need one?"

Rafe smiled. "Probably out chasing all the creeps you keep putting back on the street." He turned to Raeanne, his gaze dropping to the puppy in her arms. "He's getting big."

Raeanne started to answer, but Cinda interrupted. "No, he's lonesome."

Rafe turned to her, his brow arched. "Excuse me?"

"You heard me," Cinda said drolly. "He is lonesome. It gets lonely being home alone all day, so she's bringing him to work."

Raeanne felt silly. When he turned and looked back at her, she felt her cheeks fill with color. "I—uh…just thought once…you know."

Rafe's gaze dropped to the dog in her arms. He couldn't help noticing how she held him—her long, slender hands holding his sturdy little body with such care, such regard. Rafe glanced up again, feeling a strange, constricting sensation in his chest. "Does he eat much?"

"Anything that's in his reach," Raeanne said, glancing down affectionately at the pup. "Which includes two pillows, a potted plant and my favorite pair of slippers."

"His mama was the same way," Rafe said, reaching out to give the dog a pet. Just at that moment, Raeanne reached to stroke the dog, too, and their hands brushed briefly.

At the instant of contact, their eyes met and it was as if the world had stopped, as though time had come to a standstill and the course of everyday living skittered to a stop. Scenes came alive—recollections of places and locations, of feelings and emotions, of touching and sharing. After being apart for so long, that glorious millisecond of hand touching hand felt tantamount to an act of love.

"His mama?" Cinda asked, watching with curiosity the tense interplay between them. "This is one of your dogs?"

Raeanne snatched her hand away at the sound of Cinda's voice and Rafe watched her expression tighten. "Yeah," he said after a moment, turning back to Cinda. "After Raeanne's house was hit before Christmas, I thought she might like a watchdog."

"Good idea," Cinda said, gesturing to the three youths being loaded into the back of the squad cars. "Think these might be the same guys?"

Rafe surveyed the damage, and shrugged. "Doesn't really look the same, but it's hard to tell. Unfortunately, there seems to be more than one group 'expressing' themselves all over town like this."

Cinda nodded, her eyes shifting from Rafe to Raeanne, then back to Rafe again. "Well…" she said with forced enthusiasm. "Look, you two, I've got to be running—up six flights, to be exact." She turned and trotted for the one remaining undamaged door of the building. "See you later."

"Bye," Raeanne called after her. She turned and gave Rafe a brief glance. "Well, I better get going, too. I've got a lot of work to do."

"Raeanne, wait," Rafe said, stopping her with a hand on her arm as she started to walk away.

"No, Rafe, don't," Raeanne said, pulling herself free.

"Don't what?" he asked, defensiveness seeping into his voice. "We're not even allowed to talk anymore?"

She looked up at him. "That's just it, Rafe, we don't talk. We argue, we fight, we rub each other the wrong way. But we don't talk."

Rafe took a deep breath. "Look, I just wanted to…"

"Wanted to what, Rafe?" Raeanne demanded when his words drifted off. "To tell me something? To actually talk to me and tell me something you're feeling?"

He stared at her, surprised by the sudden burst of anger. How could he tell her what he was feeling, when he didn't know himself? "I—I just wanted to wish you luck today."

Luck, she thought darkly as she silently turned away and started into the building. She'd felt lucky once—lucky enough to hope he'd come to trust her, but not anymore. She knew now that would never happen and luck had nothing to do with that.

Thirteen

"The court calls Ethan Walker to the stand."

A buzz traveled through the courtroom, and Raeanne felt the lump of tension in her throat swell and expand. From the corner of her eye, she could see Rafe seated at the prosecutor's table. Unlike everyone else in the courtroom, whose eyes were fixed steadily on Ethan as he mounted the steps to the witness stand, Rafe kept his dark gaze riveted on her and that only served to make the muscles in her throat all the more tense. She reached for the small foam cup of water on the desk beside her, hoping no one on the jury noticed how her hand trembled as she lifted it to her mouth.

She hated tightropes, hated it when a case came down to one deciding factor, one dramatic moment that could either make or break it for the jury—and Ethan's testimony was shaping up to do just that. What Ethan said on the stand was going to be important, maybe even the turning point on which this whole thing was decided. And knowing what she did about what he was to testify to, that meant swinging either way.

She was walking a tightrope—one wrong step could spell disaster. She held no illusions that Ethan's testimony would prove his innocence to the jury, but then, it didn't have to. All she wanted was to place a reasonable doubt in their minds, a plausible uncertainty that would make it impossible for them to vote to convict. But the tricky part would be doing that without the testimony making him appear any guiltier than the prosecution already had.

She hated tightropes.

Ethan climbed the box to the witness stand. His weathered, rugged features looked stony and hard and it gave him a formidable, angry appearance. Raeanne cringed. *Smile,* she wanted to scream up at him, remembering the hundreds of times she'd asked him to remember. *Smile and show them you're not a monster.* But she understood that his dour expression sprang from nervousness. God knew, she was nervous too.

As she walked slowly around the table, she quickly scanned the faces of the people in the box. She'd hoped for a reaction that would give her a reading on what they made of this man who'd been accused of murder. But after seeing their twelve curious expressions, she realized her work was cut out for her. She had to get them to listen to what Ethan Walker had to say—but first she had to make sure he didn't scare the hell out of them.

She smiled up at Ethan, and was rewarded with a small, tight smile. She took a deep breath. So far, so good.

"Now, Mr. Walker…" she began, consciously keeping the pace of her questioning slow and deliberate. She took

Ethan step by step through the charges, reviewing the evidence and asking his slant on events. She talked in a low, pleasant voice, in an effort to relax both Ethan and the jury. It seemed to work, for even though the information she questioned him on was review, she noticed the jury listened in earnest. Ethan seemed to relax more too. He became more animated, more genuine, more *human*, and she knew that would only help their case.

An hour slipped by, but Raeanne had no conception of time or space. She concentrated her entire attention on guiding Ethan's testimony and keeping the tempo slow and relaxed. It was as though the entire courtroom had become swept up in the tale Ethan had to tell, and she wanted to keep it that way. She let him explain to the jury that he'd purchased the explosives discovered in his barn for the purpose of clearing tree stumps out of the ground, not to blow up Nick Dean's car. She then presented into evidence a police report Ethan had made days before the explosion reporting a break-in at his barn, to help support her conclusion that anyone could have broken into his barn and stolen the explosives.

"You've heard the testimony in this courtroom about the bad blood between you and Charlie Avery. Was there bad blood between you?"

"We didn't care much for each other, if that's what you mean," Ethan answered, shifting just a little in the chair.

"But it was a little more than just not caring for each other, wasn't it?"

"You could say that."

"Would you say you disliked Charlie Avery?"

"Yeah, I disliked him."

"Would you say you hated Charlie Avery?"

Ethan hesitated for a moment. "Yes, I hated him."

"Would it be safe to say you hated each other?"

"I suppose you'd be safe in saying that."

Raeanne paused for a moment, feeling the tension level in the courtroom rise a notch. "Did your feelings for Charlie Avery have anything to do with the accusation he made that your family was rustling cattle from the Kincaid ranch?"

"He lied about that."

"Well, thanks to the testimony of Rusty O'Brien, we know that now. But why would Charlie Avery lie about something like that?"

"Avery had it in for me."

"But why would Charlie Avery have had it in for you?"

Ethan glanced up at the judge, then back to Raeanne. "I…I was…friends with someone."

"Friends with someone?"

"Yes. I was…friends with a friend of his."

"And he didn't like that?"

"Right."

"This friend—was it a woman?"

"Yes."

"Was it Nan Avery, Charlie's wife?"

Ethan glanced down at his hands, which gripped the railing tightly. "No."

"Would you please tell the court who this woman was?" Raeanne pressed, ignoring the promise she'd made Ethan about not having to name the woman.

"But you said—"

"Just answer the question, Ethan," she said, cutting him off. "What's the woman's name?"

Ethan gave her a killing look, then glanced down at his hands again. "Lexine Baxter."

A loud rumble traveled through the courtroom, and Judge Matthews hammered his gavel down hard. "Order in the court!"

Raeanne glanced into the crowd of spectators, seeing Nan Avery's bowed head. She looked devastated, humiliated, an innocent victim of the truth. But Raeanne couldn't let herself think about that now. She had a job to do, the truth had to come out and people were bound to be hurt.

She stopped as she turned back to Ethan, catching Rafe's stare from the opposite side of the courtroom. His eyes were dark, unreadable and she quickly looked away. She couldn't let herself think about him right now either.

"Lexine Baxter," Raeanne repeated slowly. "She was your girlfriend?"

"Yes," Ethan whispered, lowering his head.

"You even gave her your class ring, didn't you?"

"Yes."

"So we're to assume you cared about her a lot?"

"Yes."

"Was she your mistress?"

Ethan's head snapped up. "No, it—it wasn't like that. We never…"

"I see," Raeanne said when Ethan's voice trailed off. The jury understood perfectly. "Now, Rusty O'Brien testified that Charlie Avery was involved with a woman who was not his wife. Do you know who that woman was?"

"Yes."

"Could you tell the court, please?"

Ethan took a deep breath. "Lexine was…uh…she was his…friend."

Another wave of murmurs moved through the crowded spectator's section, and again Judge Matthews censored the interruption with a rap of his gavel. "Any further out-bursts and I'll clear the courtroom." He turned to Raeanne and nodded. "Continue."

"Lexine Baxter was a friend of Charlie Avery?" Rae-anne asked when the crowd had quieted.

"That's right."

"But it was more than just a friendship, wasn't it, Ethan?"

The line across Ethan's brow deepened. "Yes."

"Wasn't Lexine Baxter Charlie Avery's mistress?"

Ethan put his head down. "Yes."

Raeanne stopped for a moment, savoring the silent crackle of tension in the courtroom. Every ear and every eye was on Ethan, on the witness stand—jury, spectators, reporters, clerks, counsels, bailiffs and judge. She smiled to herself, feeling her heart low and steady in her chest and her palms dry and hard. This was one of the rare instants, one of those sterling moments when she felt in complete control and she relished the feeling.

"That must have made you pretty mad, to find out your girlfriend was sleeping with a married man."

"It did."

"Mad enough to kill?"

Another rumble of voices echoed through the court-room, and the judge wrapped his gavel again.

"I didn't kill Charlie Avery."

"No, of course you didn't," Raeanne agreed quietly. "But you cared about Lexine Baxter, didn't you?"

"She just used me," he whispered. "Strung me along to make Avery jealous."

"She told you that?"

Ethan shook his head. "She didn't have to. She came to me one night, upset and crying. Told me Avery was drunk, had roughed her up. Made me promise not to tell anyone I'd even seen her that night, said she didn't want anyone to know. She told me she loved me, that she wanted us to be together, but she needed money to get rid of Avery."

"What did you do?"

Ethan dropped his gaze to the floor and nodded his head. "I pawned everything I could find. Gave her what I could."

"What happened after that?"

"The next thing I knew, everyone was saying she'd ran off with Avery." He shook his head. "I felt like a fool."

"And yet now we know that didn't happen. Now we know that someone murdered Charlie Avery instead." Raeanne walked across the courtroom to the jury box. "Someone, in the opinion of the prosecution's own forensic expert, of a height shorter than the victim, had crushed Charlie Avery's skull and killed him. Ethan, was Lexine Baxter shorter than Charlie Avery?"

"Well, yes, of course, but you don't think—"

"And wasn't there a lipstick and compact found along with your class ring—the class ring you'd given to Lexine Baxter—found near where Avery's remains were found?"

"Yes, but—"

"Lexine Baxter told you she wanted to get rid of Charlie Avery, didn't she?"

"Yes."

"Ethan, when you heard that Avery's remains had been found, did it ever occur to you that Lexine Baxter might have murdered him?"

Ethan shifted uneasily in his seat. "Maybe, once or twice."

"Once or twice," Raeanne repeated. "And yet you never mentioned your suspicions to the police. Why?"

"Look," Ethan said, frustrated and uncomfortable, "I don't know what happened. Lexine disappeared years ago. I don't know who killed Charlie Avery, and frankly, I don't give a damn."

"And so you said nothing to the police about Lexine Baxter. Is that right?"

"Why drag her into all this? I didn't see the need to go hiding behind the skirts of some poor, misguided woman who might be dead and buried herself by now."

"Sounds to me as though you wanted to protect her." Raeanne said, walking back to the witness stand. "You must have loved her very much."

Ethan looked away. "It was a long time ago."

"I don't believe this," Harlan muttered, shaking his head.

"What? That Lexine Baxter might have offed Avery, or that Walker was actually hung up on the woman?" Rafe asked dryly, taking a perverse pleasure in the startling turn of events.

Harlan gave him a dirty look. "You act like you're enjoying this damn soap opera."

"No," Rafe said simply. "But I don't see there's much we can do to stop it."

"Well, not when my chief investigator decides to uncover a witness for the defense," Harlan said coolly, raising a bushy brow.

Rafe leaned across the table towards him. "It's called getting at the truth. That's what we're supposed to be after here, remember?"

Harlan glanced across the courtroom to where Raeanne stood. "How can someone who looks so sweet be such a pain in the ass?"

Rafe followed Harlan's gaze, and felt his chest swell. Raeanne stood in the midst of the chaotic courtroom, looking calmly confident and in complete control. While Judge Matthews pounded his gavel, issuing orders and admonishing the noisy crowd and bailiffs rushed around ushering spectators out and scrambling for order, she coolly returned to her counsel table and quietly waited.

Ethan's testimony had been powerful, throwing the entire case into a different light. Rumors about Lexine Baxter had been a staple of Whitehorn gossip for over thirty years. The wild, unmanageable daughter of the ruined rancher Cameron Baxter had been gossiped and talked about practically from the moment of her birth. By the time she was sixteen, she'd had a reputation that had "decent" folks in Whitehorn blushing. Since she'd left town the same time Charlie Avery disappeared, rumor had had it that Lexine and Charlie had run off together.

Rafe glanced up at Ethan, who sat in the witness box while the disarray and disorder moved around him. Except now everyone knew that Lexine had had not only Charlie Avery on the string, but Ethan Walker, as well.

Rafe glanced back at Raeanne. He wished he could reach out to her, help her celebrate her triumph today. Whether Ethan won or lost, she'd been magnificent. He remembered the feel of her embrace and the silky touch of her hands along his skin.

Judge Matthews slammed his gavel down hard again, causing Rafe's daydreams to scatter.

She needed nothing from him—not even his friendship. What was the matter with him? Why was it getting more difficult instead of easier? Why was it the longer he was without her, the more he wanted her back?

* * *

"Any comment?" Sandra Wilson pushed her way through the crowd and caught up with Raeanne just before she reached the door of the courtroom. "Any indication how the jury will vote?"

Raeanne slowed her pace, the crowd jostling her. "Sandy, I stopped second-guessing juries a long time ago."

"But surely you have some clue," the *Whitehorn Journal* reporter said. "Some feeling about the verdict."

Raeanne looked up, spotting Rafe standing at the edge of the crowd. As she watched, he turned and made his way out the door, disappearing down the corridor. Feelings. She'd had a lot of feelings once—especially where Rafe Rawlings was concerned.

But she'd been wrong—her feelings had been wrong. She'd been led astray, believing in something that wasn't even there. But never again. Never again would she make the same mistake. Never again would she trust anything— or anyone—she couldn't be absolutely sure of. From now on it was either black or white, dead or alive, guilty or innocent.

"Were you surprised that the prosecution spent so little time on cross-examination?" Sandra asked, holding a small voice-activated tape recorder up to catch each word.

"Frankly, Sandy, nothing the prosecution does surprises me anymore," Raeanne told her, moving slowly with the crowd through the doors.

"Harlan Collins implied your client's testimony only showed the jury another motive he had for wanting Avery dead. That he'd murdered him over Lexine Baxter."

"What would you expect him to say?" Raeanne pushed the button for the elevator. But inwardly she cringed. "The district attorney's case was falling apart right in front of him. He was grabbing at straws."

Raeanne tried to display the same confident facade for Sandra that she had for the jury, but she knew the point was a valid one. And she'd expected Harlan to grab at it. She'd known when she put Ethan on the stand that his testimony would very likely either help him or hang him. It was a chance they'd had to take. Still, as she'd pointed out again to the jury in her closing argument, their responsibility was not to prove Ethan's innocence, just to point out a reasonable doubt and she prayed she'd managed to do that.

"Were you expecting things to wrap up so quickly?"

She looked at the reporter and smiled. "Well, let's just say I had my closing ready, just in case."

Sandra Wilson smiled back. "How's Walker doing?"

"How do you expect? He's an innocent man who's spent months behind bars for something he didn't do."

Sandra laughed. "He didn't seem too happy about testifying—almost hostile at times."

"Can you blame him?" Raeanne asked, still defending him. "He's a private man, and his whole life has been held up for public inspection."

"You make him sound like a victim."

"He's as much a victim of this as Charlie Avery is."

The elevator door opened, and with the help of several court bailiffs, who held the crowd at bay, Raeanne stepped inside.

"What's he looking forward to?" Sandra called after her before the doors slid closed.

"Having this over," Raeanne said, letting the doors close on the crowd and all the noise and confusion.

"He's not the only one."

Raeanne spun around, surprised to see Rafe at the back of the elevator. "Rafe. You startled me."

"Sorry," he said, stepping forward and reaching for the button on the control panel. "Lobby okay?"

"Yes, fine."

He pressed the button, then stepped back again, leaning casually against the rear wall. "It's been quite a day."

Raeanne nodded, feeling as though several centuries had passed since she'd seen him on the walk outside her office building this morning. "Yeah, it has been."

"I think the county got its money's worth today."

She turned around and gave him a puzzled look, feeling her defenses rising. "What do you mean?"

"From you," he said simply. "You did quite a job in there."

She quickly looked away. It was as close to a compliment as she ever expected to hear from him. "You think so?"

"Yeah," he murmured. His gaze dropped to her hand, which was tightly clutching the handle of her briefcase. It made him think of her touch, of the feel of her hands against him, of their gentle caress. Scenes drifted up from the back of his brain, of the two of them together— touching, kissing, making love. They swirled around his head like a garland of memories—a tortuous, painful crown of thorns.

"How's Harlan doing?"

He looked up, startled by the sound of her voice. His thoughts scattered. "You know Harlan. He's been busy putting the best spin possible on everything."

"Well, if anyone can..." Raeanne sighed, purposely letting her words drift.

"They really listened to you."

"The jury?"

He nodded his head. "I watched them as you gave your closing. I think you really got to them."

She drew in a deep breath. "I hope you're right."

"You have doubts?"

Raeanne lifted a shoulder in a careless shrug. "I don't know. It was a gamble. I wanted to show them a different picture of Charlie Avery—liar, cheat, womanizer. Unfortunately, to do that I also gave them another reason why Ethan might have wanted to see Avery dead."

"Ah, the lovely Lexine," he said, shaking his head. "She must have been something."

"*Really* something," Raeanne agreed, rubbing at the stiffness in her neck. She'd been running on adrenaline for hours and now, in the quiet seclusion of the elevator, the fatigue began to settle in. "Her tastes were certainly…eclectic?"

"Is that a polite way of saying she was sleeping with a married man, and a fifteen-year-old kid, at the same time?"

Raeanne smiled. "That's strange, all right."

"Walker was just a kid. I wonder what she'd want with him?"

"I don't know. Maybe she used him to make Avery jealous—or someone else. Who knows?" Raeanne said, her smile fading. "But you want to hear the really strange part? I think he was in love with her—Ethan, I mean. He really loved her. Even after all this time, all the years that had passed, he could hardly talk about it. And he kept his promise to her and didn't tell anyone about what had happened that night. It still hurt. She'd left him, and it still hurt."

It was odd, but at that moment Rafe felt a curious sort

of bond with Ethan Walker. He knew what it was to love someone, and to keep that love buried deep—hidden away where it wasn't talked about or recognized.

Rafe glanced up at Raeanne. Would years take away his longing? Would years erase the memories of her in his arms? Would they ease the pain of knowing he would never hold her again?

"If I just could have made the jury see that," Raeanne murmured, almost to herself.

"I think you did."

The look in his eyes had the small elevator closing in around her. His dark gaze saw too much, penetrated too deep, made her feel things she didn't want to. It was as though all the air in the small enclosure had evaporated, and she was left gasping for breath and for space.

"Well, I hope you're right," she said with a forced cheeriness that she hoped would mask her nervousness. "I hope it worked."

"It did on me."

She looked up at him, forgetting about her nervousness and discomfort. "What do you mean?"

"I investigated Ethan Walker, interrogated him, even arrested him on a charge of first-degree murder. I was convinced we had the right man." He pushed himself away from the wall of the elevator and took a step toward her. "After hearing your argument, I have to admit, I've got my doubts."

The elevator doors swung open at the lobby, but for a moment neither of them moved. Then, feeling dazed and probably more uncertain than she had in her life, Raeanne turned and stepped into the lobby.

"You know, you were wrong."

She stopped, and turned back to him. His hand rested

on the elevator door, preventing it from sliding shut. "Wrong? About what?"

"We can talk."

Leaning back against the wall, he let the doors slide closed between them.

Fourteen

Rafe eased his foot onto the brake, slowing to make the turn off highway 191 onto rural route 17. The big tires of the truck gripped the mud-streaked pavement, made treacherous by melting snow and slush. If he'd just switched off his radio when the message came in for him over the police band, he'd be back in Whitehorn by now, at his desk, where he belonged, instead of heading for Winona Cobbs's Stop 'n' Shop for a routine call that could have been handled by any rookie. But the fact was, he hadn't. He'd answered the alert, and God knew how long he'd be stuck there.

Rafe glanced up at the clear sky, but even the bright March morning, with its billowy white clouds drifting against a brilliant blue background, could do little to lighten his mood. He was tired, having gotten up before dawn to head for Lewistown to question a witness to a barroom brawl over the weekend that had left two cowboys dead.

The drive to Lewistown had been long, the witness's memory faulty and the trip a waste of time. Then, just to top off the morning, his supervisor, Sterling McCallum, had called him over the police radio he had in his truck to ask that he stop by Winona's on his way back into town, in response to a robbery she'd reported. All in all, it was shaping up to be one heck of a morning.

He sped along the road, passing slower-moving vehicles at a speed well above the posted limit. He thought of Winona, of how uncomfortable she always made him. He hadn't seen her since the trial, and that had been just fine with him.

The trial. After only two hours of deliberation, Ethan Walker had been found not guilty, leaving the Whitehorn Police Department with another unsolved homicide to try to figure out. It had been a controversial verdict—leaving many questions unanswered and raising some new ones. Some had agreed wholeheartedly with it, others had vehemently opposed it—and probably no one was more shocked and upset than Mary Jo Kincaid. He still remembered the strange expression on her face—a mixture of surprise and sheer panic. Then swiftly, her expression had changed to her usual mild, somewhat childlike look. It was almost as if... Rafe shook his head. He didn't want to think about the trial. Regardless of personal opinions and popular vote, the jury had made its decision and from the moment they announced it two weeks ago to a packed courtroom, it had created a scene.

When the jury foreman had read their verdict of not guilty, the place had erupted into chaos—cameras flashing, men swearing, ladies gasping and tongues starting to wag. But Rafe didn't remember much about the upheaval. All he really remembered about that day was seeing Walker grab Raeanne up into his arms and kiss her full on the mouth.

His foot pressed harder on the accelerator and the engine strained loudly as it picked up more speed. It had been over two weeks since the verdict was read, over two weeks since he'd seen Raeanne. He'd thought all he wanted was for the trial to be over, to put an end to seeing her every day in court and get a start on finally forgetting her.

Well, he'd gotten what he wanted. The trial was over, and he didn't have to see her anymore. She was out of his life. So why couldn't he forget? Why was she the last thing he thought about when he closed his eyes at night and the first thing he wanted when he woke in the morning? Why did he drive by her house at night hoping to catch a glimpse of her, or stroll through the courthouse halls hoping to run into her?

He saw the dilapidated sign for the Stop 'n' Shop, and eased his foot off the accelerator. The last thing he needed right now was to be under Winona's prying gaze. It made him feel like a bug under a microscope and he resented the intrusion.

He pulled his truck to a stop in the gravelly lot outside the place. Several cars were parked close by, and Rafe could see people wandering through the junk that littered the yard. Grabbing his down vest, he slipped it on over his flannel shirt as he weaved his way through the debris to the front door.

The bell above the door clanged loudly as he pushed it open and walked inside. At the sound, a group of women huddled in conversation at the counter stopped and turned around.

"Well, it's about time," Winona declared, stepping out of a back room, carrying what looked to be a large soup tureen in the shape of a giant green head of cabbage. "Sterling said someone would be out as soon as possible. That was two hours ago."

"I'd have thought you'd have this all figured out by now," Rafe said dryly, reaching into an inside pocket of his vest and bringing out a small tablet. "What's the matter, Winona, losing your touch?"

"My touch is just fine," Winona assured him, setting the gaudy tureen on the counter and starting for the back room again. "But I'm in the middle of this right now. *You'll* just have to wait for *me*."

Rafe started to say something, but held his tongue. She was being stubborn and it would have done no good.

"Hello, Wolf Boy."

Rafe glanced at the group standing near the counter and recognizing Lily Mae Wheeler among them. The nosy old gossip was just what he needed to make the morning perfect. "Hello, Mrs. Wheeler."

"All that graffiti at the county building downtown, that fight at the Sundowner and now Winona's place robbed. What is this world coming to? What can we do about all this crime?"

Rafe smiled. He really didn't need this now. "Well, I don't know. Crime is a problem in a lot of communities, Lily Mae."

"Well, it's a disgrace—a disgrace, I tell you," she expounded, turning to her friends. "I mean, it's getting so a person isn't safe anywhere."

"Well, it's not any better anywhere else," one of the others exclaimed. "I mean, look at what goes on in New York, or California." She shivered. "It's enough to make you shudder."

As Lily Mae and the others became caught up in their own conversation, Rafe slipped quietly to a corner of the shop, grateful to be off the hook. He was hardly in the mood to explain away the failures of the entire criminal justice system and no way was he interested in their homespun solutions.

He glanced around at the array of odds and ends that cluttered Winona's store, wondering how she could even tell if something was missing with all the junk. In his brief examination of the place, he'd been able to see no sign of a forced entry, and he began to wonder if Winona had called him out on a wild-goose chase.

As he waited, he was only vaguely aware of the discussion of the group of women nearby. It wasn't that he couldn't hear them—he could, loud and clear. It was just that he wasn't interested. As far as he was concerned, they were a bunch of busybodies, gossiping about people and things they knew nothing about.

But just then he realized there was something in their conversation he was very interested in and he listened intently.

"Well, it makes no sense," Lily Mae was saying. "I mean, Los Angeles! Look what goes on out there— murder, rape, burning in the streets. And if that isn't bad enough, you've got earthquakes and forest fires. The girl obviously can't be thinking straight. It'll kill her parents, I tell you, just kill them. Are you sure?"

"Oh, absolutely," her friend maintained. "Sharon down at the beauty parlor does Nell Riley's hair, who works down at the real estate office? She told Sharon that Raeanne is looking for someone to sublet. She plans to be gone by the end of the month."

Lily Mae shook her head. "Well, you know the poor thing lost her husband so young and that's not good for a young woman, even though I tell you that Andy Peyton wasn't much better than that drunkard of a father of his. I don't think Raeanne knows what she wants. I mean, who in their right mind would want to do the kind of work she does, working with those...well, you know, with *those* kinds of people—criminals and thugs."

"Like Ethan Walker?" another chimed in. "I don't care what that jury said, that man was guilty! He got away with murder."

"I'll say. Decent folks aren't safe anymore," another agreed in a low voice.

But Rafe couldn't hear anymore. The roaring in his ears drowned out everything else and he felt dizzy and light-headed. Could it be true, or was it just more idle gossip from Lily Mae and her friends? Was Raeanne really leaving Whitehorn?

His mind traveled back, remembering how he'd felt when she left after Andy's death. It had been hard to watch her walk away—he had suffered, mourned, but eventually he'd found a way to live with the pain. Even then, as he watched the bus carry her away, he hadn't been thinking in terms of forever. He'd told himself at the time that she would never come back, but somewhere in the back of his brain, something had made him believe there still was hope. This time...

He tried to think of his life, the long succession of days going about his everyday routines—eating, sleeping, working. Day after day, month after month, year after year. His life would be like the void he'd been existing in for the past several weeks. Except with one major difference. She would be gone. She would be out of his life for good this time. What would it be like, this method of existence, without so much as a glimpse, without so much as the hope of seeing her?

He closed his eyes. What did he do—let her go? Beg her to stay? He opened his eyes, turning to stare aimlessly out the front window. She had everything to offer a man and he had nothing to give. She deserved more from a man than a past built on legend and a future full of uncertainties. Besides, too much had happened, too many harsh words had been said, too many bad feelings had been left between them. He couldn't live with her pity and she'd made it clear she needed nothing from him.

"Okay, I'm ready now," Winona said, wiping her hands on her apron and walking around the counter toward him. But when she looked into his face, her hands stopped abruptly. "Rafe? Are you all right?"

Rafe winced and quickly looked away. He needed time to absorb all this, needed to be alone to try to sort it all out. He didn't want Winona's probing eyes on him, and he immediately tightened up. "What's this about a robbery?"

Winona regarded him for a moment, then drew in a deep breath. "Right, the robbery. This way."

She led him outside, deftly maneuvering her considerable girth through the clutter to a spot along the far side of the building, not far from where she kept her beehives.

"There," she said, gesturing to a place where several large rusted wagon wheels lay leaning against the building.

Rafe started to the spot she indicated. "What?"

"My moped," Winona said, as though he should know. "It's gone."

"Moped?" Rafe repeated. "You mean like a motor bike?"

"Yes, I mean like a motorbike," Winona said, parroting him. "It was here yesterday, now it's gone. Someone's stolen it."

It wasn't exactly the robbery he'd been expecting, but Rafe decided to go through the motions anyway. "You said it was here yesterday?"

"Yes," Winona said. Then, after thinking a moment, she corrected herself. "Well, I think it was here yesterday. Day before, for sure."

Rafe rolled his eyes, scratching out the notation he'd just made on his tablet and correcting it. "Were the keys in it?"

"Keys?"

"Yeah, you know, keys," he told her, making a turning motion with his hand. "To start it with?"

"Start it?" Winona looked up at him innocently. "Why would you want to start it? It didn't run."

Rafe's head and shoulders sagged. "What?"

"A key wouldn't do you any good," she explained good-naturedly. "The thing didn't run."

"You mean it was broken-down?"

"No. I mean it didn't run. It never ran."

"Never?"

Winona shrugged. "Not since I've had it."

"How long was that?"

Winona thought for a moment. "Oh, gosh, I guess... I don't know... Well, my goodness, that had to be about three—no, four years ago. I remember 'cause I traded with Harold Potter, lives up near the res? Took a lantern and two oil drums for it." Winona scratched her head thoughtfully. "I always felt a little bad about that, sorta like I took advantage of him, you know?"

Rafe put his tablet back into his pocket and started back for his truck.

"Wait—where are you going?" Winona called after him. "Aren't you going to investigate? A crime's been committed. My property has been stolen."

"Winona," Rafe said, turning back to her, "it was a piece of junk."

She fell back a step, insulted. "It may have been junk to you, but to me it was my moped. And it's been stolen."

Rafe stopped. His head ached and his heart pounded in his chest. He wanted to climb up into his truck and speed across the highway until he forgot about Whitehorn and gossips and wolf boys and the sounds Raeanne had made when he made love to her. But he knew he couldn't—he couldn't leave, and he couldn't forget.

"Okay," he said in a resigned voice, reaching into his pocket and pulling out the tablet again. "Let's start all over."

Winona grinned and told him again when she'd last seen the bike, how she'd acquired it and provided him with a full description. Rafe jotted it all down—including the description, which included a flat rear tire and no front tire at all. When Winona had told him all she felt he needed to know, he slipped the tablet closed and returned it to his pocket.

"Okay, Winona," he said, starting back across the yard toward his truck. "But I gotta tell you, it doesn't look good. I'll make the report, but there's not much here to go on."

"Oh, I've got confidence in you, Rafe," Winona said, walking with him and patting him on the shoulder.

Rafe looked at her, not having the heart to tell her how hopeless it was. "Just don't get your hopes up too high, Winona. Okay?"

She smiled. "You know, Rafe, I've learned that the most complicated problems have the simplest solutions—so simple, in fact, we tend to overlook them."

Rafe gave her an uneasy look, feeling as though they

were suddenly talking about something other than a stolen piece of junk.

She laughed, giving him another solid slap on the back. "Think about it." She turned and started up the steps to the door. "And keep it simple."

Keep it simple. Rafe shook his head. He kept thinking about Winona and what she had said during the twenty-mile drive back into town. Keep it simple. What had she been trying to tell him? Did she know something, or was this just another of her kooky predictions? The way he felt right now, nothing in his life seemed simple.

Still, at the outskirts of town, he turned the truck north. He wasn't ready to go back to the station. He needed to be alone, he needed to think.

He turned up Whispering Pines Road, toward the Kincaid ranch, pulling off the pavement and following the muddy trail past the old Baxter ranch. He drove until he reached the dense woods that stretched out beyond the open plains, following the path until it ended in a thicket.

Stopping the truck, he grabbed his down vest and got out. He glanced around at the familiar surroundings—the giant trees, the hard, rocky ground, the quiet stillness. Somewhere in the trees above, a bird cawed loudly, an early spring arrival who was already staking claim to a nesting site. The woods were a place Rafe came to often, a place he gravitated to when he needed time to think, or just to be alone. It was the place where twenty-seven years ago a cowboy had stumbled across a tiny baby—half frozen and crying for his life.

Sometimes Rafe thought he'd come a long way from that lost little waif who'd lain wailing on the hard ground. He'd made a life for himself in Whitehorn—he had Emma, and a family and friends who loved him. But other times, like now, he felt as vulnerable and alone as he'd been on the day he was found. What was it that he really wanted? What was it that would make him happy?

He wanted answers to his questions. He wanted to know where he'd come from and why he'd been left behind. He wanted to fill in all the blanks in his past so that he'd have something to offer in the future. He wanted to feel complete and whole and as though he belonged.

He broke off a twig from a fallen branch, poking it absently through the thin blanket of melting snow that covered the ground. He wanted all of those things, but somehow none of that mattered unless he had someone to share it all with.

No, he thought, snapping the twig in half. Not someone—Raeanne.

She was leaving—her job, her family, and…him. She was going to walk out of his life and he was powerless to stop it. He couldn't go to her, couldn't ask her to stay. He wouldn't know what to say, or where to start. So much had happened between them, they'd been pulled too far apart. There were no words that could heal the damage that had been done.

Rafe thought again of Winona's advice. Keep it simple. But how could he, when everything between them was so complicated?

He thought for a moment, sorting through all the confusion and disarray in his mind, breaking it down to basics. The simple fact was, he loved her—he'd always loved her. And despite all the questions in his life, despite all the blanks in his background and the uncertainties in his future, he wanted her with him. Because without Raeanne in his life, none of the rest seemed to matter. Without her, all the questions, all the uncertainties, all the blanks, were little more than trivial details—uneventful and unimportant. But how did he tell her that? How could he find the words?

Keep it simple. Winona's words played through his head like a subliminal message. Was that what he did? Keep it simple? He loved her. Could this whole mess between them be solved as simply as that, with just three little words?

He heard the bird cry again and he peered up through the trees to its perch on a high branch. Rafe realized he suddenly felt better. He suddenly felt like crying out himself, like shouting to the world. He turned and started back to his truck. As he negotiated the narrow trail back to the road, he contemplated what he'd do next. He wasn't sure what that would be, but he knew he had to keep it simple.

Raeanne placed the cap of the felt-tip marker back on the end of the pen and stepped back to count the boxes in front of her. Six. Six packing cartons full of Christmas ornaments and decorations. It was ridiculous. She felt a little foolish now, thinking of how far overboard she'd gone. But she'd been feeling so hopeful back then, so happy to be back in Whitehorn, back home.

She glanced around her small living room now. Boxes were now stacked high where her Christmas tree had once stood and packing materials were scattered about the carpet. Now all she could think about was getting as far away as she could. She wanted to get back to L.A., back to that lonely little apartment complex where she had lived for seven long years and never set foot in Montana again.

The past several weeks had been the worst of her life.

She'd won the biggest case of her career and yet the victory had felt hollow. She missed Rafe—missed seeing him, missed talking to him, even missed arguing with him. The void he had left in her life was more than she could stand, more than she wanted to face. Maybe she was running away, but it was better than wasting away and that was what surely would happen if she stayed.

The knock on the door startled her. Tossing the Magic Marker down on the coffee table, she ran a quick hand through her tousled hair and ran to answer it. But as she rounded the corner into the entry, she skittered to a stop. She recognized Rafe's tall silhouette through the glass and her mind raced. For a moment she considered not answering, turning around and slipping back into the living room and hoping that he would just go away. But that was stupid. They were both adults. He'd no doubt heard she was leaving and it was only right and respectful that he come by to say goodbye.

Squeezing her hands into tight fists, she took a deep breath and slowly reached for the doorknob.

"Rafe," she said, as brightly as she could. "Hi. Come in."

"I just heard this morning," he said without preamble. "I heard Lily Mae talking about it out at the Stop 'n' Shop, then I ran into Cinda at your office. She said you were looking for someone to take the puppy."

The dog. Of course, that was why he'd come. He would want it back. She felt the sting of tears in her eyes and in the back of her throat, but she was determined not to let him see. "Yeah, I've just got a small apartment lined up. He wouldn't have anyplace to run or play and I'd have to keep him shut up all day. It didn't seem fair. He'd hate that."

"And he might get lonesome."

She looked up at him, remembering their conversation on the street outside her office the day Ethan Walker had taken the stand. "Yes, he might."

"But if you give him away, won't he get lonesome for you?" Rafe asked, stepping inside.

"Maybe," Raeanne said. She wished he hadn't come in. She would have preferred that they say their goodbyes at the door—keeping it simple and light. But it looked as if that were impossible now. She stepped awkwardly through the entry and into the living room, aware that he was following. "But he'll forget about me. In time."

"You think so?" Rafe asked skeptically. He glanced about the room, seeing the boxes and shipping crates and feeling his stomach twist uneasily in his gut. "Looks like you're about packed up."

"Yeah, well…" Raeanne said, hoping she had the strength to get through this. "No sense putting things off."

"I guess not," he said, walking through the living room and checking out the cartons stacked there. "How are you parents taking it?"

"Okay," she lied, trying to force herself to smile. The effort failed miserably, so she abandoned it. "Of course, they would like me to stay."

Rafe knelt down, picking up a book from a stack on the floor. "So why don't you?"

Raeanne looked down at him, surprised. "What?"

"Why are you going?" he said, setting the book on the stack and slowly standing.

"I—I'm going because…" Raeanne shook her head, flustered. "B-because it's…it's what I want to do."

Rafe took a step toward her, feeling a little as though

he were stepping into a void. He was a big, tough cop who dealt with danger on a daily basis, but knowing how close he was to losing her forever frightened him more than anything he'd ever faced. "Is it?"

"Of course it is," she snapped, turning away and snatching up the marker. She busily began labeling boxes she'd already labeled. "I wouldn't do it if it wasn't what I wanted."

Rafe walked over to where she stood, lifting the marker from her hand. "Wouldn't you?"

"What are you talking about?" she demanded, but her voice sounded frail and uncertain.

"You left Whitehorn once before," he stated. "You thought it was what you wanted then, too."

"It was," she insisted, trying to look everywhere but into his eyes. "I wanted to go to law school, I wanted to make a new life for myself."

"And now you want to leave again."

Because I have to, she thought to herself. *Because I can't face living here, day in and day out, for the rest of my life, without you.* But she simply nodded her head.

"I'm not going to let it happen again," he said suddenly.

"Wh-what are you talking about?" she stammered, confused.

"I stood back and did nothing the first time," he said, reaching for her and holding her by the upper arms. "I was…afraid. I didn't have the courage then." He stopped, and shook his head. "Maybe I still don't."

"Rafe, what are you trying to say?"

Rafe drew in a deep breath. He felt the old affliction, felt the words stall in his throat, choking and suffocating him. There was so much he wanted to tell her, so much he needed to say. He searched for the right expression, scrambled for the perfect words, only to feel himself panic and pull away.

Then, suddenly, he thought of Winona. He saw her sparking eyes, her long gray braid, and heard the jangle of those silly crystals she wore around her neck. Keep it simple, she had advised and he finally understood her quirky words of wisdom.

"I love you, Raeanne," he said then, feeling a warmth spread through his body like the sun's healing rays after a long winter night. "I always have. I love you, and I don't want you to go."

Raeanne would probably never remember exactly what happened after that, except that she was in Rafe's arms, that he was kissing her and that she realized for the first time in her life she was where she was truly meant to be.

Somehow they had gotten to the bedroom, but she wasn't sure if he had carried her there, or maybe she had just dragged him. She vaguely remembered articles of clothing coming off, but she was too concerned about the feel of his skin against hers to notice. The telephone might have rung and she thought she remembered hearing the dog barking in the backyard, but none of that seemed to matter. Rafe loved her. He not only had told her, actually said the words, but he was showing her with every move that he made. Rafe loved her and it made her life complete.

"I love you," Rafe whispered, pushing into her and feeling her warmth surround him. "Don't go, don't leave me. I love you. Stay with me. Stay with me."

Rafe heard the words on his lips, loving the sound of them, loving the way they made him feel. It seemed strange to him now to think that he'd ever been afraid, that he'd had trouble telling her what was in his heart. It seemed so easy now. The words seemed to flow from him now. There was no way he could have stopped them.

"I love you, Raeanne," he whispered again.

"Oh, Rafe," she said with a sigh, feeling the world lose shape around her and bliss come within reach. "I love you, too."

It was a long time before the world settled back into its orbit again. They lay together on the bed—touching, stroking, kissing…loving. It was nearly dark, and the setting sun sent crazy shadows dancing across the ceiling.

"You never answered me, you know."

Raeanne opened her eyes at the sound of Rafe's voice. "I don't recall the question."

He lifted himself up on an elbow and looked down at her. "Will you stay?"

She pulled him down for a kiss. "What do you think?"

"I think I'm very happy," he said, falling back on the pillows, more satisfied than he could ever remember being. He shook his head. "I can't believe I almost let it happen again."

"Almost let what happen?" Raeanne murmured, stroking the arm that rested across her.

He turned to look at her. "Almost lost you again."

"Again?"

"I wanted to stop you the first time, after Andy died."

She shifted her weight, resting her head on an elbow. "Why didn't you?"

He shrugged. "Afraid, I guess. And guilty…"

"Guilty?" Raeanne felt all the feelings of shame and remorse she'd kept buried for so long roar to life. "What did you have to feel guilty about?"

He reached out and stroked her cheek with his finger. "Andy was dead, and I wasn't. And I wanted you *so much.*"

Rafe watched a tear fall down her cheek, and felt himself die just a little inside. He'd let her walk away once, had missed out on a chance of happiness. But, by some miracle, he'd been given another chance. He'd learned his lesson and paid dearly for it in the years he'd been alone. He wasn't about to make the same mistake twice.

"Raeanne," he murmured, pulling her into his arms. "Marry me. We belong together, we always have. I love you. Marry me."

Raeanne felt the tears roll down her cheek. "I—I don't know what to say."

Rafe smiled, brushing a kiss along her lips. "Keep it simple. Just say yes."

Raeanne let him wipe her tears away. He was right, of course. Lifting her arms up to encircle his neck, she smiled up at him. "Yes."

* * * * *

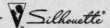
SPECIAL EDITION

DIAMONDS, POWER AND PASSION…TEXAS-STYLE!

THE FOLEYS & THE McCORDS

THE TEXAS BILLIONAIRE'S BRIDE
BY *CRYSTAL GREEN*

For nanny Melanie Grandy, caring for the daughter of gruff billionaire Zane Foley was the perfect gig…until she fell for him, and her secret past threatened to bring down the curtain on her newfound happiness.

Available June 30

Follow the biggest feud in Texas in these six titles:

THE TEXAS BODYGUARD'S PROPOSAL
by Karen Rose Smith—August

TEXAS CINDERELLA *by Victoria Pade—September*

THE TEXAS CEO'S SECRET *by Nicole Foster—October*

THE TEXAN'S DIAMOND BRIDE *by Teresa Hill—November*

THE TEXAS TYCOON'S CHRISTMAS BABY
by Brenda Harlen—December

Visit Silhouette Books at www.eHarlequin.com

SSE65463

Experience the variety of romances
that Harlequin has to offer...

Choose the romance that suits your reading mood

Home and Family

Harlequin® American Romance®
Lively stories about homes,
families and communities like
the ones you know. This is
romance the all-American way!

Silhouette® Special Edition
A woman in her world—living
and loving. Celebrating the
magic of creating a family and
developing
romantic
relationships.

Harlequin® Superromance®
Unexpected, exciting and
emotional stories about
homes, families and
communities.

Choose the romance that suits your reading mood

Romance

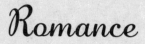

Harlequin® Romance
The anticipation, the thrill of
the chase and the sheer rush
of falling in love!

Harlequin® Historical
Roguish rakes and rugged
cowboys capture your
imagination in these stories
where chivalry
still exists!

**Harlequin's officially licensed
NASCAR series**
The rush of the professional
race car circuit; the thrill of
falling in love.

Choose the romance that suits your reading mood

Passion

Harlequin Presents®
Intense and provocatively
passionate love affairs set
in glamorous international
settings.

Silhouette Desire®
Rich, powerful heroes and
scandalous family sagas.

Harlequin® Blaze™
Fun, flirtatious and steamy
books that tell it like it is,
inside and outside the
bedroom.

Choose the romance that suits your reading mood

Suspense and Paranormal

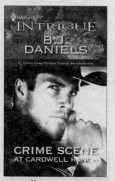

Harlequin Intrigue®
Breathtaking romantic suspense.
Crime stories that will keep you
on the edge of your seat.

Silhouette® Romantic Suspense
Heart-racing sensuality and the
promise of a sweeping romance
set against the backdrop of
suspense.

Silhouette® Nocturne™
Dark and sensual paranormal
romance reads that stretch
the boundaries of conflict and
desire, life and death.

Choose the romance that suits your reading mood

Inspirational Romance

Love Inspired®
Contemporary inspirational romances with Christian characters facing the challenges of life and love in today's world.

Love Inspired® Suspense
Heart-pounding tales of suspense, romance, hope and faith.

Love Inspired® Historical
Travel back in time and experience powerful and engaging stories of romance, adventure and faith.